WEEKEND

WEEKEND

a novel

JANE EATON HAMILTON

ARSENAL PULP PRESS
VANCOUVER

WEEKEND

ARSENAL PULP PRESS
Suite 202 – 211 East Georgia St.
Vancouver, BC V6A 1Z6
Canada
arsenalpulp.com

The publisher gratefully acknowledges the support of the Canada Council for the Arts
and the British Columbia Arts Council for its publishing program, and the Government
of Canada (through the Canada Book Fund) and the Government of British Columbia
(through the Book Publishing Tax Credit Program) for its publishing activities.

This is a work of fiction. Any resemblance of characters to persons either living or deceased
is purely coincidental.

Cover and text design by Oliver McPartlin
Edited by Susan Safyan

Printed and bound in Canada

Library and Archives Canada Cataloguing in Publication:

Hamilton, Jane Eaton, 1954-, author
          Weekend / Jane Eaton Hamilton.

Issued in print and electronic formats.
ISBN 978-1-55152-635-5 (paperback).—ISBN 978-1-55152-636-2 (html)

          I. Title.

PS8565.A556W44 2016   C813'.54   C2015-908288-9
                                               C2015-908289-7

for those who pour love in

AJAX

Logan and Ajax spooled out the miles along the Toronto lake-front, Logan's pale hand spinning the wheel of the Mustang as they sped farther from downtown, leaving high-rises, museums, galleries, Logan's roof-top condo, even buildings Logan had designed, behind.

In the backseat, Logan's Great Dane, Toby, hitched his head over the edge and drooled down the turquoise paint job, jowls bouncing, grey ears fluttering like flags. *Please don't shake that head*, thought Ajax.

It was hot—rays climbing to perpendicular, thermometer pulsing thirty-five. The day seemed half-mirage, the sun turning skyscraper windows to swimmable blue pools. Ice melted in their lattes. Ajax sweated between her breasts, under the nose pads on her sunglasses. Didn't matter how fast Logan drove, there'd be no relief with the top down; Ajax's sun-stung legs stuck to the leather seat. She harboured hope Logan might stop so they could swim.

But Logan, of course, didn't even sweat. Hard, like they'd designed themself, a skyscraper. All shiny glass and downtown angles. All boi smoulder, hard between their legs.

They'd been driving through the percolating city every day that week since Ajax had arrived from Vancouver. Passing dykes, femmes, queers, passing queens and kings and strippers and hustlers. Church Street. Suits, the high heels, the shim-mer of stockings, the coifed heads, people sewn so tight they squeak-walked. Queen Street West. Queen and Dundas. The homeless, shabby with rusty supermarket carts and garbage bags. Danforth, Bloor, Yonge, the Beaches, Baldwin. Dog walks— throwing sticks by infernal numbers into Lake Ontario, Ajax keeping her lips pressed tight about the lake's basic wrongness (pretending it was an ocean) and wishing Toby had been left at home so they could spread out on a blanket on the human-designated part of the beach instead, even though the dog was what had brought them there. Stopping for lunches and dinners, brushing the sweep of Logan's hard thigh. Cabbing to bars for Logan's poison, vodka.

Fucking on the conference table at Logan's firm. Fucking in the alley behind a sex shop after Logan stepped in alone to find something to surprise Ajax. Fucking on some barely accessible part of the beach, sticks jamming into Ajax's ass, sand fleas biting. Fucking on Logan's rooftop.

What the fuck fucking, thought Ajax repetitively; she was behaving like a kid, a teenager, locked into limerance.

Some bridge over Lake Ontario glistened as they drove past. Ajax wanted a photo, said so, watched it tool past. On her own, she would have found a way to turn around, to get back. But Logan didn't retrace their steps.

Logan's goddamned singularity spinning Ajax's head, a protractor reeling.

On the Gardiner, struggling through construction. Off the Gardiner, heading west and north out of Toronto, surprising Ajax.

"Where are we going?" A snag in Ajax's voice.

"Baby, this is your birthday surprise. Don't ask questions."

Driving. Driving.

Logan's cockeyed grin, insouciant lock of black hair loose down their forehead, their thick mobile eyebrows, their pebbled voice. It looked *good*. Toby woofed, knocked the headrest with his horse-sized head, and swung his spittle.

"I mean it, Logan." Ajax swabbed down the dog slobber. "We're going north?"

"Just taking a drive. Didn't you say you wanted a picnic for a present? I aim to please," said Logan.

North, north. Ajax hadn't realized how far they'd travelled. She noticed rolling pastures with cattle and goats and sheep. Just-shorn alpacas. Fields of wildflowers—Shirley poppies, candytuft, Dame's rocket, coneflower. Plentiful white daisies thick as butter, brown cow-eye centres. Flowers caterwauling, *This is summer! Summer! Fertilize!*

Every time they slowed for a stop sign, they could see bumblebees lollygagging in the blooms—bluebells and phlox and coreopsis—and took in the explosion of summer scents—wild grass, manure, the fruity smell of wind. It was cooling, nominally, though not enough for jackets. Ajax stroked the leather upholstery beside her leg, the bumpy texture of animal pores. Going by fast: Green fields. Ochre wheat. Rustling corn. A cornflower sky puffing with cumulonimbus clouds, horizon lined with cirrus. Ajax leaned to rub Logan's neck, feeling the urban stress go out of her too. Logan touched Ajax's leg. Willow trees leaned over streams. Horses swished tails. A family of quail crossed the road, babies round as tennis balls, causing Logan to slam on the brakes.

Woke Ajax right up.

Toby howled and shoved his drooling face into Logan's neck.

Logan pulled over. For awhile, the car idled on the side of the rural road, cows at the fence chewing cuds and mooing, Logan held Ajax's face tenderly between their palms. They feathered kisses across Ajax's chin, cheeks, eyelids, forehead.

Ajax whispered, "Don't fucking love me."

Logan said, "I think that's exactly what somebody needs to do to you. It's what I imagine doing forever."

Ajax shivered in the heat.

"And it's too late now, anyway," said Logan dropping their hands. "I already love you. Except for your gutter mouth." Logan climbed out of the car. The quail were long gone, so they let Toby romp on a short leash through the tall grasses in the ditch, now dry with summer. They bent to plant a kiss on Ajax's forehead. "Okay, even your gutter mouth."

Ajax said quietly, "I love how you ache."

"I love that you notice," said Logan.

"I notice," said Ajax. "I notice mostly your roots. A bit of stem. Some showy blossom." Ajax touched the side of Logan's mouth. "You know what your secret weapon can be for when I'm pissed at you? Just grin. Just show me that smile and I'll turn to putty."

The dog took a crap, which, even here, mere feet from cow

patties, Logan cleaned up, and the two of them, Logan and the dog, took off jogging, Toby a galloping tank as they disappeared into heat waves.

Blue wolf, thought Ajax about her partner. *Person only half tame.* She wondered if she should feel safe or scared at how serious they were getting.

A cowbell sounded close by, making Ajax jump. She jumped the ditch and gave the cows a scratch. They liked it; they pushed hard into her hands, bone close to the surface under hides. They reminded her of childhood, the field, full of cattle lowing, that had backed onto her elementary school. Smells of un-mown grass, manure, puffballs bursting spores. The first girl she liked had lived near there; Ajax remembered sitting on a three-legged stool beside a cow's full udder, Cara's hands over hers, showing her how to milk the teat, Cara's hand stroking hers to encourage the milk to let down. Shooting milk streams at Cara, Cara giggling, the sound of milk sizzling into the pail. When the pail was half full, Cara dipped a cup, held it for Ajax while she drank, milk running down her chin, her neck.

Cara licking her clean. Their first kiss.

"We should get going," said Logan behind her, slapping the hood of the car. Heavy dog exhalations.

"I'm famished." Ajax picked her way back to the ditch, leaped over it, and grabbed Logan's hand. "How about you?"

Logan unpacked a tablecloth, a basket from the trunk. "Want to have lunch with your new friends? We have plenty of time, in fact, McIntyre. All weekend."

"We're away for the weekend?" Ajax was pleased. "But I didn't pack."

"Got you covered there. I grabbed your things."

"Sneaky," said Ajax. "My meds?"

She followed Logan to the open meadow across from the pasture. The blanket billowed. Ajax settled against an apple tree trunk. In the speckled light, they dished out the food. Grapes, strawberries, cut kiwis, deli meats. Thick crusty slices of bread.

"Your meds. Of course your meds. You think I don't take note, McIntyre, but I do."

A cooler with lemonade. A steamed artichoke produced from the bottom of the basket. Gorgeous green thistle, which Logan served protractedly, dead sexily, leaf by slowly dipped leaf until, at last, the heart was exposed and cut into small manageable bites.

"We're not going home? Really?"

Logan flopped on their back chewing on a grass stalk, and Ajax snuggled in the crook of their arm.

"We're blowing that pop stand, honey. We're going north, baby, all the way north."

JOE

Elliot pulled back the curtain, grommets squeaking against the metal rod, and said, "Clear night."

Joe looked up from the nursing baby. She felt Elliot's restlessness and said, "Still?" Beaming hot day, but rain was forecast. The infant in her arms was somnolent, droopy, barely awake, and, really, so was Joe. Maybe it was hormones, or maybe the effects of the bitterly long labour. She'd been staring so hard at their baby, at her wisps of red hair, her birth-blue eyes, the button of her ski-jump nose, and the vernix gummed between her fingers, she'd given herself double-vision. Maybe she was trying to uncover whispers of some kind of message about what the hell she was doing here, in Ontario cottage country, a mother for the first time at her advanced age, a mother with *qualms*.

Too casually, Elliot rubbed her stomach. "I'm nauseated. What did I have for breakfast?"

"I hope you're not getting sick," said Joe. Without noticing, she pulled Scout closer so Elliot's germs wouldn't get on her.

"I hate my body," said Elliot, throwing herself on the couch.

"I hate *my* body." Joe's middle was distorted by birth, an unrecognizable heap. Why had she thought she'd shrink right after pushing Scout out?

"It can't *do* anything," Elliot said.

"Your body does everything," said Joe. Elliot cut a stunning muscled figure, but dissatisfaction plagued her. "Your body runs and eats and swims and fucks and, god, *everything*."

"I wanted to be Scout's mother. I can't breastfeed and I couldn't get pregnant."

"We can keep trying if you want. I wouldn't mind if Scout had a sibling, would you?"

"*Unlikely*, they said. *Heart-shaped uterus.* Doesn't that sound like somewhere a baby would *want* to be?"

"Unlikely is far from impossible." Elliot had been so moody. "I conceived and there wasn't much chance of that, either. And as for breastfeeding, you still might be able to. You could go to La Leche League. They could—"

"So the baby drinks *your* milk from *my* faux nipples. No, thanks."

"Yes," said Joe, but she thought, *Don't be petulant.* "I'm sorry you got cancer. You were way too young."

"Yes! Yes! I was!"

"... and it's not fair," concluded Joe.

Ell said, "It's not fair! I shouldn't have had the mastectomies. Do you get how much I regret doing that now, with Scout? It's not fair only you get to be close to her like that."

"I know," said Joe. "It's not fair. It's not fair at all. Honey, I'm truly sorry." She thought, *At least it never came back.* The choice back then had been lumpectomies and chemo and radiation, or mastectomies and chemo. A decade ago, but it was shocking how much something gone and done still ran their lives, how worrying about recurrence set them reeling. Whenever Elliot had a rogue pain, they ran through the chant *liver, lungs, bone, and brain*, the places breast cancer was likely to metastasize. Joe had never gotten over the sight of Elliot waking up in the recovery room bandaged with drains, begging Joe to tell her if it had turned out to be cancer, in the end, and whispering, *Yes, it was,* and then, later, after surgical recovery, Elliot flopped in the chemo recliners at the cancer agency, all the toxic warnings of the drugs they pumped into her. How she bloated, how she lost her hair, how she lay on the couch, depressed and too fatigued to move.

Elliot shrugged. "I just wish the nausea would stop. Remember after chemo I couldn't even drink water? It's kind of like that. Plus I'm having trouble swallowing."

"For god's sake then, Elliot. We should go back to Toronto; you need to see your doctor."

Elliot coughed and said, "Logan's driving up." Elliot was twitchy, a kid with ADHD; she couldn't stop herself from changing position every five seconds. Crossing her legs, scratching her head, flinging herself onto her back, sitting bolt upright.

Joe said, "I don't care. We can be in Toronto before midnight." Pain on swallowing? This was not good.

"I want to see Logan."

"With *that woman*?" Was she bringing girlfriend number 786? The current woman of the many auditioned was Ajax, a woman no doubt like all of Logan's other women, but, for all that, a woman about whom Logan had been uncharacteristically closed-mouthed. They were both used to Logan's conquests — the women who waterfalled over Logan's precipice on their plunge to the sharp rocks of reality. *Logan the Legend,* they called them to their face. *Logain d'Amour* behind their back. *Anaconda d'amour.* Joe had been crushed out on Logan since the first time they'd met. Crushed out *bad.* Crushed out so she tingled at the thought of them. Crushed out *embarrassing.*

So crushed out she'd walked into a washroom Logan was using at a friend's party and let Logan press her up against a wall and slide their fingers down her pants. She still remembers Logan growling, *Don't flirt with me, lesbian. Don't flirt and expect me to stop.* Joe's arms above her head, wrists held. It was the only time in Joe's life she'd come fast and soundlessly, lips pulled inside her mouth, biting down so as not to scream.

She was partnered with Elliot, of course—poly Elliot, who maybe wouldn't have cared, but even so, Joe had never breathed a word. She wanted to keep Logan like an amulet, all to herself, so as far as Ell knew, Joe had been faithful since the day they'd said their first *Hey you's*, because poly wasn't Joe's thing. Her partner having other women—okay. The two of them in bed together with other women—also okay. But other partners for Joe, nope.

Her personal choice was fidelity.

Except for that sneaky time with the one person about whom Ell had said, "Go ahead and do whatever your heart desires, just as long as it's not with Logan." *Not with Logan.* Because Logan was Ell's. She'd claimed that territory as her partner, way back, and they still fucked.

But for Joe, pregnant that last trimester, Logan splashed in her brain, doing a cannonball, over and over. Vivid anchor drops of the time she went behind her partner's back with not a second of forethought or guilty afterthought and did the dirty with the sexiest person on the planet. Logan, all fifties Elvis, all charm and snarl, coal hair drooping across their forehead. Logan tall and pale as early sunshine. Logan with the heartthrob fingers. Just the mention of Logan, of Logan coming up here to the cottage, *here*, to their joint property, made Joe's clit jump, minnow leaping up out of *that much wet*.

Now Scout, the baby, yawned, her delicate red mouth opening in a perfect O, and Joe yawned too. The birthing tub was still in the extra bedroom, drying, that deep blue hulk up on its side. The assemblings of a home birth—the Ina May Gaskin handbook, the nasal syringe, the stethoscope, the rope that descended from the second floor, a focussing tool she clutched in labour—those artifacts were still set up as if a second babe was on the way. Joe had dangled from that lanyard as if it was the rope ladder into the lake and relief from summer heat, while bouncing on a blue exercise ball she really had wanted to punt-kick across the room. Clutter was everywhere. Joe had her nest set up in the spare bedroom but also had gotten Elliot to drag a mattress onto the floor in front of the couch for a change of venue—she was not about to try stairs, not yet, and the couch was too deep. Change table, cradle, diapers, cornstarch, sleepers, socks, toques, bottles, nursing bras, nursing pads, soothers, teething rings, stacks of presents from friends, baby mobility playground at the ready.

Toys in their groomed adult cottage, garish moulded plastic

clashing with their taupe walls. The very brightness made Joe weary. The very plastic-ness of it exhausted her. Sometimes she'd think—*Are you kidding? Twenty years of this ugly crap? That's what we signed on for?*

Elliot leaned down and Joe expected—hoped for—a kiss on the forehead. Elliot, the architect built like a brick shithouse, broad-shouldered, substantial, who should have been the manual labourer instead of Joe, who should have been the large-equipment mechanic instead of Joe. Kick-ass, take-no-prisoners Elliot. But it was just to clean up some of Joe's baby-tending debris—tea cups, balled tissues, thermometer, orange peels.

"Wait, Elliot, lovey," said Joe, touching her arm to slow her. "Thank you for all you do for me. Just ... *thank you.* Thank you for helping me through labour. In case I didn't say that. I appreciate it all so much." She looked at the photographs on the walls which Ell had once taken of her, classic black and whites—how perfectly Ell had captured her curves, her mystery, and, more recently, her maternity. Elliot had already done a photo shoot of Scout in her backroom studio. *Preliminary photos,* she'd called these. Simple black-and-white images of Scout on a piece of driftwood. Scout hanging on the wall in a bathroom bag from IKEA. Scout in Joe's arms, smooshed in tight. Timed exposures of the two mothers nude from the waist up holding Scout.

Now Elliot surprised her. She stopped mid-gesture and smiled. "All in a day's work," she said.

And it was enough, for a minute, to fill Joe, to make her

feel cherished. At the start of their relationship, they'd done what they called "appreciations" once a week. They sat down and, for five minutes, each had said what they appreciated, and then the other had repeated it back. Maybe they needed to go back to those—why on earth had they stopped them, anyhow? After appreciations, they'd walk around in a stunned glow for half the next week, Joe remembered, surprised to find the other had noticed so many unremarkable things.

That idea, though, thought Joe—*Elliot and Logan in bed.* That thing between them that had never cooled. Joe never asked what they did, and Elliot never referenced it; Joe had never asked to join them. But Joe did use the fantasy of Logan to make herself come when she jerked off—her secret. *I've got the hots for your gf,* she could say, honestly. *I want to fuck Logan again.*

Again? Elliot would say. *What the fuck do you mean,* again? And then holy hell on earth for the lie of omission.

Elliot would be pissed, and who could blame her? Elliot would be hurt because Joe had gone rogue. Rules, spoken and unspoken, were the foundation of their house. They were the front door and the front window and the poppies in the rocky landscape. They were the baby and the theoretical white picket fence. The lines were how, over long negotiation, the two of them learned how to live, love, and stay together.

Although maybe, Joe thought weepily, the whole thing was coming unravelled before her eyes. It wasn't information yet; it was just something half-sensed around the corner—the last few months, Elliot distancing herself in a new way, Joe wary and prickly with fear, watchful. Worried that Elliot was leaving her without mentioning it, because she wanted what she couldn't have, a baby of her own. Scout was a baby of her own, from Elliot's egg, but it wasn't enough. Nothing was ever enough for Elliot—as maybe it never could be for someone who'd had cancer. Ever since Elliot had neared forty, things had gotten progressively worse; Joe was maybe just patiently waiting for her to bail. They planned to raise this baby up together and grow old and lose each other to death, however that arrived. It was a commitment they'd made and a commitment they kept making because their intimacy ran deep. Didn't their intimacy run deep? So it had seemed to Joe, until lately. Previously, troubles seemed only to bond them. Who knew? Maybe a midlife crisis trumped everything. The last few years of infertility treatments—Ell's womb, Joe's dusty eggs—had taken a toll. All the things that could go wrong between two women when daddies were plucked out of binders and IVF treatments cost $17K a pop and then often didn't work. Maybe they turned their backs to one another in bed more than they didn't.

They'd pretty much stopped having sex when Joe got pregnant and didn't miscarry. Twins, and then she lost one, so the docs said, *No sex*. Then that one remaining baby threatened to come ten weeks early, and the docs again said, *Bed rest. And whatever else you do, no sex.*

Somehow Elliot and Joe got used to the *No sex*.

How long had they tried before Scout successfully implanted in Joe's womb and stayed put? Through failed inseminations, through miscarriages for both of them—yes, Elliot, butch Elliot, even though she could never breastfeed because of her mastectomies, had done that for them, gotten pregnant—and then through more failed inseminations. Years. They could cite chapter and verse for every attempt. That was just not stuff you forgot, that you went through without incurring wounds.

If you'd told Joe that trying for a baby would cost her the vibrancy of her relationship, what would she have done differently? She knew that she was Ms Obsessive to start with, and once she was locked into something, she didn't let it go. Back then, Elliot claimed she'd never wanted kids and didn't want them going forward, and it wasn't okay to just switch the game-plan mid-stream like they were made of money—which they weren't. Babies were loud. Babies were messy. Babies were expensive. Tell her one good thing about babies that they didn't already have.

"You just fall in love with them," said Joe.

"Point for me," said Elliot. "We're already in love."

"But crazy love," said Joe. "Some different kind of love. So they say."

Elliot said, "If what we have isn't crazy love, I don't know what would be."

Joe said, "It's something unimaginable for us. We won't understand until we're there." She heaved a sigh. "What if I just long for one and don't even have a good reason? What if biology is destiny and my body knows I'm about to become menopausal and it just wants, and wants, and wants, gluttonous and primal?"

"Does it want to take back women's right to vote, too?" Joe laughed.

Elliot had said, "Even if I had a kid, it would be by adoption. Bringing a baby into this overpopulated world is repulsive. This conversation is really over before it starts, Josephine."

"Oh, god," said Joe. "I can't even talk to you. Why does it even matter *why* I want a baby, whether it's just some urge to spill my genes on the earth? When it comes down to it, how many people have justification? They just want babies. It's okay. It's not immoral. There's a lesbian baby boom out there, or haven't you heard?"

"Really? You want me to agree to have a kid because the Joneses are?" No sign of Ell's dimples. V-crease in her forehead.

"How about because it would be good for us?"

Elliot took Joe's hand in her stronger one, crushed it some. Elliot worked out with weights; it was one of the things Joe loved about Elliot—her passion for lifting, her bulk, her muscles.

"I just have a hankering."

"A notion?" Ell scowled. Joe was forever "getting a notion" and changing around all the furnishings and paintings in a room. "It'll go away when you hit menopause, and meantime, we'll still have our life."

"Just come to one appointment with me," said Joe. "Just one." *Just one just one just one.* "'Kay?"

And Elliot relented.

How does it happen that you go like that, from happily childless to miserably childless in a year? How does it happen that you go like that, from desperately against to desperate to get pregnant in a few months? How had Elliot gone from "no" to enthusiastically "yes?"

How can we help you today, why did you come to our clinic? Once they heard that, the future seemed a foregone conclusion.

Joe wondered if Ell, all these years later, would change anything, if she regretted anything. Did she regret going to that first naïve appointment with the fertility specialist? Maybe, of the two of them, Joe was the more regretful, the one who spent the most time thinking about how life used to be when it was just the two of them, before the spectre of a baby turned into egg harvesting and agonists and antagonists and false hopes and false positives and sad, sad nights sitting on the toilet shedding fetal cells, weeping. She would have, thought Joe, she would have given it all up in order to avoid all the pain and struggle and hope and dashing of hope, all the money, all the estrangement from Elliot.

Even now, looking down at Scout—the navy eyes of birth, pooched lips, mushed nose—and feeling her heart pump love, she was not completely convinced the baby had been worth it if the price was her marriage.

Elliot called from the kitchen, "I was going to work on the dock today, but it got away from me."

Joe said, "Scout's umbilicus is starting to smell."

Elliot turned and said, "What? What?" And Joe said, "The

midwife said it would start to rot and it is, it's rotting. Come smell."

And Elliot crossed the room, obediently bending over the baby and rearing back. "Jesus." She ran to the bathroom and slammed the door.

"None of this is exactly as billed," called Joe. Scout started to wail.

"You can say that again," she heard disembodied through the door. When Ell came out, she daubed at her mouth. "I'm definitely getting the flu."

"Keep your distance, then," said Joe.

"Let me just confirm: it is not as billed," said Elliot, back-handing her face.

"I know, eh? Gross." Joe squeezed her right breast, examined her nipple. "My milk still isn't coming in."

Elliot heaved a sigh. "Your milk will come in. You know it will. It just does. Day three, day four." She took the baby and jiggled her across the room, crooning nonsense. Baby-soothing motions had come on them like salsa dancing, side to side, up and down, side to side, a baby jive.

"You just said you thought you might be getting sick," Joe said quietly. Being spoken to sharply made her cry. She didn't mean to cry, but ...

Elliot didn't even hear her. "Shhh," she was saying in time to the baby's wails. "Shhhhhh, baby-o, shh. Please be quiet, baby-o. Can't you just be quiet now, sweetheart?"

This was how it was now and would be forever—the baby

an implacable force between them—a bond and a wedge. All that was joyous and funny and lazy and loving about them was buried under an avalanche of diapers and sleepers and zinc cream.

What was the distress signal of queers who used to fuck but now only watched a newborn suck, suck, suck? *You suck* seemed both accurate and unfair, but at least it made Joe smile.

"'Kay, I'm gonna go pick Logan and her girlfriend up," said Elliot. She hummed "In the Mood" to the baby while she changed her diaper. "I asked them to dinner. I can boil up some pasta, and I'll pick up salad stuff."

Joe felt a jealous twinge that she and Scout couldn't go in the boat too, not for a couple more days, anyway, until her wounds settled down. Joe was just—stuck. The little woman. The housewife. The bottom line. "We don't have a life jacket for Scout." She herself could use a life jacket, one she could wear twenty-four hours a day.

"Maybe seeing Logan will lighten you up a bit."

Lighten me up a bit? And then she thought, I wonder if I'm in love with Logan.

And then she thought, Fuck. And then she thought, Fuck Logan and the boat she was about to ride in on. "When are you picking them up?" She heard her own voice, high, thin, complaining—the voice of the shrew she didn't want to be. "I don't want to see anybody. I just want to be alone with you." But she meant alone alone with Elliot, not alone in the same house barely acknowledging each other. She meant foot and back rubs.

She meant doing things together, telling jokes, cutting up, not this moving exhausted through a series of joyless chores every day. Laundry, sweeping, vacuuming, dusting, breakfast, lunch, dinner. Boat over to get groceries, gas, supplies. Elliot either fawning and jealous or gone, gone more than she was home.

AJAX

Ajax surely hadn't realized that Elliot, the famous Elliot who once had dumped Logan, would be the first person they saw. For that matter, Ajax hadn't known anything about a cottage on an island. (*Logan owned part of an island? What the fuck?*) In fact, she'd only vaguely understood that Logan had a "shack in the woods," as they called it. That Elliot summered there had completely escaped her. Now here she was, the-ex-that-mattered, the only partner Logan had ever lived with, in the oh-so-butchy flesh. Every time Logan had spoken about her, it was with a stupid grin. In the dusk light of reunion, they both glowed before clearing their throats and pretending non-chalance. *To hell with being grown up*; Ajax decided she hated Elliot on principle.

While Elliot loaded the luggage, Ajax looked around the marina. Speedboats. Sailboats—sloops and yawls. Houseboats. Yachts. Logan's red powerboat. A mess of yellow life jackets up under the boat prow. Osprey nest on a telephone pole. Ajax could hear a woodpecker.

"Ellman," said Logan to Elliot.

"Bud. Glad you could make it up." Sloppy grin on Elliot's strong face.

"How's the new kid?"

"You know, a baby. Screams, wizzes, shits." Half smile, higher on the left, dimples, a shrug; unable to hide her pleasure in the kid's arrival. "I have a daughter. Who knew I could turn baby crazy?"

"Congratulations! That's just wonderful." A pause. "Why's it called Lake Boiling Foot?" Ajax asked, pointing at a sign

"Water's so hot you can't barely get refreshed. You'll see."

"So you're Logan's—" Low voice.

Toby crouched and peed.

"Friend," said Elliot. "Best friend. For a long time. Since we started architecture school together."

Toby shook the dock; it took both Logan and Elliot to tug-convince the scared dog to step into the boat, whereupon he collapsed in a heap with his paws over his ears.

Elliot said, "Sweet gelcoat, man," and Logan said, "Mike says two-year warranty." Logan started the engine, which emitted blue spirals of smoke before putting then shooting away from the pier. Boi talk about boat repairs as they bounced across the lake. Wind poured around the visor, relief from the heat. Forests clambered up on every shore, cottages bigger than most city mansions.

Logan lifted their chin at the bags of groceries stored under the bow, a question.

"Missus says you're expected at dinner later. Picked up some staples for your fridge yesterday."

"Thanks," Logan said. They looked out over the lake, motioned for Ajax to take the wheel. That made Ajax pay attention—she knew boats from her childhood. She canted across to take over, edged the throttle wide.

"How was the birth, man? Everybody good?"

"Intense. We're calling her Scout."

Ajax hollered to be heard. "I love Scout! I love the name Scout!"

Even though it stole her breath, she loved the wind, the jolts of the boat as it slammed into water.

"Joe was a brave sonofabitch. "

Ajax craned around. "We can't come over for dinner if—is it Joe? If Joe just gave birth."

"Haven't seen this one, though," Elliot punched Logan's upper arm, "in forever. Come, be social. Joe's happy to have you."

Ajax tried to send Logan a message, tried to meet their eyes: *No; it's not okay.* Outside of the boat's roar, the lake was placid and still. A loon called. Elliot took the wheel. The ride lasted twenty minutes. Elliot steered the boat closer to the dock where it squeaked against rubber tires. Logan reached to pull the stern to the dock, let Ajax clamber out. Sea legs.

Elliot jumped onto the dock; Logan passed up luggage and groceries. Elliot grabbed bags, said she'd see them at eight, and vanished.

Ajax cleat-hitched the boat—a knowledge-perk from having grown up on an island—then stood and stretched. She could see one house from the dock, a veritable palace—she could actually see two houses, if you counted a jutting shake wall. What had she been expecting? From what Logan had said, a shed. "It's beautiful here, Logan. Thank you for bringing me."

"I designed it, built it."

"You *built* it?" She didn't say what she wanted to say: You call this a *cottage?*

"After Elliot. After Elliot and I smashed up." They lifted suitcases. "That horrible time when you need a project, a big project so you don't mourn so loudly you lose all your friends."

"You built a cottage here, on the same property as your ex?"

"Hers was ours. She had to buy me out, and the deal was half the island. I built the second one right when I would have been happy to see her kicked off the island. Hostile, I admit it." Logan laughed and kissed Ajax's nose. "But you know what? It's worked for us for a lot of years by now. Can you just wait for me down here while I take this stuff up?"

Ajax picked up some of the lighter grocery bags but Logan reached for them. "You sit yourself down and put your feet in. Tell me if the water's cold. I need a report."

They looked at each other; a challenge. "I like to do as much as I can," Ajax finally said firmly but quietly.

"Just indulge me. No carrying. I know your challenges. May I quote: *Carrying anything uphill.* So not on my watch, McIntyre. This weekend is all about being taken care of, for *me* to pamper *you.* Let me just put our stuff away and get ready a little to welcome you."

Ajax swished her feet while Logan made several trips. It was warm, almost hot—like Elliot had said, Lake Boiling Foot, liquid sluggish air—not like BC waters at all, more like the

Bahamas. Water slapped the pylons. Fuck being ill; being ill sucked. Finally Logan was back and kissing her neck.

A pathway was partly delineated by in-ground solar lights. The house loomed, half log, half river-stone mansion. Logan set down the last bags. "I'm carrying you over the threshold, McIntyre."

"Logan, you built a *log* cottage?"

Logan grinned. "Logs from the property, as it happens. With a bit of help. Well, okay, substantial help."

"Wow," said Ajax. Logs stained dark brown. Accents of red and white. A wide porch. A clothesline. Chaise longues. A lengthy outside table. A fire pit. A meadow of poppies. They startled a deer, which had been investigating geraniums on the porch; it clattered away. Flashes in the dusk, like phosphorescence in BC waters, discombobulating, winking, until she realized what they must be.

"Fireflies!" she cried. She hadn't seen fireflies since she was little, in Ontario visiting her gramma. They didn't see them in Vancouver.

She hugged Logan tight.

"Everything's gone blue," said Ajax with wonder. "Wow."

"A van Gogh painting just for you," said Logan.

"*Starry Night* with fireflies." Blue tree trunks, indigo light, yellow bugs like a hundred spinning planets. She wasn't crazy. She spun in the half-dark. Couldn't she go out like this, at least, in love with Logan, addled with fireflies and a northern sultry night?

Logan leaned on the porch railing and said, "You realize this was how I fell for you, right?"

Ajax had her arms out as if she'd be able to grab the dusk and keep it in a jar. Stunning beautiful useless happiness.

"The way you're open to everything. The way you notice. The way you haven't lost your childlike glee." Logan carried in the bags and reappeared. "Come on. I'm starving. Jump up. I want to get dinner on."

Ajax swatted them, laughing as Logan tried to lift her. She probably had fifty pounds on them. "Don't be a freaking idiot."

Ajax pecked them all over their neck, but then she was in Logan's arms like a solid sack of potatoes while Logan—they couldn't fool Ajax—staggered over the threshold.

"I want to shower you in gifts for all your life," said Logan.

The cottage was lit with dozens of fat cream candles.

"Wow," Ajax said again. "Wow, Logan. Just wow."

JOE

Elliot sauntered in with sacks of food, waking Joe, still in the jammies she'd worn for two days, naked from the waist up. "Whoa," said Elliot as Joe sat sleepily up. "Your knockers."

Joe covered them. The size of cantaloupes and crazed with sensations—buzzing and soreness and prickles near her clavicles.

Elliot said, "That's what you want, right? Baby sleeps, you nap, your boobs grow. Milk coming in. It's kinda fascinating. Can I touch them?"

"Hey," said Joe and she could hear the loneliness and vulnerability in her voice. She patted the mattress. She didn't dare sit on the couch—it swallowed her so it was hard to struggle up, her arms around the baby, plus she was worried she'd leak blood. "Sit with me a sec?"

This house: rubbed woods, sun-faded slipcovers, worn carpets.

"Just let me put these groceries away. Logan and Ajax will be here at eight."

Joe felt the itch of sudden changed emotion and raised her voice. "Ell, wait. I'm filthy and weepy and I can't take a proper shower with my stitches. I can't even sit at the table yet." Elliot had had to walk her to the tub, steady her under a handheld spray. "I need to wash my hair. I feel gross. Your daughter has peed and pooed on me."

"I'll help you shower," called Elliot from the kitchen. Cabinet doors slammed, the fridge wooshed open and closed.

"Never ... never mind," Joe called. The baby was still conked out in the rocking cradle, so Joe felt safe enough to wobble to the shower without help. She grabbed furniture, the walls, as she went. She felt infirm crawling over the edge of the claw-foot tub, but soon she stood under the faucet's soft flow. That, at least, felt good, even though it stung her stitches.

She wanted to see Logan, but she wanted to see them because of her dumb schoolgirl crush and to show off Scout—as if they'd be enchanted with an infant. Here she was with everything she had ever asked of life at her fingertips, everything: a beautiful summer home, a semi-detached in the Beaches, a kick-ass wife who designed houses for chi-chi Toronto clientele, a healthy baby girl, her own challenging job fighting through thickets of sexism. There wasn't a solitary thing she was missing, except maybe milk in her breasts, which, despite Ell's optimism, she still didn't have; she was worried the baby must be starving; all babies got before milk was a few drops of colostrum.

"Why did you invite them over here?" she said at the kitchen door, pulling on a T-shirt. Elliot hacked veggies for salad. "Why on earth tonight? This is our first week as a family. I need ... I don't know. More of your attention. I don't think I should have to ask."

"I haven't seen Logan for ages," said Elliot.

"Battle of the butches?" Joe too was scorched with jealousy these days. Or was it even jealousy? She felt something, maybe wariness? Because they'd had a baby?

"Don't call me a butch, please." Elliot's voice was dull. She didn't turn around, was careful not to display her reaction. Lately, Ell was thinking of following Logan toward transitioning; she'd been a butch three months ago, but now identified as genderqueer, using "she/her" pronouns. Joe had scarcely adapted to the change. She herself was probably genderqueer but despised labels and swore the descriptor would never tumble from her lips. Did everyone have to be so PC and predictable? *You're showing your age,* she thought.

"Boi battle?"

Scout whimpered, waking in her cradle; Joe turned to check, smiled when she saw it would be a while before the baby yowled. She had a minute or two.

Elliot stopped chopping, carrots sliced into an orange mountain, and regarded Joe. "It's not. We're buds. We fuck hard sometimes. You don't like to peg me; they peg me. You know these parameters. But lately, you're—" Elliot struggled to express herself. "You always do this. You say you're okay with me being poly and then you're not, not really. Not the times I actually spend time with Logan."

"I'm just feeling vulnerable. Insecure with us, Ell, because we haven't been close lately." Joe hated Elliot having orgasms with Logan; she was possessive of orgasms. She said, "Maybe it's some rose-coloured fantasy I have of new parenting, but shouldn't we be bonding now? Shouldn't we be nesting, just you and me and Scout, is what I'm saying? Can't we get together with Logan and Ajax tomorrow instead?"

"Tomorrow Logan's popping the question," said Ell. This

made Elliot smile—naturally straight and white teeth, such seductive armour, while Joe's were a snaggle in her jaw that required an every-night dental appliance.

Joe drew in her breath. "Oh!" she said. Grabbed the counter.

Elliot frowned, regarded her. "Why 'oh!'?"

"Doesn't it seem awfully—" She looked for the word. "Awfully *rushed,* to you? Didn't they just meet? I don't even know which one of them's going to get hurt, but this has hurt written in wet red letters. Or maybe S.O.S. Throw them a life preserver. I'm not kidding."

"Remember Liza and Kate; *they* got married after less than two weeks. People can be happy," Elliot said, back stiffening. "Not that *you'd* know anything about that."

Ouch. Joe blinked back tears. Lately there was a lot of this—Ell's frontal attacks, stones slingshotted at Joe's Achilles' heels. There'd never been any convincing Ell to just say things out loud, bluntly, face them frontally rather than letting her hostilities ooze and leak in damaging ways.

Joe watched her scoop celery and carrots into a salad bowl and started to cry. "*Aren't* we happy? Oh god, what am I saying? I *know* we're not."

Was it wrong to crave a means to fold Elliot back in? She heard mewls as Scout came alert in the living room. Joe was moody these days; she acknowledged it. It must be hell being around her. She could cry over finding the toilet paper roll empty. But past that, *why* was Elliot turning away? This was a finished puzzle with a now-missing piece.

She looked around the kitchen: vintage appliances, salvage finds, copper pots, bead board panels.

"What's wrong *now*?" said Elliot, her voice a warning, a push away. She crossed the kitchen to pop a baby carrot into Joe's mouth. "Eat."

Joe felt guilty complaining. *I want more, I want more.* She blinked back tears, set her mouth. How could she begin to express herself to Ell cogently and reasonably? Put into words the swirling, chaotic mess she felt? At the first demonstration of emotion, Ell put up walls. "No, no, honestly, I was just admiring this place. I was just appreciating the eye candy you made for us."

Across at the other house, she heard Toby woofing, voice foghorn deep.

But Elliot didn't like Joe when she was calm and systematic either, these days. She just didn't like Joe was how it was shaking down. Her kindnesses now seemed to be flukes, one-offs, and Joe never knew when they were coming, which destabilized her.

By now, Scout was working herself up into a state—done fussing, she needed help, solace. Joe lifted her from her cradle, where smells of baby powder and urine blended to rise in a baby cloud.

Joe didn't want to use disposable diapers, but the cloth ones soaked through in record time, too quickly for the baby to have anything resembling a nap. She'd grown up working-class, but now that she wasn't, she wanted every iota of pleasure and ease that Elliot's money brought—even the ease that was environmentally conscious disposables. Yes, this made her feel guilty. Yes, of course she knew cloth diapers were best. Yes, of course none of this was supportable—not her longing, not the ecological damage of disposable diapers, because even if they were biodegradable, they went to a landfill first. Yet, yet, yet. Scout in cloth diapers might as well have been a doll from childhood—bottle in its mouth, pee streaming out the other end.

Babyhood was wet. It had caught her off guard. Pee and liquid yellow poop and spit-up and tears and blood. If the baby had woken up with green pea soup sluicing from her pores she wouldn't have been surprised.

Was Scout going to interrupt every conversation she and Ell had for the next twenty years?

Logan Logan Logan, Joe thought. She ruminated on Logan just so she didn't have to think of unsolvable problems, marital problems. Lately Logan moved through Joe like a wildfire, like the fires set in the fields around town every summer when she was a little girl, the controlled burn-offs, the smoulder and smoke. Men in helmets hefting hoses. She needed dousing. She fantasized about sleeping with Elliot and Logan together, which she probably could do if only she asked them; she never had because she knew it would be dangerous for her to bed Logan.

She changed Scout and carried her into the kitchen, jiggling her. Watched Elliot chopping broccoli. Scout was Elliot's mini-me, with scruffs of Elliot's hair and Elliot's almond eyes. The same thin lips.

Elliot kissed the baby's head, popped more carrots into Joe's mouth.

"My breasts are buzzing," Joe said. She felt a wash of relief. Her milk coming in, at last? She wouldn't be pointless any longer—she'd be a font of nourishment. There was a sensation up near her clavicles trickling down toward her breasts.

Relief, but also a recognition of how bizarre her body was that it could do this.

Everything about pregnancy and birth and now, having an infant, was unexpectedly freaky. She wanted to be all *I got this*, but she didn't have it, she didn't have it at all.

The doorbell rang. Joe went to answer it.

"We can't come for dinner," Logan told her. "Sorry to be so late saying so."

They stared at each other—Logan's always frank appraisal, half-challenging stare.

Don't, thought Joe. *Stop it. Just stop it.* "Sure," said Joe, "we get that you guys are busy." Joe's breasts started leaking. She felt it, milk skiing from her shoulders to the moguls of her breasts. To her horror, it oozed through her shirt, a spreading dark stain. Milk bubbles appeared on her pj shirt and began to pop.

"This is not awkward at all," Joe said, looking up at Logan with an embarrassed grin.

Logan's mouth fell agape, their gaze fixated.

Joe was pretty sure not too many women had caused Logan's mouth to fall open. She felt some rueful satisfaction in that, at least.

Logan looked up, finally. "Jesus," they said, "you really do have a baby."

"Say hello to Scout," said Joe and jiggled her.

Logan nodded, stepped inside. "Well," they said. "A baby. Congrats."

"Elliot's cooking already. Trout with lemon and almonds." She led Logan to the kitchen.

"Girl wants to be alone," said Logan to Elliot. "Girl says this is *our* weekend. I kinda maybe didn't tell her that I had a cottage to begin with, let alone that I co-owned the property with my ex or that my ex was picking us up in the boat. You know. A few missing deets. I had a blueprint and didn't share it." A look shot between Logan and Elliot; the world of things bois didn't mention to their femmier halves. The secret world they moved in, the tree houses: NO GIRLS ALLOWED.

Elliot said, peeved, "Logan, I'm half done here." She'd set the table, lit candles, picked a bouquet of roses and poppies.

Joe felt the currents between the two. Not just a morning paddle, but rapids.

Joe pushed on her right boob, hard, with the palm of her hand, watched milk weep through her fingers. Elliot passed her a tea towel, draped a loose arm around Joe. "Look at that, would you? You go."

"I'd better feed her," said Joe, "now that I can. I can't believe seven million women have already done this."

"Her boobs are getting enormous, that's one good thing," said Ell.

"Elliot, fuck off." Joe laughed. "But true. They are the size of two small houses." She sat down to feed Scout, staunching her flow on the right and feeding with the left.

Logan stared. "That's wild."

Joe said, "I feel like I should live in a barnyard."

"Just call Ajax and tell her to come over," said Elliot. "Please? Do it for me." She took Logan's elbow to turn them to face her.

For me? thought Joe. They had language like *do it for me?* Logan's hair fell into their face.

The two went into a clutch that made Joe uneasy. The baby slurped. She could feel the child's rhythmic pull—so earthy and elemental. Elliot's hand rubbed Logan's ass, slow and sexy. "Um," Joe said as milk squished out even past the cloth, "you guys, please, get a room."

Could a person re-negotiate polyamory after years? Could she say, *Look, Elliot. I need us to be monogamous from here on?*

Did she even mean *get a room*, or did she mean, *hey, guys, you've got partners?* One of you has a new baby and the other one is about to propose. Those are serious relationships to be fucking with.

Ass-rubbing. Joe made a disgusted noise and left the kitchen.

Dinner was a quick meal of cold cuts artfully assembled—dolmades, asparagus, olives, cheeses, breads—delicious, but Ajax wondered if they should have accepted Elliot's offer.

After the dishes, Logan wandered outside to build a fire, taking horse-sized Toby along. The screen door slapped behind Ajax; a long squeal, a woody wallop.

When Ajax had the last plate dried, she wandered out—but not before slathering herself in bug juice—toward the orange glow. She leaned to smell nicotiana, white bugles on tall stalks. She turned back to look at the cottages, admiring the chimneys, the screened porches, Logan's boot scrape in the shape of a Corgi, the herb garden raucous with mints and rosemary, the field of Shirley poppies waving on their hairy night stems. Did Logan even know that poppies were her favourite flower?

In the clearing, at a bonfire on the lake's edge, Logan choked in a cowl of smoke, poking at their struggling fire. Toby, curled on the ground, sighed, stretched, cracked a tired, red-limned eye, didn't get up for Ajax. Ajax stood downwind and waved a bag of marshmallows. "Dishes, check." She kissed the top of Logan's head. "Lovely as hell to have food prepared. Thank you." ·

Logan smiled. "Every time I ask you on the phone, you're always eating cauliflower."

Ajax laughed. "At least it's vegetable; It could be fucking marshmallows." Flames came off the wood like excited insects, orange-blue, tracing skyward toward the paint spill of the milky way in the sky.

Ajax thought the sloppily romantic *Logan gave me the stars.*

Logan used their Swiss Army knife to sharpen a stick and passed it over. "Do you think about where this is going?"

Ajax pushed a stick into a marshmallow. She bit down on what she wanted to say, that she'd love Logan forever, that Logan didn't have to earn it. This was it. She leaned into her lover's shoulder, shrugged, and said softly, "I'll go where it goes."

"I wish you didn't live so far away," said Logan.

Ajax swatted at mosquitoes. "Doesn't it make every second count?"

"It makes them hard," said Logan. "Knowing I'll lose you again."

The smell of burning sugar rose. The sky was bright, except for clouds hovering at the horizon. Ajax yanked her marshmallow out, blew out the flames, ate it charred. The goo inside stayed on the stick, white and melting. Ajax couldn't afford to travel east; Logan couldn't afford the time to travel west. Logan had their aging mom to care for in Toronto; Ajax had two grown daughters; one in Vancouver and one, pregnant, in the Bahamas. Ajax and Logan had just three options: end the relationship, travel to see each other, or move, and most of the time, to Ajax anyhow, none of those seemed manageable.

"Whoa, sweet," said Ajax, biting into the marshmallow goo and offering it to Logan.

Logan motioned her away. "Too much sugar for me."

Toby snapped at a bug. Ajax moved across the clearing, leaning back onto Logan's legs. They watched the fire catapulting, listened to frogs croaking and logs snapping. Mosquitoes dive-bombed, buzzing irritatingly beside their ears, so that their evening was punctuated with slaps. "I'm glad I brought you up here," said Logan.

"I get so wrapped up in the city, I forget this exists, you know," said Ajax. "The wilderness. Basic pleasures like these."

Logan squeezed Ajax's knee. Across the lake, they could hear shouts and laughter from other properties.

Ajax stroked the back of Logan's hand. "I should go in and get a sweater," she said but didn't move.

Logan said, "I want to keep on doing this for a long time. I'm crazy about you."

"My back is freezing and my front is burning." Ajax got up to sit in a chair.

Logan turned their ball cap backward. "I don't want to stop, is the thing."

"It's way too early for us to be having this convo," said Ajax. A frog chirred. *Way too early.* She didn't know what to say to Logan anyway—the distance wouldn't vaporize by wishing it so.

Logan leaned forward, stuck a stick into the fire. "My buddy Mark said that people just *know*. I felt that way about you, Ajax, when I saw you again in Montreal." They sounded almost ashamed by the admission.

The fire cracked like underfoot twigs. Flames shot up.

Logan continued. "I knew. I knew when you came around

that pillar and said my name." They gave the marshmallow to Ajax.

"Thanks," said Ajax. *And I still don't know what we can do about it*, she wanted to say next. She'd been in Montreal for a painting award. "All that night when we were walking around, I was thinking *Fuck, fuck. I still like them.* I didn't know you liked me back. Why would I imagine that? I had a crush on your shoes."

"You and your shoe fetish," said Logan, slapping their arm. "I'm getting eaten alive."

Ajax laughed. "Come on, *brogues.* You're sartorially endowed is all I'm saying, and I noticed."

Logan squeezed hard. "When we caught each other's eyes at the drag show."

"Yeah." Crowded room. The bar's anniversary show. Ten, maybe twelve drag queens on the stage at once. Perfume, makeup trowelled on. Good and horrible voices raised in song.

"When we were lying together on your bed looking up my ex on your computer," said Logan. "I wanted to kiss you so bad."

Same hotel, one night of overlap. Ajax remembered the surprise of sexual tension. "I didn't want you to go back to your room. I almost went after you in the hallway, except I couldn't make the first move. Then you texted me from the train something like, 'I know one thing: your eyes smile when you laugh.' That's when I got it."

Logan grinned. "Remember I texted, 'If you're looking for a

bottom, that's not me'? And you texted back, 'If you're looking for a top, that's not me?'" Logan laughed. "Then I asked what you liked in bed."

"And I told you!" Ajax grinned, embarrassed.

"I liked that I could think about what I wanted to do to you and know it would be what got you going."

"I do like all that; I'm a kinky little thing. But as long as you're clear that I'm not a masochist outside the bedroom." She was sometimes; she knew it. "Or if I am, it's something in me that needs squelching. If I see any disrespect or get a sense that I am less than equal, poof, I'm—" She turned to look at Logan.

"I'm getting lectures now?" Logan smiled.

"I just want respect, Logan. I want you to know how critical a piece of things that is for me—after my garbage ex."

"Have I been less than respectful?"

"I'm just saying. For the future. Eventually, we're going to be mad at each other. That's what'll test our mettle. How we behave then."

"I just love to twist you sideways," Logan said.

"As long as you keep it in the bedroom, baby," said Ajax. "You can twist me any which way, as long as it's sex. That's all I ask. Exclusively for sex."

They looked at each other in the flashing firelight, frank gazes that made promises. They'd had several long-distance months together before this trip—months to find out everything. And so far, so good, so very good.

They didn't feed the fire. Ajax watched Logan staring up

at the stars as it died, said softly, "You're very handsome."
She realized how fleeting the weekend would be, how soon
she would be flying back to BC, how quickly love, and all of
this—the trees, the lake, the bugs, the blow jobs—were likely
to disappear.

JOE

Joe felt an argument brewing. She knew she was silk-sensitive and should just button her lips, but—"You're in love with them," she said. "Aren't you?"

Elliot took two places away from the table settings. "Oh, for god's sake, don't, Joe. How is it that you spend years coping with my lovers and then now, at this late date, this bullshit?"

"You are. You think you're not, but I see you around them. I see how you light up. Anyway, come *on*. What are you referring to, 'late date?'"

"For crying out loud," said Elliot. "I can't even stand that you're starting this crap." Joe was trying to nurse, but so unsuccessfully, milk squirting, that Elliot, done with the table, grabbed the baby, walking her as she wailed, in a football hold they'd seen friends use. According to their midwife, no soothers were permitted at this stage in order to force the baby into developing a good breast latch, in order to compel a habit of needing just breast.

"Hello, you little butterball of goodness," said Elliot, bringing Scout close up to her face where the baby finally soothed—perhaps in surprise? Elliot sounded deliciously fond. "Hello, you scrunched-face alien. Are you MaPa's little baby from Mars? You are, aren't you? You're MaPa's little baby girl from Pluto."

Joe melted. Her breasts let down. Lord, when it started, the milk thing, it just wouldn't quit.

She was already regretting what she'd said, but at the same time, she wanted to say more, similar things, lots more, and furthermore, she couldn't stop herself. "I can't even tell that you're my wife anymore," she said, tears waterfalling down her face. "You've barely looked at me since Scout was born. I'm a person! I'm real! I have feelings!"

Elliot looked away from Scout, exasperated, looked back with a cleared expression. "Aren't you MaPa's scrunchy-wunchie?"

Joe sniffled and said, "Something's going on. There's something you're not telling me."

Maybe the baby was glad to hear Ell's voice. Maybe she'd been missing the way Ell used to talk to Joe's stomach when she was in-utero. The loving massaging hands, the cooing voice, old rock 'n' roll songs, "Jailhouse Rock," "In the Still of the Night," "Maybellene."

Joe scraped her face with tissue. "I'm sorry. Just come over here. I can feed her again and we can cuddle."

"Joe, I'm getting ready for dinner. I'm cooking, the water is boiling out of the pot," said Elliot. "The birthing pool is still up. There are three piles of laundry. I can't do everything around this place and mollycoddle you, too."

"*Mollycoddle* me?" Joe heard her voice rise dangerously.

"Oh, stop it. Unless you're on some kind of stupid pills, you know perfectly well what I mean. I don't mean you're an asshole and I've never loved you. I just mean the chores are spiralling out of control, and there was a lot I was supposed to be accomplishing over the summer and I feel out of control and you know I hate that."

The architect in her. It was all about straight lines going straight up. Could she at least acknowledge that the blueprints were changing?

"Those guys aren't coming over, right? You were willing to stop everything and visit with them," said Joe, rising to take Scout back. "So visit us instead. Come on. How are you feeling? Still flu-ish?"

"Not flu-ish. It came, it went." Elliot slumped beside her, brooding and resentful. She watched Joe's clumsy attempts to get Scout latched and drummed her fingers on the coffee table. Scout fussed when she couldn't quite figure out the nipple. The milk drips started again which made latching harder. Joe opened her mouth at the baby to mimic what she wanted: wide open, guppy-lipped. And Scout responded. Silence reigned; the baby suckled, and Joe winced at a new pain she supposed was good news.

"We should watch the latching movie the midwife gave us," said Joe.

Elliot drew in a sharp breath.

"What I said earlier. You really could think about breast-feeding, Elliot."

"Do I have to remind you I don't have nipples?"

"Now *you're* being intentionally stupid."

"I'll be back at work in the fall," said Elliot. "You're off for a year. You have the freedom." Ell looked small and vulnerable suddenly. "And Joe, if it's okay, could you maybe not mention my deficiencies again, please?"

Elliot suffered phantom pain and numb skin. *Can you feel that?* Joe would ask, trickling her finger across Elliot's chest or arm. *No,* Elliot would say. *Now? No. Now? Maybe, sort of.*

"God, you're crabby. You don't have to be mean, Ell. I'm just trying to do the best thing for Scout." She paused, thought, didn't resist. "Also I don't see why you have to sleep with Logan anymore."

Ell rose. "You asked me to come sit with you and now you're attacking me. Can I say anything right?"

Joe thought about that. "Probably not. Probably no, you can't."

Elliot said, "Look, please, for fuck's sake, don't pick a fight with me when you don't mean to." She tickled the baby's cheek.

"I might mean to," said Joe, tears tracking down her cheeks. "The book even says you are not supposed to leave me alone this week, not once, not for an instant. You read it, I know you read it."

Elliot shrugged. "You're not *alone* alone. I don't want to argue. I wasn't trying to do anything against you. Or us. I'm happy about Scout."

"About the baby, but that's where your interest here stops."

"Well, I don't want her to grow up hearing our fights, Joe, I don't. We're patterning the experiences she'll gravitate toward later on. I know you don't want to hurt her future chances either."

"I don't, but—"

"I am pulling with you, Joe. I am. I'm just overwhelmed with some things, some things I wasn't expecting, that I'm having trouble dealing with."

"See? See? I knew it!"

"Don't go off the deep end now. Don't. You do this. You explode into a fervour when I haven't said anything to rile you up."

"Okay, fine. Okay. What things?"

"Nothing things. Work things, some of them." Elliot shrugged. "*Things,* okay?"

"You need to show me you care, is all," said Joe.

"Don't I show you? Isn't cooking for you showing you?" Ell did almost all the cooking. A lot of the cleaning. She was no slouch around the house. And no slouch as a partner either, most of the time. Most of their years.

"I need you to notice *me,*" said Joe. There were small snuffling noises at her breast, but Scout kept falling asleep instead of nursing and coming off the nipple open-mouthed, head canted like a drunk—finally food comatose. Could babies feel the stress between a couple? Was Scout right this moment imprinting on her mother's misery like a whooping crane following a light plane?

"I need you to notice *me,*" said Elliot.

Joe blinked in astonishment.

"All you see is Scout. Sometimes I feel that's all you wanted me for was to have a baby, and now that you have her, you have no use for me."

Oh, that was insane, insane! All she did was notice her! Dropped everything when she was around to smother her with attention! Joe felt as if lethal gasses were expanding inside her, pushing at her skin. "But I love you, Elliot! I'm wild about you! All I do is consider your welfare!"

Elliot pushed herself up, tucked a weary fist into the small of her back. "I admit, I am not as patient as I usually am. I'm sorry."

"No, *I'm* sorry," Joe said, lifting bleary eyes. "You're not entirely wrong. I'm absorbed with her. And I've been shrill with you, demanding. This experience is, I don't know, consumptive." Joe's left arm was aching from Scout's weight. "It's how crappy and vulnerable I feel physically, the stitches, the fact that I can't get more than two hours of sleep in a row, and then all the worry about getting her latched to establish breastfeeding, and is my milk ever going to come in—"

Elliot laughed. "I think your milk is definitely in." Joe's shirt was soaked to her waist. "I'm sorry you're hurt," said Elliot, relenting, wrapping her arm around Joe, pulling her as tightly in as she could without pushing up against Scout.

"Tell me you love me."

"You know I do," said Elliot, kissing her cheek. "I'm married to you, aren't I? Obviously I love you."

"It's the best," said Joe, sighing with pleasure, quelling the inner voice that said, *Hey, wait a second!* Snuggling down, she rested her head on Elliot's shoulder. She could smell her own milk, sweet, sour. It was true that she was no kind of wife these days. It would be six weeks until they could have sex. And even then it might not be what she'd had before, since in birthing, somehow in all her magnificent pushing, her clitoris had torn. What was Logan, what was anyone else, compared to this, compared to the three of them becoming a family together?

Campfire next door, and Elliot said they should go. She'd been twitchy through dinner. "It's not far. Do you think you can walk it if you hold on to me?" she asked Joe. "I'll carry Scout." They navigated across the rocks down to the campfire pit between the two houses, met Toby waggling his tail partway. Lightning bugs blinked on, blinked off, blinked on, blinked off. Joe realized that it felt amazing to be outside, even just creeping along as they of necessity had to, her arm slipped through Ell's elbow to help steady her, the U-pillow huge and geriatric around Ell's neck, the babe snuggled into the crook of Ell's low-hanging free arm. It even felt amazing just to realize that she didn't have to exist within the bubble that was their living room and spare room for perpetuity. Elliot gave the baby over, slung the U-pillow onto a stump for Joe, then stood behind her so she could lean for support.

"Y'all," Logan said. "Take my chair, Joe."

While they switched, Toby flopped down, a woof coming out of him as if he'd moved a great weight.

"Ajax, this is Joe, and baby Scout. Joe, Ajax," said Logan.

Joe was seeing if she could sit comfortably on the pillow. It smarted, but then her stitches hurt no matter what.

Logan stoked the dying fire.

Ajax said, "Scout is a great name. I'm happy to meet you, Joe. May I hold her?" She walked around the campfire jiggling Scout, rubbing her back and patting her bottom.

"You must have kids?"

Ajax told them about her kids.

Though Joe had been hoping to avoid a feeding, Scout got hungry so she fiddled with fixing the tiny voracious mouth to her nipple. Crackles from the fire, the sound of the baby slurping. Preamble gotten through; how they all knew each other. How Logan and Ajax had met twenty years earlier and lost touch and met again. When she sat down, Ajax leaned into Logan as if she'd known them always. Joe had half a mind to say, "Wait a second, that's *Logan* you're talking about," but it hadn't been Logan's hand on Elliot's ass, but the reverse—Elliot's hand on Logan's ass. Joe was surprised that Ajax was older—Logan usually dated down, dated thirty-year-olds. Ajax, she said, was turning fifty; it was her birthday weekend.

Toby musically shook his collar, put his large head on Logan's lap, and Logan petted him as long ropes of spittle fell. He didn't sit long before he melted into the ground, his big head tucked onto his paws. Logan offered Dos Equis; Joe couldn't, Elliot begged off, and Ajax didn't.

Logan said, "Sure am glad to be up here again. I didn't know when I was going to make it back." Logan hugged Ajax close. "Was waiting for the girl to be able to come with me."

"I thought we were going for an afternoon's drive," said Ajax.

"Oh, Logan is a real card," said Joe dryly. "All about romance and true love."

"I think they really are," said Ajax, beaming over at Logan.

"Let me tell you about love. Here's what I know about love," said Logan. "My cousin Miranda met this woman when she was young—nineteen. She met Daisy straight after she broke up with this loser dude she'd been dating in high school. She was in college at the time, taking a two-year program in insurance brokering. She wasn't worldly. She hadn't travelled. She didn't really excel in school, and she certainly didn't make any real friends, not in all those twelve years. Miranda was still living at home with her mother, but she worked at a foot-long shop, mostly for tips, and this woman came in a lot. She always ordered a BLT sub, and it got so my cousin was excited to have her come in, you know, looked forward to seeing her? She was always in nice clothing, and she flirted. I don't know at what point Miranda figured out that Daisy was married and had a newborn, but by then she was in love. We all said, don't hold your breath; she is not going to leave her wife. Go out with somebody else. But she couldn't. She slept with Daisy in Daisy's marital bed when her wife was out. She slept with her year after year until, eventually, yeah, Daisy left her wife and they moved in together. But then she caught Daisy having sex with other people—"

"Well, we all do that, pretty much," said Elliot. "I mean, speaking for myself as someone poly."

"We're not," said Ajax and reached for Logan's hand. "Right, hon?"

"We're not," Logan confirmed. "I'm not anymore."

"It's a question of what a couple promises each other,"

said Ajax. "It's a question of being honourable. Pretty much if you're keeping an element of what's going on hidden from your partner, you're about to be sucked under on the honour thing."

"Exactly," said Logan, raising her beer. "So Daisy did the opposite, and my cousin found out, but she was still really young, and she believed Daisy when she said it wouldn't happen again. She liked to believe people were basically good at heart."

"How very World War II," said Elliot.

"So she got married to Daisy and it happened again, of course, and Miranda finally left Daisy. Then Daisy got into a bad car wreck, and my cousin took her back. Daisy couldn't work anymore, but she could still philander. So she philandered. And Miranda found out and, kaboom! Apart. Again. Then Daisy messed Miranda around."

"Physically?"

"Yeah, uh-huh," said Logan, uncapping another beer.

"That should fucking just never happen," said Ajax. "I know that it does in our community, and lord knows, I had my own trouble like that with an ex; we've all had our experiences with controlling, angry partners, but—"

"That is over the top. That's not love," said Elliot.

It was humid, the night pressing in on them, pressing, it seemed, their sweat to their skin. Logan saw a shooting star and pointed too late to share it.

"What's love, though? They would have said they were in love," said Logan. "Even Miranda, when she was being battered, she would have said she was in love. And Daisy probably would have said she was in love. You know you have it when you have it, but other people can't assess your heart to say you're right or wrong. Is love a feeling or is love an action?"

"We have it," said Joe. "It's a feeling and an action."

"It's a feeling," said Logan.

Ajax said, "It's an action."

"I guess we have it," said Joe. "I mean, I'm happy when Ell's around. I light up. I mean, I have my moments, and this week there have been lots, but ..."

"She's maybe been a little cranky," said Elliot, patting Joe's knee.

"You try pushing a watermelon out your hoo-haw," said Joe.

Logan made a face.

The fire spit sparks.

Elliot took the baby from Joe and wrapped a blanket tightly around her, covered her head, swung her up to her shoulder to pat her back. "If you're talking about love, you could talk about this. Four days ago, I didn't even know Scout. Now I can't imagine life without her."

Aww, thought Joe.

"Daisy was completely obsessed with my cousin, is what I am getting at. She wanted to know everything she was doing, everyone she was seeing, you know. And maybe that was a kind of love." Logan took a slug, drew Ajax closer.

Joe said, "That's not love!"

Ajax said, "Having a planned baby is love, for sure."

"It matters to me that Joe would put herself through that," said Elliot. "Labour was hard. But, I mean, look what you get."

Ajax grinned at Logan and stroked their leg.

"Maybe love is just the ability to get along together, day to day," said Logan. "To stand each other's foibles. Maybe that's all it comes down to. Maybe it's understanding that if you break up, you have to take yourself along and that's who you'll be dealing with—again."

"Speak for yourself," said Elliot.

"Maybe it's loving unconditionally," said Ajax. "I loved my ex unconditionally, but she didn't love me the same way. Really, I doubt she knows a thing about love."

"But fighting can be good," said Elliot. "Things build up between us, for instance, and then we fight, a good walloping yell, and then things feel better afterward. That's love too. There's no reason that can't be love."

"If it's not rage. Melt-downs and suicidal ideation. If it's not violent," said Ajax. "If it tips into violence, that's not love, I'm sorry. If you're manipulating the other person, no. That's just not love."

Logan said, "I give you that. Fights are important. Fights are sometimes just as important as getting along. But not always. My mother married her first husband in Morocco, and they had two little boys. That man beat my mother, he beat her to a pulp. She was a PhD, you know, and he was a medical doctor, but he still got home and beat her every night, and this one time, she just ran. She ran as far as she could to get away from him, which in this case was to southern Spain, and she abandoned my brothers."

"Not you?"

"I wasn't born yet," said Logan. "And my brothers aren't in my life."

On Elliot's shoulder, Scout burped and fell sound asleep.

AJAX

"Is this love?" Ajax asked. "I dated this woman who went on about frogs in cook pots, right, how they won't jump out as long as the water heats slowly, how they won't protect themselves from a slow boiling? I dated her for maybe three fucking weeks, and then I made some crack that I'd been trying to drink more since I divorced. I'm basically abstemious, not because I've chosen to be, except behind the wheel, but because I don't particularly like it. I was striving to be a little easier with it generally, to learn to enjoy a glass over dinner. This girlfriend was an alcoholic, years sober but still going to AA every day, pretty much, and she said she wanted to break up with me because of what I'd said. She said she couldn't respect someone drinking to impress someone else. She said I was probably an alcoholic, just not drinking yet. She said she knew all sorts of people who'd become problem drinkers at my age. I was upset. She basically gave me an ultimatum: quit drinking or we were over. A little red wine is good for my heart, I said, and she said no, uh-uh, not on her watch. I said, but I'd be quitting because she had a problem with it, not because I did, and it seemed to me that if, after decades of abstinence, she still had this large a conceptual problem with alcohol, it was still fucking controlling her as much as when she drank, still wrecking her relationships. I quit for her, but every date from there on she grew increasingly hostile, and she'd show up with lists of all the things I'd done wrong since our last date. It was easy to see where her kind of punitive anger was going, long-term, like turning up a burner, right, under that frog in a pot? I was almost a freaking frog who didn't know when to jump."

"That's not love," said Joe, swatting a mosquito. Her stitches were throbbing. She wished it would cool down. Maybe a fire in the heat was a bad idea? She'd push back her chair, if she could. "That's control, maybe. But that's not love."

Logan built s'mores and handed them out—graham crackers, chocolate, marshmallows. They laughed as they tried to eat without dropping them. Toby came back to life, sitting on his haunches, waiting, diving on spills.

"We lasted about four months. She thought my friends were bad influences," Ajax continued. "She hated my best friend. She thought my friend was getting in between us. She told me I shouldn't be allowed to choose my own friends since, obviously, I did a poor job of it. I had, for instance, another friend who was suicidal and needed to talk to me once while my girlfriend was over. She couldn't tolerate me being on the phone or on the computer, even if I was too sick to sleep. She would wake up mad that I wasn't in bed. And she called that love."

"Do you know what we talk about when we talk about love?" said Elliot, tossing her hair. "We talk about the things we can tolerate, maybe, the vast list of things we give up for companionship."

"You see it that way?" asked Joe, readjusting herself. She licked her sticky fingers. "These s'mores are good. A vast list?"

"We talk about lust," said Logan.

"We talk about lust *and* sacrifice," said Joe. "We talk about family bonds. About nurturing those who are dear to us." She took the baby back.

Elliot said, "We ought to talk about never making too many sacrifices."

"We talk about the things that we build," said Joe. "I can feel that sugar rushing through me."

Ajax raised a beer. She too felt the sweet claw into her brain. "The architects won't disagree."

"It's still too hot out here and I'm fading," said Joe. "Communities, I meant."

"Or how about this one? I dated this woman who asked me to buy a dog cage for her to sleep in. I was, like, whoa, outa there," said Logan.

Ajax thought about that. Kink was kink; was that kink? She said, "When I first came out, I put women on pedestals. I thought, as a dyke, I wouldn't experience any crappola. Boy, was I wrong."

"She got slugged by her wife," said Logan.

"Shit," said Joe.

Ajax felt a burr of wariness that Logan was discussing it. "That's not true, exactly. She didn't hit me. She paralyzed my arm. She grabbed me and bruised me dozens of times. She used a lot of intimidation tactics to get me to behave the way she wanted. A lot of gaslighting etcetera, etcetera."

"Maybe I don't know what love is," said Logan. "But I've got enough experience now to know all the things it isn't."

"You do, honey. You do. This is love," said Ajax, squeezing her tight. "Love is treating your partner and your friends and family with respect and admiration. Respect, yes. And love is kindness. It's honouring your partner even when times are challenging."

"Well, *maybe* that's love," said Logan. "Or a facet of love."

"Don't make me fight you," said Ajax. She put up her dukes. "'Cause I will. I will box you into the ground to prove kindness is love." She laughed.

Elliot said, "Or maybe love is self-love just as much as any of those other things."

Joe looked at her. Was she as self-centred as she sounded? "Sorry to s'more and run," she said, creaking up, shooting Ell a glance.

"I have to get these guys home," said Elliot. "Forecast says storm."

Logan looked up. "It's clouding over."

Ajax and Logan watched Elliot help Joe climb the hill, Joe slow and measured and in obvious pain.

"I *will* wrestle you," said Ajax quietly as soon as they were out of sight, slipping onto her knees in front of Logan, pulling down their zipper. "What are you wearing?"

"It's good," said Logan. Logan changed five or six times a day, different dicks for different purposes. They spent more time in the washroom than Ajax did. A packing cock. Cock for anal. Big Albert for when Ajax craved a stuffing. Cock for sleeping. Cock for showering. Dude of a Thousand Cocks. Ajax pulled this one into her mouth, began to move on it, thinking how it was better than it had been eons ago with guys, thinking she wasn't so worried about her teeth. Logan said, a hand on the back of her head, "*This, this* is love."

Logan did up their shorts. They damped the flames, pushing dirt atop them.

As the fire sputtered, Ajax sat back on her heels and said, "Let's go swimming!"

"Now?" Logan said, gathering their supplies.

"Sure, now. Why not? Water'll feel perfect at this time of night. What about Toby?"

"He won't wander far. There's not far to wander, come to that." Logan kept damping down the coals. "I don't swim at night. Clouds are rolling in. See that, to the west?"

"Except for the great white lake sharks, it's completely safe." Ajax slapped Logan's leg. "Come on, you'll love it."

"Can I just hold your towel for you?"

"Chicken." Ajax reached for Logan's hand, tugging them up.

"Cock, not chicken," said Logan. "I ain't scared a *nothin'*."

They picked their way down to the dock, where Ajax stripped. She took Logan's clothes off too until Logan was down to their skivvies and loafers. Logan pulled the binder off, stripped gaunch, held tight to their harness. Ajax wavered on tippy-toes on the edge of the dock.

Logan wrapped their arms around Ajax, bending to kiss

the back of her neck. Small tender kisses. Squid ink sky, long creaking dock. "You taste like sweat."

"You know what Sartre said to de Beauvoir?" Ajax said. She leaned back into Logan. "He said, 'I love you with the window open.' I want to love you like that, Logan." Ajax turned. "Without expectations and jealousy. Loving the full person you are." She petalled kisses on Logan's face, forehead, eyelids, cheeks. "Swim with me. Will you swim with me?"

Toes over the edge, they held hands, swung arms. Big leap of faith going where they couldn't see anything—the water was emptiness, blacker than sky, a void. They could hear it, though, against the pylons. Slapping.

"I see the Big Dipper," Logan said, pointing. But rain clouds were pushing in fast, cowling the sides of the lake.

Faintly, faintly, the barely rippling sky-ladle off to the right. Ursa Major. Dubhe, Merak, Phecda, Megrez, Alioth, Mizar, and Alcor, each fifty-eight to 124 light years away, unimaginable.

Ajax said, "That light has travelled 50,000 years to get to our retinas. My dad used to teach me about the stars."

"You go first," Logan said.

"Both first. Together."

Bats dive-bombed them, flicking black spectral arrows. Across the lake, the trees hulked dark against a lighter sky.

"Sharks, you said?"

"Many, many sharks, all nocturnal," said Ajax, lifting her arms to shape her dive. "Hammerheads. Basking sharks. Even whale sharks. Okay. One ... two ... three!" And she went over.

The lake was warm, even bordering on hot. As her head broke the water, Ajax thought, *Love badly, then love well.*

Logan cannonballed, shrieking.

Ajax laughed. She could barely see them in the dark. But she could hear them.

They came up sputtering, said, "This is truly weird and bizarre."

"It's my favourite thing, Logan. I don't feel there's been summer till I've swum naked at night."

They floated on their backs holding hands like otters; even this late, the lake was too warm for their nipples to erect. Ajax narrowed into an inverted bowl of stars and the inside-out sound of her wonky heartbeat drumming. That beat of life that had gone off its own rails, and above her the flash and pizazz that was their galaxy. The world narrowed just to her heartbeat and stars, Logan's hand an umbilicus leading her back home. Reality spun her on her axis three times three times three.

"We're in the suburbs," said Logan, "of the Milky Way. In case you didn't realize."

Ajax lifted her head. "What's it like downtown?"

JOE

Some vaguely recalled dream about parenthood being a terrible mistake. Joe struggled awake, found, to her great relief, Scout curled up beside her, absolutely fine. Heart pounding, she wondered what had woken her. At first, she thought maybe the noise was a raccoon knocking over trash cans. It was murky here in the guest bedroom, just a night light in one wall to help guests find their way to the bathroom, otherwise a stumble through tar blackness. The island wasn't like the city. Up north, with no ambient light, darkness was absolute. Joe worried the baby had slept too long, but she realized that when Scout cried, she thought that went on too long too.

She was lonely and nervous. She needed Elliot. Elliot was getting normal nights' sleep, because one of them might as well.

She felt the outline of Scout, patted her.

The idea that she could form a family with someone ... She was raised in the heart of the city with no siblings and parents who fought before separating. What hubris to think she could do something different, break the chain, offer her child a different outcome. It wasn't possible. One parented as they had been parented. The best she could offer Scout, she supposed, was parents who were at least present, flawed and full of idiosyncratic foibles. She couldn't even promise that they wouldn't fight, since they were already hissing at each other. Was that something she wanted to tell her daughter about love?

Joe was being held captive by maternity in a way that Elliot just was not. Elliot had been pregnant, and had miscarried—would it be the same if that fetus had grown to term, and Elliot was the one chained by maternity? Joe suspected if Ell had been the bio-mom, Joe would still have been the one strapped to the domestic—being further toward femme in the gender spectrum, having a less lucrative job. Perhaps even by inclination.

Did she hear Elliot retching in the bathroom? Apparently Ell had picked up that bug going around.

Maybe she'd overlooked the fact that, before Joe had wanted a baby, Elliot had cautioned, *Why rock the boat?* But, eventually, Elliot had clutched the IVF life preserver every bit as hard as Joe did. She carried, Joe carried, they both miscarried, bang, bang, all in six months. So much loss. Boats taking on water, boats foundering. Bloated women sinking below the waves, babies gone to fish. They'd had one embryo left, suspended in liquid nitrogen, and Joe, without even telling Elliot, had made steps to have it implanted, a final try.

Joe breathed slowly, deeply, trying to calm herself. What *had* she been dreaming? Intellectually, she knew Elliot was just as committed to Scout as she was, and not being at Joe's side every minute didn't imply that she wasn't. Might, in fact, be more of a comment on Joe than on Scout. But in her heart, Joe fretted. Her marriage, and now Scout too, were the most important things she'd ever had.

Once, long before the IVF upheaval, just after they'd gotten together, Ell'd sat Joe down.

"You know I use het porn," Elliot said. "I still find guys sexy."

"Okay," said Joe slowly. Het porn—blech. "Right. So what's the pragmatic fall-out to that?"

Elliot claimed there wasn't one. Then she blanched and said, "I might be bi."

Joe laughed. Elliot had slept with whole baseball teams. And was truly butch.

"No, Joe, don't mock me. I think I have to go back to men. I've thought a lot about this. Being a lesbian just isn't working out for me. Whatever I thought it would give me, it's not giving me. It didn't fix anything."

Fix anything? Was being queer supposed to *fix* something? "Can you maybe talk about this, please?"

But Elliot withdrew. Joe thought to give Ell some room before revisiting it, before she collapsed in sorrow, but two days later, when she again inquired, Elliot claimed never to have said it.

Joe said, "You know perfectly well what you said, and if you're thinking that way, it's my business because it threatens us as a couple. I've been mulling, and now I need to talk about it, to find out what its edges are, to find out what you meant and why you told me and why now and what you plan to do about it. Do you want to peg men, is that it?"

Elliot again said that she hadn't said it. Joe was just—Joe did this. Made up stories.

"I didn't make it up," Joe told her firmly.

"You know you do this," said Elliot.

"I'm calling you on something distressing you said. Don't make me lose respect for you, Elliot."

Elliot raised her hands palms forward. "I just never said it, Joe."

Eventually, over time, when nothing came of it, Joe had more or less forgotten it. More or less. It only flickered through her brain during insecure moments. *Really* insecure moments.

If Scout stayed asleep, if she could transfer her to the cradle, maybe Joe could sneak upstairs and surprise Ell, curl up, bask a little in the breeze from the fan, admire Elliot's honed muscles. Her earthy smell. She hadn't done stairs yet, except for outside. She gingerly transferred Scout to the cradle and crept up the stairs. When she reached the door, she saw Elliot, back arched, mastectomy scars white, bringing herself to orgasm in front of the TV to the sight of herself being pegged by Logan. In the video, she still had breasts. Ell stifled a cry as she saw Joe, and stuttered into an orgasm at the same time. Joe's own clit twitched helplessly.

"You have *sex tapes?*"

Did Ell still need to see old footage? Maybe the breasts were incidental. These were the sorts of questions they never asked each other. In some sense, Ell's life was her life, and Joe's life was hers. She missed the intimacy of their brand-new time, the spontaneous dancing in the kitchen, the wrestling, board game nights. Now they sealed themselves up behind individual screens—not even TV, which at least they'd watched together. *What are you watching? I'm on FB. What are you watching? Harold and Maude.*

Elliot just looked at her, exasperated. She'd wrecked the orgasm, Joe guessed.

Joe sat down on the bed. She half thought, *I should just have joined her. I should have seen what footage of the two sexiest women in my life together would do to me.* "Are you okay? I heard you in the bathroom."

"What? Go 'way, no. You're embarrassing me."

Joe walked herself down the stairs while Elliot ran after her, hopping to get into her pajama bottoms. "I'm really sorry, Joe. It's not what you think."

Joe turned from the banister. "What do I think?"

"You think I don't want you. I know you think that. I wish—"

What do you wish? thought Joe. There were more broken sentences than finished ones these days. "I just had your baby, and it's still not me you're fantasizing about. What the fuck am I to you, Ell? Just some brood mare?" White hot anger flicking in her veins. "Fuck you. Fuck you and fuck Logan and fuck motherhood. This sitting around leaking from my breasts with stitches in my cunt while you have sex with someone else? Hoop that. Uh-uh. I am not a moron. And while we're at it, someone ought to go over there and tell that poor woman Logan's planning to marry that she had better fucking say no because Logan is never going to be any good."

"You *like* Logan. Come on, Joe, you know you do." Elliot had her pants up and strode after Joe.

"So what? That's like liking crystal meth. Sooner or later your teeth are gonna rot."

"You're not fair to them, Joe."

Joe coughed. "Fair? Like Logan needs me in any capacity to be fair?"

"They don't have many friends. Logan needs us to be there for them. We have to do more than just share property."

"They really don't, Elliot."

"They do—and you know what? I don't even understand why you're huffy about this."

"You know what, Ell? Fuck off into the sea."

AJAX

Though the temperature had dropped with the encroaching storm, it was still hot. Logan cranked the air con, built a fire: paper, kindling, bigger logs. They patted the couch, handed Ajax a snifter of brandy. Toby dragged his ploofy bed toward the heat; Ajax laughed, snuggling in while Logan rotated their glass. "This is the epitome of horrible for the environment, you know," said Ajax. "Making it cold so you can heat it?"

Logan shrugged.

Ajax sighed. Should she object? Did she always have to object to everything? "I'll just pretend it's snowing out there." She raised her glass. "I don't know if I'm hot or cold, honestly. Okay, imagine we're in Whistler at a romantic ski chalet."

"Poof!" said Logan. "It's winter."

"It almost is in here now," said Ajax. After the lake, her hair was coated and filthy. She'd pulled it into a mass on top of her head, but the curls hung heavily. She broke out in goosebumps. She said, "That just makes me think of how I miss you when I go home."

"We should fix that," Logan said, wrapping Ajax in a bear hug so they fell back together on the couch. Logan pulled off Ajax's shorts and top. "We should fix that really soon." Logan softly kissed her, exploring her mouth, her puckered nipple tips. They stood Ajax on her feet, stood up and freckled delicate kisses across Ajax's shoulder blades, her breasts. They sat, slid Ajax's panties down her legs, kissed her hips, turned her around and nibbled her ass. Ajax shuddered. Her hands roamed Logan's face, reading Logan's skin like braille, as if she could take in everything that had happened to Logan before tonight: their infancy, their teen years, their lovers, their disappointments, their delights. Ajax touched Logan's mouth, pinching their lips as she kissed them. Logan licked the side of Ajax's lips.

"Fuck me halfway to heaven, honey," said Ajax.

"Nuts to purgatory," said Logan. They stood, grabbed the top knot of Ajax's hair, pulled back hard. "I'm sending you to the moon."

Logan turned off the air, damped the fire, threw open the windows.

The antler chandelier swayed, and on the chunky pine table, ivory candles sputtered.

Ajax noticed a peculiar pressure in her ears.

Ajax watched Logan turn off ordinary life, become the prowling, haunting top Ajax needed. "Hands over your head," said Logan, eyes narrowing.

Thunder rumbled distantly, lightning electrifying their windows, making Ajax startle. She was on alert anyway when they had sex—instantly open, wanting, but also on guard because Logan changed things up so she never knew what was coming her way. She lifted her arms.

Logan's eyes bleached to the lightest wolf-grey.

An ornate French mantel clock ticked out seconds.

"Up against the wall," said Logan. They walked behind

Ajax, cupped her elbows, pressed her hard. "Keep your arms up. Legs apart. Eyes closed. Don't look."

Ajax could hear Logan moving around the room and moaned.

Minutes later, Logan's nipples contacted Ajax's spine, stroking Ajax's back on either side of her spine. *No binder.* Logan spun her, rubbed nipples to nipples, fullness to fullness. Then, kneeling, pushed legs wide to rub a nipple over Ajax's clit.

Ajax pushed toward her.

"I'm going to enjoy fucking you."

Ajax said, "Now, now. Oh, please."

Crickets falling silent. Thunder, the cracking lightning. Logan's tongue slid across Ajax's leg, the insides of her thighs, continued higher. They pushed Ajax down, ran their nipple over Ajax's mouth, told her she couldn't close her mouth on it.

"Remember strippers' rules?"

Logan had taken her to a Toronto strip club, to the private, low-ceilinged red rooms for a lap dance. The cubicles had looked like first-class airline seats, except for its decrepitude and the rhum in the air—Logan and Ajax squeezed into one cubicle.

Sweethearts, the dancer said. *You are, aren't you, you two? You're lovebirds. You a fella, Mister, or you a girl?* She ran her hands up Logan's binder. *Honey, you got sweet boobs. Where're you from? I'm from Vancouver.*

I'm from Vancouver, too.

Get on out. Burnaby.

Harsh whisper in Ajax's ear: *Never tell a stripper anything true.*

They watched her dance, her platforms six inches of gleaming plastic. Ajax scanned up her legs, to her face-level crotch: silver lamé thong, shaking bells. Pasties.

Don't fucking tell her anything, whispered Logan again.

I got me some lesbians, she said and Ajax giggled. They could be lesbians; why not?

The dancer ground on Logan, moved to Ajax, tweaked Ajax's left nipple, hard. *You are such a relief from my usual clientele, I can't tell you, honey.*

Ajax laughed.

Stop laughing, hissed Logan.

But Ajax couldn't stop. The tiny-breasted stripper yanked Ajax's shirt up and then slid up her body with her own until her nipples—big, brown—ran across Ajax's face. Then into her laughing mouth. A raspberry-nipple brushed her tongue.

Logan said, *Don't you dare suck that. If you suck that, we'll get the boot.*

The stripper said, *Spank me.*

Logan said, *You can do what she asks you to do, but that's it.*

You've been here before, darlin', the stripper told Logan. *You do it.*

Logan spanked her.

Spank me, she said again to Ajax.

Ajax could not stop laughing. She slapped her.

Oww! the dancer cried and rubbed her ass.

McIntyre, that is not how you hit a woman, said Logan. *You cup your hand like this.* She hit the stripper again. *It makes a sound but it doesn't hurt.*

The stripper crammed Logan's cowboy hat onto her head; her hair slapped Ajax's face. She pulled back and gyrated. *Ride 'em, cowgirls. Keep them doggies moving.* She stopped grinding on Logan a minute and confirmed their cock. *Yeehaw!*

Now Logan dragged Ajax back into the present. "Remember that? Strippers' rules. You can only do what I tell you to do."

Weak-kneed, Ajax said, "Please, please, please." She could smell her cunt on Logan's nipple. She opened her eyes. "Oh god," said Ajax, lowering her arms. She thought nothing besides *I want you I want you I want you.*

Logan stood back. Moved her to the wall. Watched her, said, "Did you open your eyes without permission? Did you lower your arms? Don't you even think of moving again."

"*Asshole,*" said Ajax cheerfully; she pressed her knuckles to the wall obediently. Longed to touch. Everything was hot, suddenly, too hot—the waning fire (what was with all the fucking mid-heatwave fires?), her skin, Logan's ears where the tips flamed red. But a breeze was coming up—the wind was chilly against wet skin.

"Dirty-mouthed thing," said Logan, frowning. Toby moaned and rolled over.

"And if I am?" Ajax's chin lifted.

Logan slit their eyes. "I might punish you. You've already been bad."

There was a pause while the possibility hung in the air. Every time Logan wet her nipples, the wind slid across them like fingers.

"Or not." Logan smiled.

"Oh god, Logan, fuck. Logan, fuck. That is so not fair." Fire guttering. Candles side-waving. Growing darker. Logan nude but for black leather harness with buckles, black cock. Boobs surprisingly round.

"Anticipation suits you, McIntyre." Logan flicked Ajax's left nipple, making her jump. "See what it does to you, how hard your nipples are?"

"Logan, fuck me. Come on, touch me."

Logan stroked their cock, added lube.

Ajax pressed her breasts toward them.

"Back against the wall, Ajax. Believe me when I say that I can out-wait you any day."

"But think of the time wasted."

"Yeah, Ajax? I'm wasting time? How wet are you?" Logan slid a finger between Ajax's thighs so it came up shining. "As it happens, you can wait longer."

"I can't, I can't," said Ajax. "Fuck off."

"If you're so eager, touch yourself," said Logan, running hands across their own breasts, squeezing their nipples tight. Sliding their hands along their cock.

"Please, please, please. I'm fucking out of my mind."

"I'm touching *myself*." Meandering fingers, Logan rubbed their clit, put their fingers in their own mouth. "I can come like this; I don't need you." But still, they ran their fingers across Ajax's lips.

Ajax licked her lips, tried to capture Logan, but Logan pressed her back, a firm hand on her shoulder. "Don't you move."

"Or what?"

"Make your clit wet. Make it stand up. Rub it for me, honey." Logan pinched Ajax's left nipple.

Ajax gasped.

Logan said, "Do what you're told when you're told to do it. Do it now, Ajax."

But Ajax couldn't.

"I'm not pleased," said Logan. They produced alligator clips, slid the rubber tips over Ajax's nipples, fastened them—it hurt significantly. The chain dangled cold between Ajax's breasts. Logan took it like it was reins and drew Ajax to the couch, placed Ajax in front of her. "Spread your legs. Tell me what you want me to do to you."

"I don't know, I don't know." Ajax didn't know. Anything.

Logan yanked the nipple chain.

Ajax spread her legs. Heard moisture crackle between her thighs.

"You do know what you want. Now *I* need to know. Have you been bad?" Logan huffed hot air between her legs. "You've been bad, Ajax, haven't you?" Logan reached a tongue tip to Ajax's clit. Just that, the barely rotating tip of their tongue. Kept it there while Ajax gasped.

With a toss of wind chimes, rain boiled into the lake. Logan would, no doubt—no doubt—soon strip her raw. If only more lovers realized the devastating power of softness. It would make what was coming both worse, and so much better.

"Say it," said Logan, releasing Ajax.

So Ajax said it, but quietly, hushed from stubbornness. "I've been bad." Crotch zap in response.

Logan raised a hand. "You don't sound convinced."

Ajax shook her head—not *No, I'm not convinced*, but *No, I refuse to succumb. Make me.* "I've been bad, Logan. I don't mean to be bad, but I am, I'm bad." The reluctance with which she gave in. The reluctance with which she abandoned equality.

"And what happens to bad girls, do you know? Here at my cottage?"

Was the cottage the same as every location they fucked? Because if it was, she knew what her role was, what her next line of dialogue might be.

When she didn't say anything, Logan tugged the nipple clamps harder, bent, and ran their tongue over the protruding bleached, bloodless brown tips of Ajax's nipples. "Bad girls have to be punished, don't they?"

"I don't know."

"You do know." Logan stared hard with their etiolated eyes. The floor-length red curtains jeté'd into the room.

Ajax thought, *Play along, play along, play along. Games belong in the bedroom.* But it was dastardly hard to give in.

"Okay," said Ajax, resistance in her tone of voice. "Yes. Bad girls need to be punished."

"And who's been bad?"

That cunt smell. Sharp, demanding. Smell of the lake. Maybe a star-smell, too, elemental. "I have been."

"Ajax, we either do this, or we don't do this. All in. Game on."

Ajax said it more resolutely. "I've been naughty."

Logan grabbed her by the hips. "What have you wanted me to do to you?"

"Spank me." Ajax took a huge breath. "And sodomize me."

Logan raised their eyebrows. "What did I spank you with?"

"Oh god."

Logan ran their hand up the sides of Ajax's body, smacked the side of her right breast. The sound of the slap.

"Your hand."

"Were you bent over a table?" They pointed. "That table?"

Ajax turned to look at the dining room table. Where they'd eaten just hours earlier. *Fantasy*, she thought. "Over your knee."

Logan's hands trickled up Ajax's back, whispers of touch.

"Did I spank you with anything else?"

"No. Yes. A wooden paddle."

Logan nodded, said, "Why? Why should I?"

Ajax bit her lip. Why *should* she spank her? Why *would* she spank her? Stay in vanilla because this wasn't PC? Stay in vanilla because a white woman wailing on a black woman was clichéd? Do it because it was hot? Do it because she was a bottom? Do it because she was a bottom with a top that screwed on just right? Cunt juice dripped down her thighs—she could feel it. She knew what it looked like from watching former lovers—it slid milky as pearls. She wondered if she'd ever see Logan's cunt. Was the very expression "Logan's cunt" a misnomer? They didn't have a cunt as much as a *difficulty* between their legs, and it wasn't something they cared to share. No chains of pearls here.

"You just should," Ajax said. She kicked herself for leaving the moment—for thinking. If she wanted to come, and she did, if she wanted to make that bond with Logan, she needed a blank brain, or an effectively fantasizing brain, at least, but definitely not this, this analysis of what her lover had gone through/was going through/would go through, if, as Ajax suspected they would, they officially transitioned. Or the wave of clit-deflating sadness that always followed imagining Logan's pain.

Shitballs on speed. Shut up, brain.

"I asked you why." Logan stopped touching her, raised their eyebrows, the right higher.

"I've been bad," Ajax repeated, swallowing. Even clamped and blanched, her nipples hardened further in a waft of wind. They grew numb. Bad, because she knew where Logan taking the clips off would take her.

"Have you?"

"I need you to spank me." And this time, in a surge of desire, Ajax meant it. She really, really fucking meant it. Desire thumped, a beat inside her.

"It's going to hurt," said Logan leaning forward to grip

Ajax's hips. "It will be for punishment. Do you understand that?"

What had she fucking done wrong? Nothing. Insignificant shit. *Nothing nothing nothing.* As if that mattered one whit. Ajax took a breath. "Hurt me then. Hurt me so good." Giving permission to be hurt made her groan. So often in her life—in her marriage—she'd been hurt without consent. This was better. This was so much better. This took nasty kinks and ironed them.

She wasn't naïve about this, its pleasures and utilities. Neither was she well-practiced, as she assumed Logan was.

"You have to be corrected," said Logan. "In your fantasy, how did I fuck your ass?"

Big breath. Working to stabilize herself. Heat thumping irregularly—a constant accompaniment for Ajax during sex. "Me on my stomach, ass in the air."

Logan put the chain of the nipple clamps in Ajax's mouth. "Tug," they said.

And Ajax obediently did. The clamps pulled, sending out shocks. Her own pain, her personally caused pain. Which fucked her mind.

Logan stroked themself. "With this cock?"

"Too big," said Ajax, gasping not at the impossibility but at the realization that sodomy was certainly on tonight's menu.

"Have you taken cocks up your ass before, Ajax? Other than mine?"

"Yes."

"Smaller ones?"

"Yes."

"You like it up the ass."

"Yes." It was true. She always had; her ass gave her more pleasures than her cunt, which themselves were not insignificant.

"Does it hurt to have a cock up your ass?" Logan lubed their hand, ran it around the tip of their cock, moved it down and up.

"It does hurt," said Ajax. "It makes me come."

"So you like pain, Ajax?"

"I like the edges of pain. I like domination more. I like surprises during sex. I like voice." Ajax was about to say that the nipple clamps were too much—but they were only *almost* too much, the knife-edge where pain nearly morphed into pleasure. She dealt with pain all the time because of her bad heart; decades of angina, months of unstable angina, two heart attacks. She knew more than most people about how to absorb and transform agony.

Logan looked at her sternly. "Bend over my knee."

Ajax stood there. There it was. The order. Could she? Could she allow herself to do it? Even her *desire* to obey, to be this raggy-boneyard of anti-feminist compliance, humiliated her. Which was the point, surely. *Subjugate, McIntyre.*

Logan released their cock. "Jesus, you're disobedient. You need training. Turn around, right now, hands over your head." A tone brooking no opposition, though Ajax had to wonder what would happen if she refused—if she used her safe word or just said, *Um, hey, sorry, not into it after all*. What would

Logan do to her if she *didn't* bend? Logan's voice low, growly: "Do what I say right now."

Ajax spit out the chain, turned and lifted her arms, which caused the nipple clamps to pull differently. She waited, but Logan didn't do anything. Ajax tried not to mutter. Logan could guess every goddamned puke-wheeling button she had—even while doing new things. They made her stand there wondering. After minutes—three, five? too many—she felt Logan's breath mist across her buttocks.

Here was how it was supposed to play out: Logan insisted, Ajax obeyed—those were the rules. Top, bottom. How tops got off; how bottoms got off.

Ajax wished the window was closed, that the drapes were pulled. Not that she imagined Elliot or god knows Joe prowling around the cottage in this weather. She wished—what? *Oh, turdballs from hell.* She didn't know what she wished. That they were back in her beloved Bahamas fucking on a private beach with surf galloping toward them?

"Such a bad, bad girl," said Logan. "Will anything make you good again?"

I could write an essay, thought Ajax cheekily. It was the punishment she'd usually meted out to her children. *Write 100 words on why what you did was wrong; include a sincere apology.*

"I'm sorry," said Ajax, feeling precipitously, actually, contrite—more for leaving the scene in her mind, again, than for any imaginary crime. "I'm *really* sorry." Should she say *Go easy on me* when she didn't want that? A good quarter of her wanted to say that, wanted to run to her childhood bedroom, slam the door, and fling herself onto a flouncy bedspread. Power dynamics were fun (except when they weren't).

"Bend over my knee, Ajax. No more bullshit. Do what I say, and do it right now. I've been letting you off easy."

"Okay."

"And what do you say?"

"I said okay," said Ajax, half resentfully. Toby lifted his head, whined, shook his muzzle, and settled back down.

"You say, 'Yes, sir.'"

She searched Logan's pale spooky eyes for a hint of indecision, but didn't find it, so she said it: "Yes, sir." And then bent. She felt silly, clod-hopperish; she was not the smallest woman, and she felt too big for the thighs that meant to hold her. But Logan clamped her in, one of their legs over one of Ajax's. The temperature was dropping. Logan's cock pronged into her stomach.

"This is going to hurt a lot. I'm going to give you thirty-six with my hand, and then I'm switching to a paddle."

"Thirty-six?!" Ajax tried to get up. *Ouch.* Lamely, she said, "But you'll hurt your hand!"

"You want this. Tell me again that you want this."

Was it always a question of this, of saying *yes yes yes*? Of relenting over and over? Control and powerlessness. The power of powerlessness. She said it again.

There was a long moment when nothing happened.

"Do it," Ajax said, gritting her teeth, caught between excitement and nerves. "Go ahead. Do it. I want you to hit me."

Logan's hand came down hard.

The second the pain registered, the slap heard and absorbed, Ajax's eyes bugged. She jerked, gulped, consciously held her position, bracing palms on the floor.

The dog let out a single yip.

Don't think about Logan's carpet, she warned herself, eyeing it, noticing its colours.

Logan's fingertips trickled softly across the skin they'd hit. Wonder in their voice, they said, "I can see exactly the shape of my hand. In red."

"Against my brown ass? Nah," said Ajax. "No, sir."

Logan said they were taking a photograph.

"Um," said Ajax. "Consent for kinky sex and consent for images are two different things and that would be a no, sir, no, thank you."

Logan said, "You have no say in what I do to you." The camera apparently was already easily accessible. Logan stroked her ass. There was no sound of a shutter.

As soon as Ajax's flutter against Logan's invasion had been sweetened into complacency, when she finally expected the tender touch to continue and the next slap not to come, thought that maybe Logan had relented, Logan spanked her again. Ajax yelped. And loved it loved it *loved it.*

Logan spanked Ajax five times on each cheek. Every swat was a ladder rung Ajax had to climb, the stakes rising.

Logan dipped their hand. "Why are you so wet? Did I say you could get wet?

"You make me wet." Ajax pushed her ass higher. "This spanking makes me wet."

More slaps, brisk and unyielding.

Logan hit stung flesh. "Wait, wait, Logan, it's enough. I've had enough."

Logan ignored her, continued. What was Logan experiencing from their side? Were they horny? Near to orgasm?

Ajax said, "No!" and put up a hand to protect her ass.

Logan pressed Ajax's wrist to her lower back, the restraint serving to ignite Ajax's capitulation. "Honey, there are dozens more just like those ones, and they're coming your way now. What do you think a punishment spanking is? When I'm finished all of that, I'm paddling you for getting wet, and when I finish that, I'm taking your ass."

"Oh, for fuck's sake," said Ajax, partly wounded, completely aroused. "Jesus."

"And if you come without permission, believe me, you'll be getting extra. And leaving the scene? For that, you also get extra."

Ajax could feel the slide into orgasm. "Please," said Ajax again, lifting her ass, moving it. "Spank me. Please hurt me good. Hurt me more."

"Does it hurt, baby? It ought to hurt. I hope it hurts." Logan rubbed her ass, then touched her clit so softly that Ajax nearly burst. "You're deeply maroon."

Ajax repeated that it hurt. Her voice sounded disembodied, but she was anything but—for the moment, she was all body; nipples, ass, and cunt. She began to weep from the pain.

"You are not going to be able to sit down," said Logan, spanking her, not waiting between slaps.

Even after Ajax rose and Logan caught sight of her tear-streaked face, they harboured no mercy. They ordered her to bend over the arm of the couch. Ajax balked—out of instinct more than objection; she could not seem to force herself to fold for more. Whatever she had meant by asking to be punished, it was not *this*.

But, of course, it was exactly this. And it was also pain, for once, with a positive outcome. Pain with the O of exclamatory bliss.

Logan sighed, cranky. "Tell me again why we're doing this? Why I bother?"

Ajax folded her hands. "I was bad."

"You were bad, what?"

"I was bad, *sir*," said Ajax.

"You were bad what?"

And it came instinctively from her mouth. "I was bad, *Daddy*." She thought she would try this terrible word.

"What happens to naughty girls who anger their fathers?"

She reached around to gingerly touch her ass; she could feel it swollen and burner-hot. Was the pain soon to become worse? Where would worse pain take her? "They need a lesson, sir. They need to be taught manners and correct behaviours."

During early childhood, in her one-room schoolroom in the Bahamas, kids had been strapped at the principal's desk under photographs of Queen Elizabeth.

Logan released the clamps on Ajax's nipples. The pain was momentarily so dense that Ajax squashed her breasts hard. She'd been brain-stabbed. Logan said, "That they do. So bend, McIntyre. Do what you're told, and soon this will all be over. I'm sure you want my cock up your ass sooner than later, don't you?"

Probably Logan knew that Ajax would go over. Sooner or later, Ajax would submit. Ajax gritted her teeth and bent. The arm of the couch offered better security than Logan's lap had, was padded and more rounded to fit her body, but that quickly became little reassurance when she considered why she was there. She felt even more humiliated than she had when she'd been over Logan's lap. Because of Logan's vantage point?

But she noticed a difference. She was finally letting go, moving toward where the sensations controlled her as much as did Logan.

Her nipples sharply hurt.

"Legs apart," they said sternly. When Ajax didn't obey, Logan jammed their knee between Ajax's legs, forcing the issue. "You're wet down to your knees, I swear. It's unbecoming." Knowing Logan was looking at her privates nearly sent Ajax spilling over some edge. Logan pushed Ajax's shoulders to the seat cushion. "Put your face in your hands and think about why you're here. Think about how bad you were and what's coming."

Logan dripped lube onto her bum crack. Pretended they were going to penetrate her. Moved their fingers near Ajax's asshole but didn't enter. Moved away. Teased more. Penetrated just through the sphincter. Pulled back. Widened the sphincter, let it close. Repeated until Ajax pushed her ass into it. Showed Ajax the paddle with which she would be hit—rectangular, blonde wood—and ran it cold across her body, up and down her arms and legs, chilling her ass. It lulled her, too, into the false sense of security that Logan was seeking.

When the wood first hit Ajax, she jumped and sobbed.

"Don't," said Logan. "Don't jump. I can't allow that."

Twelve fast impacts hurtled Ajax out of summer into some winter darkness, some cold isolation, some icy rejection—and at the same time, built for her a snow palace. Logan slipped fingers into Ajax's ass. "Do it, Ajax. Come now. Squeeze my fingers, honey."

Ajax sobbed outright while she came, a long chain of orgasms that followed one after the other in kaleidoscopic outburst. Her toes shrilled pleasure.

Logan pushed the head of their cock against her asshole.

"Say you want it," said Logan. "Tell me you want me up your ass, Ajax."

"Fuck my ass. Please fuck my ass. Please, Logan. Please. Now. Don't make me wait any longer, baby."

"I'm gonna fuck your ass."

Logan gripped her hips and ground in, the head of their cock achieving a tantalizing slow entry, pausing before the rest followed, like pushing down a French press. They were fucking Ajax's orgasms. As they went deep, their pelvis was cool against Ajax's inflamed ass cheeks.

Logan reached around to twist her nipples, and Ajax yelled from the stupendousness.

Logan came yelling, "Deep in your ass, baby," grunting and pushing, their pubic hair prickling against Ajax's damaged skin.

AJAX

That night, Ajax dreamed of Logan colouring her, only in the dream, Ajax didn't have a body; she was two-dimensional, flat. Logan had crayons, a box of thirty-six Crayolas — Atomic Tangerine, Blue Violet, Inchworm, Jazzberry Jam, Mauvelous, Tickle Me Pink — and was hard at work, but they coloured outside the lines, and every time they spread wax where Ajax ended, Ajax expanded. Scritch of crayon against paper. Ajax could feel the crayon stick, the thick paper, see the name Razzmatazz in black on pink. Fingertips so close Ajax could see whorls of a Fibonnaci spiral. She could see the orange dunes of Namibia, the blue holes of the Bahamas, the Grand Prismatic Spring at Yellowstone. She saw bison, polar bears, cassowaries, sloths hanging from Cecropia trees. Longitudinal stretching, icebergs calving into blue growlers. She saw Logan like she'd never seen a person before. Logan's chin, Logan's throat, where Ajax could track the hot pulse of their jugular vein, the sinewy ropes of their sternothyroid muscles. Logan's hands seemed, somehow, to be creating her, to be actualizing her from a crude charcoal sketch until she was animating, moving in place, then free and fluid. Logan's fingers were stained with colour, a smudge of green across their cheek. Logan's earlobes, Logan's reckless lock of hair slipping past an eyebrow. Logan an artist, pinning Ajax in place then moving her out, making her spill over, a northern glacial waterfall, moss on slippery banks, rivulets of sugar. Making Ajax's eyes skate off the sides of the page, desire fogging out her edges like steam, like geysers, the whole room turning to cloud mist.

Logan wasn't in bed when Ajax woke; Ajax could hear them in the kitchen, smelled pancakes. She stretched in the mussed white sheets. Pretty bedroom—taupe with coral. Comfortable bed, memory foam.

Do you remember what you did last night? the mattress asked.

She found a vase of poppies on the beside table, a card saying happy birthday. She'd forgotten! She was fifty today—a half century. She felt a blur of love, wondered what else Logan had planned.

"Hey," she said at the door of the kitchen, tying up her robe. "I dreamed you coloured me into existence or something."

Logan wrangled bacon in a spitting cast-iron frying pan and lifted their cheek for a kiss.

"It was kinda romantic," said Ajax, smiling. "Kinda spiritual, too, for an atheist."

"Happy birthday, gorgeous," said Logan. "Mind feeding Toby? Just open that can and dump it in his bowl and freshen up his water."

"Remember that other dream I had when we first started going out?" said Ajax, turning the can of dog food in her hands. "That dream where everything felt right instead of traumatic? It was like that, sort of. Same affect, right? Saying I'm safe with you. I'm bigger with you than without you. More me."

After feeding Toby, Ajax set the porch table, helped carry

plates. Tiny vases of flowers and scattered confetti dotted the tabletop. Red floor, green/blue table with peeling paint. Toy boat in the corner, sail faded pink. Wicker furniture. "I'm touched," she told Logan, swimming her finger through confetti. "I like this place. Very shabby chic."

Logan buttered their pancakes. "Different than my condo, right?" Their condo was stainless and leather mixed with antiques. Here, there were five double beds on the second storey plus a raft of bunk beds—country at its most relaxed. "Accommodates twenty, actually, pretty comfortably."

"Wow," said Ajax. She sat, rearranging herself gingerly on what she thought was a feathered seat cushion. Pain was not a memory—she carried it with her. "Tell me how you came to build it. You broke up with Elliot ..."

They could hear the scrape of Toby's collar on the food dish. "Elliot turfed me out on my ear," said Logan. "I'm an old battle axe; I handled it." Logan shrugged, dotted their mouth with the napkin. "Ell and I wanted a place where people could gather. I think we were thinking dishevelled weekends, music, booze, campfires, s'mores on the barbie, orgies. You know. We did some of that, or I did, and Ell joined in when she felt like it. She was—busy elsewhere most of the time." Logan sounded wistful. "So ... How's it feel to turn fifty?"

Ajax picked up the maple syrup bottle with its log cabin graphic. "Not as sweet as maple syrup."

Logan laughed. "Consider the alternative."

As if Ajax ever forgot the alternative. Fifty or death.

Excellent on the choices, world, she thought. She wondered whether she was glad to be fifty—glad to be in what people called her second half century. Which in her case was more likely to be five years or ten or fifteen—fifteen if she was exceedingly fortunate. At what point did one's physical ailments win? Not just the body-battle, but the battle for one's mind? When did being in continual un-chosen pain cease to be worth it? She could imagine a time when she would be ready to stop. She was not sure why Logan—why anyone, really—would love her at her age and general state of decrepitude. Inside her, nothing worked well. Cranky kidneys, cranky heart, brain addled from TIAs—transient ischemic attacks, or mini-strokes. Angina— the squeezing of the de-oxygenated heart. Heart failure; an organ that could not pump well enough. Hypertrophic heart, enlarged past common sense. Peripheral vascular disease giving her de-oxygenated limbs. Arrythmias. Her body was bad on the outside, too: Crappy ankles, knees, hips, lower back, rotator cuffs. Osteoarthritis. Generally in bad shape. She heaved a sigh. Getting old was not for the meek. Hell, *living* was not.

"Thanks for cooking again."

"You can cook anytime," said Logan.

"I will." Ajax reached over for Logan's hand. How could she tell them that when they'd drawn her off the page, they had, in some crazy way, set her free? How could a fifty-year-old woman with a very sore bum even say that? At some age, didn't getting drawn off the page make you redundant?

Fifty!

"Not this weekend, though. This is my weekend to coddle you." Crinkly smile.

Ajax grinned back. Maybe to other people this would seem like a big birthday; to her, it seemed like a life crisis. To her, it was hardly something to celebrate. "My ass really hurts, by the way. In case you were wondering."

Logan grinned. "I can see that. To be expected. I can't really say it breaks my heart. Perhaps the next time, you won't be naughty. Perhaps you'll mind your p's and q's."

"Fuck right off." Ajax laughed.

"Indeed," said Logan picking up a piece of bacon. "Indeed, I will do just that, as soon as I get that robe off you."

JOE

Joe came blearily awake to Elliot talking in the kitchen. Where was Scout? She couldn't see her baby, who surely had been sleeping right next to her, and stumbled up in a blind panic, pajamas askew, hair no doubt a mess. She found the baby tucked over Elliot's shoulder in the kitchen, trying frantically to chew her fist—relief, a flood of it—while Elliot poured coffee for ... Who the hell was she pouring coffee for? Some butchy teenager wearing a tool belt and a half-clean T-shirt with rolled-up sleeves, someone Joe might've been hot for twenty years ago. Joe was acutely aware that her pajamas were wet from a let-down; she probably stank.

She backed away, sticky and gross, reluctant to make a bad impression.

"This is Scotia," Elliot said. "Scotia's spending the summer north; she's here to help me fix the siding." Elliot in paint-streaked pants and a tool belt.

"How do you do?" Joe said, wishing she had a robe to pull around her. "Ell, can I talk to you, please?"

The girl said, "Pleased to meet you, Ma'am."

Ma'am? Joe thought. *Ma'am?*

Elliot grinned at the carpenter. "Milk? Sugar?"

"Elliot, a minute?" Joe yanked Elliot into the hallway, taking Scout off her shoulder. "Why the hell are you having work done now, with the baby brand new, and why didn't you give me a heads up?"

"I told you a few days ago," said Elliot. "Anyway, we won't be long." She held her stomach. "I won't work long; I'm *still* sick." Peeved voice.

Joe hissed, mad but quiet. "Carpentry, for god's sake. This can wait, Ell. This can be done next month. Next *year*." Joe's mind went to sex, Elliot and Scotia. Because apparently she was the worst poly-partner *ever*.

"This was Scotia's only open window. Don't get your shit in a knot. You know it's not good for you, and it's not good for my baby. You know stress hormones go right to your milk."

"Did you honestly just say that?" Joe opened her mouth wide in outrage. "*My* baby? I am so tired of being patronized. And Scout is just as much mine as yours."

"I'm not patronizing you, and I'm perfectly aware of Scout's parenthood. I'm just saying you could monitor your moods. You're hormonal, so why not just let a few things slide?"

Joe's mouth dropped open.

"If you need me, I'll be outside. You can text me, and I'll be at your side in thirty seconds. That's fair. You have to admit, that's fair."

Scout let out the piercing but wobbly cry of newborns, but Joe ignored her and whispered fiercely, "This is not about being fair, Elliot. She won't be little for very long."

The house was already warm, the sun laddering up the sky, a yolk in its sizzling blue frying pan.

"I was keeping Scout quiet so you could sleep in. How about just saying thanks?"

"You want an award? For mothering your child?"

"So should I tell Scotia to leave? Is that what you want?" When Elliot got angry, her mouth changed shape, the middle of her upper lip plunging.

"Please go fix the siding," said Joe. "Because that's what our lives hinge on. By all means."

"We'll work fast. We'll be done by three with two of us."

Joe wanted to give Scout back to Elliot to tend now that she was crying. "Just take her for a few minutes while I pee and brush my teeth."

"What? I can't—"

Joe passed her the baby and walked away. Elliot went back to Scotia; Joe heard her laugh self-consciously over the baby's wails.

All day long she heard sawing and nailing; it felt like Elliot and Scotia were hammering into Joe's skull. She looked around: diapers, wet wipes, baby powder, zinc cream, sleepers, breast pads in nursing bras, leaking tits, the smell of the baby, the baby's fine red hair, the whorls of the baby's ears. A glass of water on the TV stand. Tousled blankets. Bird song. Heat. Thermometer. Fan. Half-eaten breakfast. Half-eaten lunch. Half-eaten apple. Half-eaten peach. Banana peel. Coconut cream for her sore nipples. Lactation tea. Wasps and flies buzzing. Stink bugs. Flour moths. Facebook and IMs when the Wi-Fi worked. Doing pretty much everything one-handed because she had hold of Scout in the other arm. Outside the window, hummingbirds dipped into nectar; around the feeders were spotted towhees and chickadees, and, sometimes, the long sharp call of a flicker demanded suet. As the day wore on, Joe got more furious instead of less.

Why had Joe married someone poly to begin with? Because Elliot was Elliot, with her ready laugh, her confidence, her intelligence, her spark, and, let's face it, her wealth and the comforts and safety it brought. Poly was the deal—take none of the package or take everything. Poly had seemed like freedom to Joe. If she hadn't used it but the once, did that mean she should expect or demand that Elliot change? This week, since the birth, and for a few highly pregnant months, she had needed Ell to become someone she was not. She needed Ell to be sloppily romantic in a way she never could be.

Joe had changed, not Elliot. This was not on Elliot.

Joe put on her baby wrap and tucked Scout inside. The baby seemed positively octopedal—all those limbs—Joe in her flip flops picked her very careful, slow way down to the dock, glad that they had put in railings the year before (carpentry, yes, carpentry they had actually needed). For the first time, she realized she was a mother in the world with an infant to protect, and this state of affairs wasn't going to go away. She tucked the two of them under the floppy green umbrella, then fretted about whether refracted sunshine could hurt Scout's tender skin. Could you even use sunscreen on newborns?

Except for the banging up at the house behind her, the morning was lovely. Ravens poked through the boughs of the cedars imparting the raucous news of the day. In the rookery a little farther around the tip of the island, herons squawked and gabbed, and the young, nearly fledging, assumably fan-flapped their wings. In the shallows, frogs leaped. From where she sat, Joe could see minnows and trout fry circling in murky lake water. Blue jays screamed through the branches.

Something made her turn. Logan and Ajax picking their way down to the dock, Toby a small horse behind them. Toby stayed on land, refusing to step onto the dock, and sometimes woofing his abandonment. Joe's breath caught when she saw Logan.

"I'm so glad you came down," said Ajax. "May I?"

Joe hadn't even realized her arms were sore until Scout was out of them. Ajax situated herself so that the sun wouldn't touch Scout's fragile skin and crooned, "Oh my god, Scout, you are the sweetest. She's so small and perfect, Joe. Logan, honey, look how adorable this baby is."

"And strong," said Joe, "and capable." How could a newborn be either strong or capable? But it seemed important to surpass stereotypes.

"Strong, yes!" said Ajax. "Ferocious! Look how solid her neck is! Linebacker shoulders, I can tell. You can see her moms work out. Totally." She winked at Joe.

"What on earth is Elliot hammering at now?" said Logan, spreading out a towel. They shucked down to a sports bra and swim trunks, slathered on sun protection. "It's Saturday. July. Can't she and her friend just come join us?"

"I completely don't know the answer," said Joe.

"Let me get that," said Ajax. She handed Scout back to Joe before spreading lotion across Logan's back.

"Elliot's at loose ends," said Joe apologetically. She watched the tenderness between the couple enviously. Would they make it? Logan a playboy and Ajax old and, from what she'd heard, fragile. Logan a bald eagle; Ajax a mouse. Joe doubted that Ajax was likely to stand up for herself against the high-rise that was Logan, the force of nature that was Logan. Maybe Logan hadn't been upset with Ajax yet, but they had a sizeable temper, a sarcasm that unwound mortal women, and Elliot had once implied they were capable of physical violence—whatever she meant by that. *Did they hit you?* Joe had asked, but Elliot had gone mute. "Ell can't handle pat leave. Three weeks and she's already snaky."

"You guys here all summer?" Ajax asked.

Joe nodded. "Some idiot's romantic idea of a home birth and forty days of keeping the baby close." She grinned and shrugged. "Okay, my idea, though why I thought labour could be romantic completely escapes me now. I thought of it as warm and candlelit, the babelet delivered to the waiting warm arms of her moms. Ha! It was nothing like that. Abso-freaking-lutely nothing."

Ajax laughed, moved on the dock. In the lake, a fish jumped, striped bass or carp, maybe.

"Plus the romance of parenting went out the window pretty quick when I couldn't figure out how I was supposed to pee. I can't even pull my pants down carrying her. Maybe if I had a kangaroo pouch. Scout would fit with a little redesign"—she grabbed her postpartum paunch—"but alas." She kissed Scout's head. "I'll bet you Ell wants to go back to the city by next week. She'd probably build a suburb here, if she could, just to have something to do." But the problem was deeper inside Joe's wife than that, more serious than restlessness, Joe suspected. She just didn't know what it was.

"I'll eat my hand if I ever see that woman satisfied," said Logan.

"Well, Logan, you don't have to shake on the salt and pepper at this point. Problem is, I go around feeling like I've got an anchor in my stomach. Something heavy thrown overboard. I've been weepy and sad and needy, and the baby cries, and it's all a big mess at our house," said Joe. "I caught Ell watching sex tapes last night, and I blew up at her." She did not say: *Sex tapes of you.* "I don't even know what I expect from her. I really don't even know. And could she give it to me if I did? All those years in fertility treatments—we've both been wacko, I know. Now I'm in a mash-up of jealousy, registering some threat, and it drives me *crazy* that she's got Scotia here, because, is *that* it?"

"Elliot is not easy," said Logan.

"*Hard but worth it* is how that goes, right? This is not a good week." Joe tried to bring logic to bear. "I mean, obviously, except for having had a baby. Scout is pretty great."

The sun was high overhead and hot even through the umbrella. A fringe of water lilies bobbed beside the reeds, and far out on the water a Canada goose paddled with its chain of goslings.

"Ell ought to smarten up," said Logan.

"I'm sorry to be dumping on you," said Joe. She moved her nose across Scout's head, the soft red hair like feathers. "But Ell's an idiot."

"You know you probably have a touch of postpartum blues, right? She pretends that she's so tough, but she wanted that baby."

"We tried to get ready, but we weren't actually. We weren't prepared. We had no freaking clue what it would really be like."

Ajax said, "Adapting takes time, is all. Six months from now, when infancy is over, you two will probably feel like you were always mothers."

Ajax crossed to kiss Joe's cheek. "Too hot," she said. She dove, broke the surface, and yelled for Logan to join her.

Joe and Logan watched Ajax. Joe whispered, "Ell told me about tonight. We'll make ourselves scarce. Congratulations. So awesome."

Logan smiled. "Hey, she didn't say yes yet."

"Think she might not?"

Dragonflies motored through the water lilies. There was a weight to the heat now. Logan moved back under the umbrella.

Laughter silted from the cabin; Elliot and Scotia.

"I can understand why she wouldn't." Logan pushed back in the chair, arms behind their head, puffs of armpit hair. They didn't have their binder on, and Joe could make out the outlines of breasts through the sports bra. Thought, *Don't go there.* "But I really like her, Joe. I've never felt like this."

"I can see that," said Joe. "The way you look at her. It *feels* different."

"I guess ... I never thought I'd feel love, Joe. I got pretty used to that, one superficial relationship after the other. You know me. I carouse. I drink too much. I give women a rough time—I choose the wrong ones, I never call them when I say I will. I lose interest. I don't seem to choose people I'd want to take to firm events—they don't travel well. Ell was the best of the bunch, which is saying something since all we did, I think, was drink and fight. But Ajax is different. She's not a pushover, but she's kind. She's smart, she's funny. But she does what I do—keeps choosing people who treat her poorly. I think she's easy to treat badly because she's guileless. Even at fifty. I guess I'm not that far behind her, but—fifty. It seems so old." Logan waved to Ajax, who was now out in the middle of the lake. "I'm just—I'm sweet on her. Sweet on her like a teenager. She's sick, is the thing. She might just say no to save me from that."

"Sick how?" Joe had heard, but only in vague terms. A dragonfly took a nip out of Joe's leg and she cursed, jerked with the baby in her arms, which half-woke Scout. She jiggled her back to sleep.

"She doesn't want me to try to save her, and she might think that's what the proposal is, and what the fuck do I know, maybe it is, in part. I really do want to look after her. She's had a lot of rotten luck. Enough bad luck for four people."

"She's fifty years old though. She's not twelve, Logan."

"No, I know, and she'd say that too. She would."

Scout cried, her neck slick against Joe's arm, and Joe lifted her top, worked at getting Scout latched. "I guess I mean, be realistic. She has vulnerabilities, but you have to feel she's your equal or forget it, it won't work. Do you?"

Logan watched her nurse. "I hope Ell knows what she has with you, Joe."

"I don't know why she let *you* go, frankly. Or why you let her."

"We were a mismatch from the get-go," said Logan. "All sex fizz."

"Sex be good," said Joe. She grinned. "I think I remember that."

Logan had a spot of white sunscreen on their nose that hadn't been rubbed in.

Joe said, "Don't sleep with Ell again, okay?"

Logan looked at her. There was history shooting between them, things said with eyes and yearning. "I'm not sleeping with Elliot or anyone else again, Joe. If Ajax says yes, I'm pledging fidelity tonight."

There was a long pause while they listened to the baby suckling. "Well," said Joe finally. "I really hope she says yes."

They sat like that for a minute, listening to the hammering up at the cottage.

Joe said, "Isn't this just completely Elliot, how she tries to be helpful and she *is,* only not in the way that you need? Look at these stupid life preservers attached to the dock. If someone was drowning, do you think we could get them loose soon enough? So Elliot."

Logan laughed. "That time I broke my leg, she spent a day looking for the perfect crutches instead of being with me." They scratched their head. "I'll keep the baby if you want to swim."

Joe looked at them. Logan with a baby—oxymoron. "Here," she said, passing Scout over, standing, stretching. "Just jiggle her a lot. I will swim."

She stripped and dove in. Wished it was more refreshing—it was tepid, nearly hot, and her stitches burned something awful. Still, it was good. Good. And she needed more good.

AJAX

Ajax and Logan spent the rest of the day flaked out on the dock slathered in sunscreen, staying as much under the umbrella as they could. Every time the heat boiled toward them, they floated out on huge inner tubes. Once they snoozed, marooning themselves in lily pads. Ajax wore a bathing suit to cover up the sex damage—which she'd showed Logan was fully purple, an ecchymosis, a spectacular bruise. Whatever else happened between them, she would not be repeating last night every day of her life. "I must be careful with my lover's skin," Logan had said, patting her bottom softly. "Because my lover is precious."

Logan hauled out a third inner tube and an anchor; they floated out in the warm water with the third tube carrying an ice chest of lemonade and vodka coolers, their flotilla roped.

"There's such a thing as true love," Logan said, nodding, head back, eyes closed.

"Maybe," said Ajax. How true could love be when it would invariably crumple and die at some future juncture?

Logan half-opened an eye. "You're a cynic, McIntyre."

"There's a whole goddamned lot in this world that works against relationships going forward." Ajax chugged her lemonade.

"Like what, for instance?"

"I don't know. Infidelity."

"I'm monogamous." Logan said this with absolute clarity. *Always?* Ajax wanted to say. *Are you always monogamous?*

Bull-pucky. "Look, I don't ask for monogamy prior to commitment, so you do what you want. But ... money. Money is a big fucking issue."

"I have enough. And there's always more where that came from."

"Those kind of disparities—your income, mine. You being a top and me a bottom."

"We fit," said Logan.

"Yes, it fits, but it's a big power imbalance we've got going here, Beaumont, and incongruities like that have a way of rising up later to whack one across the face."

Logan stirred, shielded their eyes to look at Ajax. "You're not exactly chopped liver yourself. You do pretty well, you know. I thought this was a love affair. I thought it was a birthday celebration. I thought we were up at the cottage on a lake on a blistering summery day. Do you *always* have to fret?"

Ajax sighed. "Point taken."

"Give your heart a little break. Just relax and love me."

Ajax pulled another can from the inner tube, popped the lid, swigged.

"Just float," ordered Logan.

So they floated.

A couple hours later, Scotia and Elliot threw themselves off the dock amidst much merriment. Ajax thought how Joe would feel left out, maybe even crushed, and she wished Elliot would stop being a kid and just go back inside where she was needed.

Logan passed Ajax a colander full of warm peas. Ajax sat on a cushion on the stoop in the sunshine shelling them, rubbing her fingernail along pod seams. Logan blared swing music. Peas round as musical notes fell into Ajax's lap, rolled out along the paint-chipped stair boards. What came to mind was a little girl she'd loved when she was seven, on a back porch forty-some years ago, shelling peas in her Gramma's strainer. Eating more than went into the bowl. Shucking corn, ripping back husks, plucking off the silk threads stuck to the kernels. Racing barefoot to offer up husks to the neighbour's horses. Running back to beg for sugar cubes, which her grandmother dispensed from an orderly cardboard box. Horses' heads large and sweaty, skulls pressing the skin. Twitchy ears, swishing tails. Hair sweeping down over their faces, eyes brown and round with long lashes. Maggie was always nervous but Ajax led her forward, showed her how to hold the sugar cubes with a flat hand, fingers tight.

The sun dipped low toward the beams that photographers called sweet light; slanting in, it turned red blossoms orange.

Logan cooked Memphis-style barbecued ribs, and Ajax prepped veggies and potatoes. After dinner, under a banner that read "Happy Birthday," Logan pulled out a cardboard hat sprinkled with glitter and set it onto Ajax's head. Made her close her eyes and wait. Logan re-appeared wearing a tuxedo, carrying chocolate cake and special ice cream they'd brought from the city, and singing "Joyeux Anniversaire." They presented Ajax with several wrapped packages.

"Blow, blow!" said Logan.

Ajax laughed. "Do I still get a wish if it's a sparkler?"

"*C'est une jour spécial*. You get fifty wishes, and they all are guaranteed to come true." Logan grinned at her. The kind of grin that made Ajax long for them again.

"I wish I could turn fifty every day, in that case." Ajax made a private wish for the protection of her children, both of whom had called.

"I like you, McIntyre."

Ajax smiled. "Only because I'm young and cool."

"Oh yeah. Definitely young and cool. That's what I think when I think *Ajax*. I think, *She's so young and cool, such a stud.*"

Ajax cut pieces of cake, licked her fingers. "Maybe you just find it exciting that I could die at any moment."

"Maybe I do." Logan shrugged, started to eat; the cake was dark chocolate, not sweet, good with the sugary ice cream. "Or maybe, sweetheart, that one thing alone breaks my fucking heart over and over."

Ajax cocked her head. "Please don't start having a rescue fantasy. Because you can't rescue me."

"You don't have to remind me," said Logan. "Fuck rescuing you. Just don't get sicker. Promise." Logan scraped their plate. "Pinky swear."

Ajax tore into her gifts. Logan had bought her shoes similar to their European brogues. She slipped into them, admired her feet—perfection. "I love them! Very fetish-y indeed. Now you can also like me because I have über cool feet."

Logan surreptitiously wiped their eyes. "I want you to feel fetish-y every day. I want to make you feel special for the rest of your life."

Gift certificate to a garden store in Vancouver; certificate for a spa day in Toronto. Ajax said, "I'm too sexy for your shoes. Too sexy for your cake. Way too sexy *pour ta copine*."

"*Ma copine, elle est bonne. Mais, est-elle une femme? Elle s'identifie comme une femme, mais je pense qu'il est peut-etre un garçon.*"

"*Oui*," said Ajax.

"*Et ne te l'oubliez.*"

"How could I?" Ajax laughed. She sobered. "Logan, damn, what do *you* want from your life at this point? What's important to you? What makes you weep? I need to know these things."

Logan met Ajax's eyes and said, "I wasn't a popular kid. I'd get picked nearly last in games even though I was a decent athlete. I was lonely a lot, solitary."

"That must have hurt your feelings."

"Don't you know yet that I don't have feelings." Logan grinned.

Ajax stuck out her tongue. "You'd like to think that, wouldn't you?"

Now Logan snorted. "You think you're so all-seeing."

"You were a vulnerable little kid. You got hurt."

"I got used to rejection quickly enough, because, well, no choice. Standing there thinking *Pick me, pick me, pick me.* Feeling shame like a blush stealing over me as more and more kids joined the teams and I didn't." Logan shrugged. "I guess every kid goes through that in one way or another. I was lucky to be good with grades, at least, if not popular." They scratched their nose. "Okay, fine, if you want to go digging, here's something I vaguely remember from when we lived in South Africa. I had a pet dik-dik named Sally."

"Oh, like a miniature antelope? They're adorable!"

"I was so young. It's hard to know if I remember her or I just remember my parents talking about her. I think I remember sharp hooves. There were baboons around, and my mother said I got pretty scared once when one tore the kitchen apart. They're the size of adult men, the males, with pretty crazy teeth. Not that baboon encounters are anything rare, in those parts. They're terrible citizens, very canny and highly aggressive and not afraid of people."

"I would love to see a baboon. A dik-dik, for that matter. Why were your parents in South Africa?"

"My father was employed by a resource extraction company, my mother taught Italian at the university."

"You're lucky. I grew up on a farm in a town without stoplights. First stoplight I experienced, I was maybe ten or eleven. I didn't really understand that restaurants existed."

"I was positive I wasn't a girl, but they said I wasn't a boy, and nobody knew what to do with me—least of all me. Tomboy didn't quite fit, especially when I started ... you know. Boobs. Kids were cruel. No beefs against Paris, but ... When Mom got a job in Montreal, after she broke up with my dad, I was fifteen, the worst age to move. Hell for a queer trans kid, I can tell you. But moving out, university—that made things better."

"Did you and your mom always fight?"

"Pretty much, yeah. Let's just say she didn't appreciate my kind of person." Logan reached to stroke Ajax's arm. "Still doesn't for that matter."

"I'm sorry."

Night slipped toward them.

"She wants me to be someone else. It wrecked me. I was already an outlier, and she just made it harder. My dad was better; my dad seemed to like me no matter what, but then he and my mom would fight about it—what I could do to fit in, how I was going to find my way in the world, if they could have done something differently when I was little, if I was ever going to find happiness in my aberrance. When I brought girls home, my mother would just freak out. *Freak out.* Once, she walked in on me and a girl in flagrante delicto; the girl was giving me a blow job, but I think my cock at the time was a stuffed balloon held on with elastics."

"Jesus," said Ajax, laughing.

"It's a bit more solid these days."

"A wee bit," agreed Ajax.

There was a lengthy pause. "Sit in that chair." Logan pointed.

"As compared to this chair?"

"As compared to this chair," Logan said, raising their eyebrows.

"Okay," said Ajax slowly, reluctantly, frowning.

"Not asking," said Logan, "telling."

"Okay," said Ajax. She walked to the chair Logan was pulling away from the wall, sat, winced.

"Pull off your shirt," said Logan. They paced.

Ajax did, a slow peel, licked chocolate from her fingers.

"Bra," said Logan.

She yanked her sports bra off.

Logan had her strip completely before they offered her a pillow. "Don't move," they ordered.

Logan bent to kiss Ajax's neck and throat, special places under her ear. Logan told Ajax to bend forward, then grabbed her wrists. "Safe word."

"Nitro," said Ajax. "And put it right beside us, because if I say it, I'm going to need it fast."

Logan sat across from her, cockless, and opened themselves where they were raw and vulnerable, touched themselves. The two of them masturbated and sparked without even touching each other. Ajax saw that they could not stay in one piece. They would love hard, until they broke themselves on it.

The chair hurt Ajax's ass.

Finally, Logan took her to the bedroom, asked her to lie on her back on the bed. Logan straddled her head and lowered themselves onto Ajax's mouth, and Ajax licked and sucked them and carefully slid her fingers inside Logan and Logan climaxed, crying out.

When Logan came back to themselves, they said, "It's not easy for me, fucking *sans* cock."

"I know," said Ajax.

Logan went down on Ajax, kissed her, said, "You snuck up on me from behind."

Ajax started to cry, rolled onto her side away.

"What, Ajax? What'd I do?"

Ajax shook her head. Her voice was small and full of tears. "It meant something to me, being inside you. I'm sorry."

Logan rolled onto their back. "Sex with girl bits is always going to be a just-occasional thing."

Ajax said, "I can't be a masochist, you know."

Logan looked at her.

"And you can't be a fucking sadist with me, all the time." Ajax said loudly. This was a bit ripe, she realized, coming from a woman with a swath of purple-blue on her ass. "I mean, of course you can be, but ... I can't be a masochist. I don't want to be a masochist. I'm *not* a masochist. You've probably given me more bottoming than I've had in my lifetime, and I'm already stuffed full of it." She ruefully smiled. "As it were. This needs to be a sometimes thing because I love vanilla sex, too."

"You love *all* of this. You love the way I touch you." But Logan had pulled back and sounded hurt.

"Yes," said Ajax. She didn't want Logan to think it was their skills that were being questioned. "You please me completely."

"Why do you have to label it, then?"

"It's just that it looks a lot to me like I'm a masochist and also, not to put too fine a point on it, apparently heterosexual again."

"For god's sake," said Logan. "No, you're not. That is an impossible interpretation."

Ajax rolled onto her back. "I'll bend toward you as you bend toward me. But understand; I'm queer; I'm not into guys. I've been screwing women for decades. I can't go back to just hetero sex, only with a trans guy. Boobs turn me on. Cunts turn me on, way on. I *like* fucking women. But I like fucking your power. I like your power fucking me." She turned onto her belly. "I'm confused, is all. I'm just confused."

"Really, get this through your skull: I'm not a trans guy. I don't know if I'll ever take T. Think more: Logan, dude with boobs."

"You call yourself trans sometimes, and I think we both know it's a possibility. A dude with sometime-boobs and basically no cunt. I get that," said Ajax, but she felt lonely. Very lost and afraid suddenly, because of all she might be giving up to stay with Logan, all the unknowns ahead. "It's not your gender. It's that our sex is so cock-centric ... I love a clever dick, but it's not all there is."

"I don't want you to be unhappy, Ajax, but I won't change the way I want to fuck. What gets me off gets me off."

"Bend toward me," said Ajax. "We'll both bend to the edges of our comfort zones. Maybe it's not a natural fit—I don't know. But it's what we have to work with."

"I promise I'll bend toward you," said Logan, "but I can't promise how often I'll bend toward you."

"I will bend often," said Ajax. She could feel pressure

building in her ears. "I'm comfortable bending. I'm not unhappy. My birthday has been perfect. I'm worried we won't be able to shut off kink outside the bedroom—'cause you know and I know that we are going to go further with it. I'm worried it will bleed over. As it were." A small cough, a grin.

"We can make this relationship anything we want it to be, Ajax. In bed or out of bed."

"Of course, but ... " She was going to say, *It's not you getting fucking hit with the paddle. Lean over my lap and then tell me the same story.* But she thought about that paddle, and it just turned her on. Regrettably. How could she really convince Logan of what she meant when, truly, she loved being punished?

Logan said, "I wish you wouldn't worry. We can play any way we want to play. Safely."

Ajax rolled closer. "That was hot, what you did last night, but that's never going to be all I want."

"Nor me, either." Logan laughed and said, "So why are we even having this discussion?"

They climbed from bed.

"Come outside," said Logan. "The rain's stopped at least for right now." They fetched canning jars with holes pounded through the lids. "Just sweep it through the air." They showed her, capped their lid. In the dark there were five tiny lights, strong enough to read by: magic.

Ajax did the same thing with hers. "Did you know the artist Caravaggio spread the powder of dried fireflies on his canvases to get a photosensitive surface? Crepuscular bioluminescence."

They swung their jars like lanterns until Logan poked Ajax, Ajax shrieked and tickled Logan, and the two of them ran, yelling and laughing. They stopped and hugged hard, Ajax's heart pounding.

"Smell the world, Logan. Petrichor."

"The thing is, Ajax, you notice things about me. Things you weren't supposed to notice."

"That you're gentle?"

"I am sometimes."

"That you care for your mother even when she irritates the hell out of you?"

"She irritates the fuck out of me."

"You're a great architect. I'm proud that you made that happen in your life, that you went back to school."

"Hardly anyone notices. It was a lot of work."

"That you're letting love build a world inside you."

Logan didn't reply.

"No? Am I wrong?"

"Sugar," said Logan.

They watched the bugs circle in their jars until finally Ajax took pity, released them, and watched them climb into the sky.

"Give me five minutes," said Logan.

When Ajax went back in, Logan took her to the bedroom, where they'd scattered peony petals on the bedspread. Vases of peonies and poppies stood on the floor, the bureau, the TV stand, the bedside tables.

"Happy birthday, honey," said Logan.

"Oh, god," said Ajax, her hand on her chest, eyes welling, taking Logan's hand, leading them to the bed, curling up beside them in the silky petals, the fresh scent, the sudden sound of rain on the roof. "Logan, thank you. Thank you so much. When the hell did you do all this?" They must have had the vases already prepped somewhere, hidden. "This weekend is precious to me."

Logan looked at her across the white pillows. "You open me." The words were right, but Ajax noticed they were twisting a handkerchief.

Ajax said, "Me, analog can opener. You, can. You never know what'll come out."

"And that, my dear," said Logan, "would be why I love you."

Ajax grinned drunkenly at them. "Maybe yellow wax beans, asparagus tips, maybe artichoke hearts. If I'm extremely lucky, balloons. Have you tried canned balloons?"

JOE

When she heard the shouts, Joe struggled up from the couch to see Elliot and Scotia stripping down on the dock, Scotia pushing Elliot into the lake, jumping in after, legs raised, back-flopping nearly on top of Ell. So much for Elliot having the flu ...

Scout had taken maybe three minutes to ramp herself up and then hadn't been able to calm down; she'd been crying for half an hour. If Joe could hear shouts at the lake, certainly Ell and Scotia could hear Scout wailing in the house through open doors and windows. Joe had tried what she could, but still the baby's cries escalated, and Joe's helplessness and panic escalated with them. To have Elliot romping with some kid when she could be in here helping—no, it was beyond the pale. Joe stuck her crinked baby finger in Scout's mouth to give her something to suck, but now that Scout had been trained to expect nipple, the finger infuriated her. She was now too agitated to latch. Joe already knew trade tricks—how to encourage her to make a wide mouth, get her to press her small tongue down against the bottom of her mouth, how to try changing her, irate and exposed on the change table, so that nursing would seem like refuge.

Joe grew frantic. The baby's cries cut into her, buzz saw.

She'd assumed Scout would be an exceptional child, a child who could prove that even moms who'd had childhoods with difficult parents could be raised healthy and whole, but what hubris that had been—already Joe could see that that wasn't how parenting worked. Parental flaws were a fungus in the air their kid breathed. Nobody had been raised by wolves, but instead by imperfect, angry, neurotic humans. And they were *passing it on*. Anger was a mist in the air of this house, a mist that Scout breathed. Joe didn't imagine that the child understood this, but assumed it would become part of her tapestry of the acceptable, the known, the familiar—what she, in later life, would turn toward. And now, this shrill inescapable cry from the face that Joe had fallen for, this face screwed up tight and red, not even aware of her mother's attempts to soothe her. Not even noticing her mother's desperation.

Not even noticing that, on the dock, her other mother was cavorting with some—kid. Joe didn't know if Elliot was likelier to come back up to the house or jump in Scotia's skiff and go off with her. Still, still, this child was Elliot's too, and she had to step up. Right the fuck up. Now.

Joe wept, the tears dripping off her chin, landing on Scout's onesie.

A little while later, as Joe was working up a head of steam to go outside screaming, she realized Elliot and Scotia were gone. Vanished. Had she missed the sound of boat engines?

If *she* bailed the way Ell felt free to do, guess what? Scout would die.

Joe panicked.

Walked and panicked.

Panicked and stumbled.

Scout wouldn't shut up and wouldn't shut up.

The entire cottage reverberated with her jackhammer screams.

"Be quiet, baby, be quiet, baby, be quiet, baby," she repeated, but no way her voice was audible over the cries. She yelled it, "Be quiet, baby!"

Scout appeared to be completely unreceptive, her face accordioned with rage.

God, why won't she shut up? thought Joe. For a filament of a second, Joe considered shaking sense into the baby, forcing her to listen, but it came to her: *That is how parents kill their kids.*

She rushed to tuck Scout into the cradle. Better she cry it out than that Joe went anywhere near her again.

Joe realized just by having thought the thought, she had become, to some tiny degree, a threat to Scout's life.

Someone who could snap.

Full of shame, Joe considered other ways out. Rooftops—Logan's high rooftop in Toronto, the old Bloor Viaduct, pills—how many she had, what they could be used for—ceiling fixtures.

Postpartum depression?

Maybe it was.

The knock came so quietly, Joe wasn't sure at first that she'd actually heard one. She struggled up from her nest—clothes half on, sweaty, stinky, her stitches barbed wire across her clit. Ajax stood outside with a nodding bouquet of Shirley poppies, pinks and reds.

"Hi," Joe said.

Ajax—still in bathing suit and flip flops, grinning lopsidedly.

Joe said, "Hi, um. I guess. Hello. Come in. I'm—" She wanted to say, *I'm crumbling.*

"I heard the baby screaming," said Ajax. "I know what it's like being stuck alone at home with a newborn and I wanted to see if you're okay, if you—you know, need anything. If I can help. At least let me get these poppies into water."

Joe felt the burn behind the eyes, the heat around her eyeballs. "Scout's asleep. Wore herself out." *As if it wasn't obvious.*

Ajax swished past her, found the kitchen, a vase. "Is Elliot home?"

"I haven't seen her all day," Joe said. "Ajax, I'm so scared!" Her hands shook; she looked at them like they didn't belong to her. Thinking about hurting her child had been the scariest moment of her life. "I wanted to ... I don't know what I wanted to do when Scout wouldn't stop screaming!"

Ajax drew her in for a hug.

"I know exactly what you mean. Roseanne Barr once said something like, 'If the kids are alive at the end of the day, I've done my job.'"

Joe laughed and pulled away.

Ajax said, "It's just lucky they make them cute."

"These last years—oh, I don't know, since we started trying to have a baby, or before that, maybe, after Ell had breast cancer, did you know Elliot once had breast cancer? I don't know. She's just not herself. She's distant. She's uninvolved, like she's detached herself, like she's left me without telling me." Joe turned away, said in a strangled voice, "I'm sorry. I know that's maudlin. I don't even know you. I shouldn't be telling you this." *Instead, should I tell you,* Joe thought, *that Logan and Elliot have sex sometimes? That Ell masturbates to images of the two of them from back when she still had titties?*

She let Ajax take her into her arms again and lead her, still weeping, toward the sofa. "I'm sorry," Joe said, "I'm just so sorry. I don't know why I'm—"

"Honey, it's *supposed* to be like this," said Ajax. "Just because women don't talk much about the first three months of parenting, doesn't mean it's not a bloody disaster for all of us. You're a train wreck of hormones right now and you're supposed to bawl your head off because life just sucks and you're so fucking in love with this baby and also you wish you'd never given birth to her and you hate her guts and you're in love with your wife but she's an asshole and life sucks and nothing is okay no matter what anyone says about it."

Joe looked at her in amazement. "How do you know all that?"

Ajax smiled. "You're not re-inventing the wheel. All mamas go through it; the vast majority of us live to tell about it."

Joe wept while Ajax enveloped her, which felt to Joe like being held together. She didn't want Ajax to loosen her grip for fear pieces of herself would fly around the room.

"Let it out. It's okay to be upset. It's really hard. It's okay to cry."

"Why is it all on me? I thought parenting was something Ell and I were going to do together!"

"I know," said Ajax. "It's okay. Shhhh."

"She's Ell's baby, I mean, her genetic material. Her egg and the sperm from our donor, and now, now, why isn't she here with us? Any excuse to get into the boat and away from me."

It went like this, back and forth, with Ajax soothing and Joe sobbing and blowing her nose. "There's lots to be upset about," said Ajax. "But you're strong, Joe, and you'll get through it, I promise. I know you will. That's what mamas fucking do. We get through shit. If we can't do it for ourselves, we do it for these little gumdrops we love at least while they're sleeping."

"Can I clone you? Where are you when it's three a.m. and I'm pretty sure I'm the only queer mother on earth?"

Ajax held Joe out, two hands on her shoulders, then patted Joe's face with a tissue. "It's a really hard adjustment. It gets easier when they move out of infancy because you get more sleep and they get more entertaining."

"I thought Ell and I would be so smitten with Scout that all we could do was walk around with smiles on our faces, beaming like idiots, but it's not like that at all, Ajax, it's anything but that."

"No, it's not like that. It's not like that for freaking anyone. I mean, think of labour. How do you communicate just how bloody brutal that is? How would you communicate *any* of this?" She waved her arm at the mess and evidence of chaos — used diaper bin, clothes heaped from the dryer, clothes tossed toward a laundry basket, abandoned tea cups, Joe's pajamas. "I have no ruddy idea. So of course people don't know. It's a lot of crying, diapers, spit-ups, vacant staring, mess, loneliness, and resentment, and, often, a quite unsteady love that only grows better with time."

"I think I love her," said Joe. She looked at Scout in the cradle and felt absolutely nothing.

"Love evolves. We expect it to be stable, but it's a spring plant, edging up slowly, exposing its stem first, finally sticking out tiny lime-green leaves. It checks out the temperature, stops growing if it's cold. It takes a while for it to be big."

"But what about you and Logan? You seem big quickly," Joe said.

Ajax said, "Maybe we're big with love, but maybe we're just madly infatuated. It's too early to know for sure yet."

"Are you taking it slow, though?"

"I'm more than cautious. I'm pedalling in reverse, even. Pushing them away so they can't get really close." Ajax rocked on her bum.

"They don't seem like they're letting you push them very far away," said Joe. "They don't often bring women here to begin with."

"No?"

"Some, sure. I mean, and obviously Elliot's here. One or two others through the years. And, you know, they're Logan. There are some parties. They've had a lot of women. I'm sure you realize that."

"I know that. But I do too."

"I just meant to say that Logan thinks the world of you if you're here. If you're here, they're probably pretty gone on you." Joe sniffled, blew her nose.

"I hope we're both hopeful," said Ajax. "I hope we do make it. I have impediments to love, though. Besides history, I mean. I'm not able-bodied."

"Oh?"

"I guess I look okay, in my aging, decrepit way, but I have a bad heart."

Joe put her hand on Ajax's knee. "I'm sorry. That's shitty."

"For twenty years now. At least I'm aging into the disease. It isn't as embarrassing to admit at fifty as it was at thirty."

"Embarrassing, why?" *Ell, Ell, Ell,* Joe thought.

"I don't know," said Ajax, "I found it so goddamned humiliating. Because it made me stand out? Other dykes were leading these carefree lives, and here I was, black in a city where there are no blacks, alone with two kids and heart disease. I didn't fit in. My life was a different thing. Clubbing? No, not clubbing."

"Wow," said Joe.

Ajax shrugged. "You grow into yourself eventually. I got the chance. I got to see the kids mature, and in the end, they didn't have to manage without me."

"I'm glad you're still here. I'm really, really glad that you guys are here this weekend."

"Speaking of," said Ajax looking at the clock. "I guess the boss awaits. With that cockamamie dog and his endless slobber."

Joe wanly smiled. "Bossy hound dogs, the both of them."

"'Kay, sweetness," said Ajax, kissing Joe's forehead. "You'll be okay, you know. Sooner or later you won't be feeling this rotten even when Elliot's being a total cretin. Things will ease."

"Voice of wisdom. Thank you. Really."

"Call me anytime. We're just in the next cabin, you know, if you need something. Even if you just can't stand another minute alone."

JOE

The baby slept and slept—far longer than ever before. Joe wasn't used to not changing diapers, not breast feeding; she guessed she should feel cheerier about a break, but she didn't. Her throat was thick and she felt lost. She worried Scout was sick. *Do something*, she told herself. She sorted laundry and, wary of bending over her stitches, started a load. There was still no sign of Ell and Scotia, but the two boats were definitely gone; looking out the window again and again didn't change that. Bad but also weird that Elliot hadn't checked in. The idea of Elliot with Scotia, with fresh, unblemished, uncomplicated Scotia, only made her feel worse.

Joe made tea and settled back on the couch, thinking, cynically, *Lactation tea.*

The phone rang and she grabbed it. Linda, an old friend from Nanaimo in BC, wanted to catch up on baby news before she announced to Joe, sotto voce, that her first partner, Dree, had died in a car accident.

"Whoa," said Joe. She braced herself on the couch.

"I'm sorry to tell you."

At first, Joe's voice wouldn't come, she produced sound but not words. Then, "Do you know what happened?"

"Driving drunk. Driving stoned, maybe. The tox results will be a while. Wrapped herself around a tree. I don't know; gossip says maybe she wanted to, maybe it was on purpose."

Slowly, Joe waited for the news to penetrate. She said, "She was always threatening to kill herself. This is—I can't—Poor Dree. This is really horrible."

"I remember she was suicidal," said Linda.

Elliot had never threatened suicide. Joe'd forgotten what a shitty piece of manipulation suicide threats could be when someone was just using them to get what they wanted. Joe thought back to the drama, the meltdowns, the scenes, the hysteria. "Why was I with Dree, for god's sakes, Linda? Why did I think that kind of behaviour was okay? Love at first sight, I remember. And I'd had skin cancer on my back a few months before we met, went through all that treatment baloney, and she told me that she'd had uterine cancer, far worse than what I'd gone through, and it'd spread inside her abdomen. She looked at me and I looked at her—and that was it for the next five years. It's a wonder I ever got my mechanic's ticket, I was so distracted."

"And the lying," said Linda. "Remember?"

Joe made a strangled noise, said, "Know how you knew Dree was lying? Her lips were moving."

Linda giggled.

Joe looked around the cottage, but it was suddenly a Dali painting, dripping, the clock hands running in goo down the wall, the table legs liquefying. Her life now and her insane life with Dree bled together. "She used to steal things," she said. "I tried everything to get her to stop. I told her how embarrassing it would be if she got caught and I had to tell our friends. I begged her. I tried giving her money, buying her stuff to stop her. And she was addicted to codeine. Lord, tell me please, why was I with that lunatic?"

"She was funny," said Linda. "Really fucking funny."

"She *is* funny! She's so funny!" Joe realized her tense was wrong, sighed. "I loved how funny she was. And warm when she wanted to turn her charm your way. But oh god, the lying, Linda! I remember right off she said she'd reimburse my plane ticket when I flew to Saskatoon to see her, and we went out shopping and she wanted a bunch of clothes and she said she'd pay me back if I used credit, and then, of course, none of that happened. Her cancer diagnosis was like dice in my brain, rattling. If there was a ninety-percent chance she'd be dead in five years, could I commit to loving her *no matter what*, could I take a chance on a woman who was probably going to die, soon and badly?"

"Yes," said Linda softly. "I remember that."

"After she moved in with me, she took over the chore of picking up my mail from the post box I had because I moved so often back in those insecure rental years, when I was always having to leave because the landlord was renovating or selling the place, or my girlfriend had left me. One day, Linda, I saw the bag Dree always took into her office, hanging on the doorknob, open, stuffed with mail. I looked; letters to me, bills mostly. I spilled them out in a way that could suggest the dog had just bumped into it—you know, a reminder to give them to me. When she got home, she just put them back in the bag, so I knew she was withholding my mail. I sat her down after dinner and called her on it. Usually I just had a wobbly case against her lies—some vaguely formed suspicion—but this time I had proof. I confronted her, and she fought me on it for four unremitting hours. She had crazy tactics! She tried chastising me: *How dare you think so little of me!* She tried loving me up: *Oh, sweetie, I would never do anything like that. Why on earth would I? Does that make sense to you? Does that make even a smidgeon of sense?* And of course it didn't, at all, and ordinarily I would have folded. I did fold in similar arguments because she had such good points—the bad stuff never made sense, so it couldn't be real, right? I was a battered old fiddle, and she was a bow. She was good at manipulating me. After that tactic didn't work—and I remember, she gave that one a good hour—she switched to anger: I set her up! How fucking dare I, a fucking student, accuse her, a pharmacy tech, of lying? I ought to be ashamed of myself because, who was I, who was I? I was an asshole, that's who I was. She wished she'd never met me. But I still stuck to my guns. What I remember now is my firmness: *No, you lied. You took my mail. No, you lied. You took my mail.* And her relentlessness. The conversation for her wasn't about stealing, it was about winning. Finally, I got up and went to bed and told her she was not welcome to join me and that I'd give her one last chance in the morning, and if she didn't come clean then, she should pack her bags and move. In the morning when I got up, she was gone. Not her stuff, just her. And there was a note that said, 'Joe, I did steal your mail. And also, I never had cancer. I hope you can forgive me.' "

Linda said, "You never told me this before."

"I'm not sure I've told anyone," said Joe. "It was just so bizarre, and it seems even crazier looking back. I was young and vulnerable. I'd had female lovers, but I'd never been in love before Dree." Joe considered. "Because we'd both been ill, I thought I'd met a kindred spirit. I thought, *Wow, two women, recovering from sickness together. We can do this.* And then, that morning she announced that the projections I'd built our future on—all the joy and tenderness and good wishes and hope and palliative care at the end, you know—all that was bullshit. She'd stolen my mail and she lied to me about having cancer. She'd had endometriosis, not cancer. I didn't know what to do, Linda. I felt so shattered. I felt dirty and used."

"Yes," said Linda. "Of course you did." Linda talked for a minute about Dree's current partner, Eileen, how crushed she was, her erratic behaviour as she tried to adjust to Dree's loss.

Joe said, "Dree came back to clear out her stuff, and I wasn't mad anymore, just hurt and broken, and I saw her and hugged her. Because I had thrown my lot in with her, and under all the bullshit, what she'd told me was good news, right? Dree wasn't dying! She wasn't dying!"

"I know," said Linda. "The best news you could have gotten—that your partner was going to live. But also, for you, the worst."

"We were in Vancouver then. Dree wanted to move back to Nanaimo, and we'd lost our housing because our landlord had sold out from under us, and I just said, *Fine, let's go back, whatever. Whatever you want. It will help you stay off codeine, right, and stop stealing."*

"And you moved here."

"What a con woman. What a bullshit artist. I can't even count the number of other women she got involved with while we were together."

"I'm sorry," said Linda. "I wonder if it's been that bad for Eileen all these years and no one had any idea. They were together a long time. Sorry Dree was such a complete waste of space. Sorry she's dead."

Elliot had rigged a simple rope pull to the cradle so that every time Scout fussed, Joe could rock her without getting up, but Joe didn't dare send her back off to sleep because she'd been under so long after her cry. "Do you know she was the number one reason I agreed to a poly relationship this time?" Joe felt a cinch in her heart about Elliot and Scotia. "So all the shenanigans would be above board. I'd know. Every goddamned time my spouse fucked someone else, I'd know all about it. Because of Dree, really."

"And how's that working out?" asked Linda.

Joe laughed. Scout started to cry, and Joe's breasts let down in response. "Up, you know, and then it plummets, pretty fucking far some weeks. Like, really, this week. I guess I thought she'd change, you know, with the baby, but she's been drifting lately, and we're, I don't know, estranged?"

"Fuck," said Linda.

"Although thinking about Dree certainly makes me glad

for what I have now." Joe had once become Dree's frog in the boiling pot of water. Now was she Elliot's?

Joe sent out texts to Elliot, knowing most of them would bounce back due to bad connectivity, but hoping something might get through.

Once Scout was suckling, Joe telling her to *open wide, guppy-latch*, pulling her firmly to the boob, all she could think about was Dree and what a strange, deranged woman she'd been, and how Joe had loved her to pieces even so, and how she was shattered, and shattered that she was shattered. The kinds of things Dree had done were straight out of the personality disorder checklists: shallow emotions, situational morality, entitlement, lack of sense of self, but back in those days she hadn't understood that. She'd stood up for herself that once, about the mail, and then never again because never again had Dree made such a transparent blunder. She embarrassed Joe in Nanaimo, stealing, creating divisions between Joe and people she'd never even met, between Joe and her friends. She screwed up special occasions, started scenes in restaurants and parks.

Those were bad old days.

Joe had still been shaky from Dree when she got together with sane, ordinary Elliot. All Elliot—smart, accomplished Elliot—had ever wanted to do was be able to sleep with other women, and she didn't want to lie about it or go behind Joe's back. She hadn't manipulated Joe. She hadn't lied, she hadn't stolen. If she was sometimes self-absorbed, if she wasn't as romantic as Joe might want, if she wasn't attentive, Joe would take that any day over what had happened with crazy Dree.

Dree, who'd finally hit a tree.

AJAX

"Part of what I love about you, Ajax, is that you were raised in the Bahamas."

Woof! said Toby, shaking himself. Logan rose to let him out.

"Only until I was twelve." At the table, pushing around a maple syrup bottle.

"Still. It's more European than Canada is, surely." Their thumbs in their short pockets.

Ajax stuck her finger in a pool of syrup, licked it absent-mindedly. "That wasn't my experience, really, Logan." She'd grown up poor and scrabbling. Her parents had worked for a dive resort and had emigrated because life in the Bahamas was dead-end. Nowhere to go but sideways and eventually into old age. Ajax's grandmother had sponsored their move to Canada. They'd landed in a Toronto blizzard, and that had been difficult, the few months shivering through winter while her parents bickered (her mother was glad to be back, but Ajax and her father couldn't handle the cold in the land or the people)—but carrying on to Vancouver hadn't made it much better. Warmer, with beaches both familiar and strange—same water, more or less, but cold and mountain-backed, and the weather was no great shakes. Her parents had edged her away from painting, wanted her to become a professional—a doctor, a dentist—but she'd stubbornly attended Emily Carr and earned a certificate that lead to ... well, they'd been right: it hadn't led to much. A hand-to-mouth life as a portrait painter. She and Logan, no matter the laboured parallels Logan wanted to draw, were not from the same side of the tracks. Logan's mother had taught at universities—in South Africa, in Paris, in Montreal, in Toronto. Logan's dad had been a CEO for a gold-extraction company. Logan didn't have a clue about class stratification. Saying, *You won't have to worry about anything if you're with me,* which they had said a hundred times, was baloney, a sentiment rather than a fact. She'd learned her lesson about getting too dependent with her ex.

"But it's a Commonwealth country."

"So is Canada, Logan." Ajax was annoyed; was Logan looking for her to be something she wasn't? Educated? White, maybe? The curtains lifted in the same breeze that had been captivating the night before. There was something so achingly summery about them—about everything here—that Ajax could almost close her eyes and imagine herself back in the Bahamas. And right now it irritated her.

"But it's more aware of being a Commonwealth country."

"Have you ever even been there, Logan?" Ajax had grown up on a peripheral island and attended a one-room schoolhouse. She moved her fork through the syrup. "The standard of living is not high."

"But you learned manners."

"We learned colonial manners, that's true. But I barely wore shoes the first decade of my life."

"We moved a lot," said Logan.

Were they trying to equate their immigration experiences? Had Logan also moved into a too-small house in a rural suburb of Vancouver which had been already overcrowded with people? Ajax thought not.

"I never felt at home. I never made friends. I always knew I'd just be uprooted again." Logan poured themself a vodka tonic.

Ajax stood to take dishes to the kitchen. "Moving is hard on kids."

"My little barefoot goddess," said Logan, bussing her as she gathered plates.

"Don't," said Ajax, lifting their plate. "Now you're just ticking me off." She bumped into a life preserver on her way to the kitchen—was suddenly annoyed by the kitsch on the walls. Hung paddles, old rusty lanterns. Things that said, *I am rich. I hired a designer. My house could appear in* Cottages North. *I will never need an actual lantern.*

"Hey! Hey! I didn't mean to offend you. I'm just trying to say I like you."

"Right," said Ajax, tightly. "There is some awful something happening right now, right here, that I am just going to cross out because I don't want to get into it with you. Not this weekend. Can we defer?"

Logan said, "I just like you. I like everything about you."

We'll see how long that lasts, thought Ajax. Logan was pushing close to buttons: poverty, race, emigration, resettlement, hunger. Her past life wasn't something Logan would ever understand. She filled the sink with hot, soapy water, plunged in her hands. Quintessentially, she and Logan had almost nothing in common. Which had essentially no bearing on love.

"You'd be wrong to expect differences aren't an issue for me, Logan," said Ajax in bed where they'd found each other again after breakfast. So much divergence between them. Ajax had lost her parents; Logan's were still alive. She had kids, Logan didn't. "I just want to be sure there's enough to go on with if our attraction wanes."

"You already said that," said Logan. "You've said that ten times. Do you think I'm not listening? It's not like I can do anything about any of this. You come from where you come from. I come from where I come from. You think it's relevant. I don't."

"Don't be snappy. These are my preferences and expectations, extensions of what I value in *my* life. I just—I need to discuss it more. I need to talk about what it means, what it signifies, how it changes my life to be with a rich white person, to be taken as half of a heterosexual couple." Ajax heaved a sigh. "I shouldn't care what other people think, I know. At my age, people don't even notice me anyhow. But it's embarrassing for me to feel straight." Logan shot her a look. "It's like stuffing myself back into that closet I escaped from."

"Oh, come on," said Logan. "Really."

"I know, I know. I'm not exactly proud of this. Defensive, yes, but proud, no."

The screen door slammed—the dog, letting himself back in. They heard his nails click across the wood, him slurping water.

"Me with a transman. I just never thought."

"I say it again: Don't label me. I'm just me."

"You're not a woman," said Ajax. She thought of women as water, and Logan was definitely not water. Not wet. Not flowing.

"Obviously."

"I signed up for loving you," said Ajax. "So this is just part of the equation when I think we might get more serious. You're white and you're trans."

"But this *is* who I am," said Logan, irritated. "White, Germanic heritage. And not born a girl even though I have girl bits."

"Please don't get mad." A pause. "You're mad."

"I'm not mad." Logan rolled away, stiffened.

"You are mad, I can tell." Ajax thought, said, "But lesbian sex is different."

"How is it different?"

"It's not ... It's not focused as much on ends." She thought back to lovers who took four or six or eight hours to make love, lovers who came a dozen times, lovers who never came (nor seemed to care). She thought about sex with Logan: dirty, hot, enflamed. But not so much an exploration—nothing much to explore with Logan's body nearly always going to be out-of-bounds. Or was she missing something? A language the two of them could speak that was contained in this kind of sex? A cursory guide to BDSM would suggest she certainly was missing things—if that's where this went. And for certain she'd never been this physically opened or wet with anyone before. Logan didn't explore Ajax's nuances, either; Ajax wasn't sure Logan was capable of nuance. "A lot of the time," she offered, "making love can be as sultry as laundry on a tropical clothesline on a breezy day."

"You want sex to be like laundry? More tumbling?"

Ajax laughed.

"You think you know so much." Logan sounded put out.

"I do know so much, and you're mad, and maybe I'm wrong to bring this up again. Maybe it sounds like I'm saying *You're not enough.* You've fought to be who you are with freedom and dignity and now I come along and imply I need you to be someone you're not and never could be. I'm just thinking out loud. Ruminating. Do you get that? I'm not building a skyscraper here—like, this is the floor, this is the ceiling. Tell me you get that. I'm not saying this is how I have to have things, that I have nothing to learn from you and how you fuck."

Stiff nod.

"Maybe I should only talk about my qualms with friends. But grant me this: We both arrive here with that dreaded 'baggage.' Like, me being sick changes your entire life, Logan. I need accommodations, and you have to make them if you want to go forward with me. Well, it's the same for me. You need accommodations for this thing about you, and I have to make them if we're going to go forward. Do you see?"

"I don't see why it doesn't just matter that I love you."

It went through her in shivers, Logan's love. "Your being a boy presses me closer to being a girl, and I don't want to be a girl. It's not who I am."

"Why does it?"

"People read by one's company, too. As you read more masculine, I read femmier."

"Good."

"Good if I wanted to look or be femmier. We're the same, really. You're just farther along the gender curve than I am."

"No curves for me, if you don't mind."

"Ha!" said Ajax.

"Well, I feel so cherished." Logan sat up, their voice hollowed. "Basically, you've said I'm bad in bed and I'm not unique and being with me is a kind of agony for you."

"God, no!" said Ajax, pulling them back, meeting their eyes. Such deep, cold eyes when they were mad or hurt. "God no. For fuck's sake, not in a hundred years. My thing is negative and your thing is neutral. I get the difference. But your thing is so hetero, Logan. And what if you start taking T?"

"Isn't it queer if I'm queer? By definition? Plus I'm not taking T," said Logan. "I'm not planning to take T."

"What if you get your boobs taken off?"

"What if I do? I probably will when Mom dies."

"Boobs are a major turn-on for me," Ajax said. "If I'm going into this, with all that I am, I need to know what I'm capable of accepting and embracing, what my limits are. I need to know whether I can handle it if your breasts are gone, you're on T, and you're getting a moustache and goatee. If I don't 'pass' anymore as gay because you've become ... an actual guy."

Logan's chums? thought Ajax. *They were already straight men, almost exclusively.*

"You know what it means. It means I'd be allowed to use washrooms everywhere I go."

"I know that," said Ajax. "I wasn't talking about bathrooms."

"Well you would be if you'd been the kid going home with wet pants because you were taunted when you tried to use the girls' room and you'd already been banned from the boys' room."

"Oh, honey. Honey, I'm sorry. That's horrible. Scarring."

"I'm *glad* you don't have a clue."

"I get harassed often enough as it is and I look like this." She motioned toward her large breasts.

"You don't get harassed. You don't know harassed."

"Well, when my hair's short, I've had women lurch across restaurants to keep me out of the ladies'. I've had women come into washrooms while I'm cleaning my hands and go back out to look at the door to see if they're in the right place. I've had women say, *Sir, did you know this is the women's washroom?*"

"My sweet girly girl," said Logan.

"Not to het women, I'm not. I'm transgressive, even if you don't notice it. Just because I'm a bottom doesn't mean I'm not butch."

Now Logan laughed out loud. "My wanna-be butch baby."

"I applied, but I failed the entrance exam."

"Shut up and kiss me."

"Yes, sir," said Ajax.

"Now," said Logan.

JOE

When Elliot wandered in again, it was after dinner time, and Joe immediately noticed she was famished.

"Hey," said Elliot too casually, hanging her keys.

"Wife-mo," said Joe. "Where were you?"

"Didn't you get my note?"

Her note?

"In the kitchen."

"Ell, I've barely been near the kitchen today."

"You didn't eat? Make tea?"

"I didn't eat, no. I've been waiting for you. Where were you?" That skinny thread of complaint in her voice. Scout at her nipple, hoovering.

Elliot dropped a kiss onto her part so lightly that she might as well not have bothered. Joe smelled sweat, and something else. Musk? "I went by my parents'. I called."

She hadn't called. "My old girlfriend died."

"Dree? You mean Dree? Dree died?"

Joe nodded. She was trying to make it real: *Dree was dead.*

Elliot said, "Oh, no! What happened?" Ell threw herself on the couch behind Joe, massaged Joe's shoulders while Joe, perennially sore from the new ways she was called to hold her body, moaned.

"Dree in a tree. She wrapped her car around a tree."

"Oh, god, that really sucks. Are you—okay?"

"Anyway, Dree sucked." Joe couldn't control herself. Her

voice sounded thick; she was crying, sort of. The kind of crying when a person you once loved and escaped from dies. When you are heartbroken because redemption is finite. Now Dree would never apologize and Joe never would, either, for whatever her part was.

"Didn't you think that she was basically a good egg?"

"I believed ... in her redeemable heart. Yes, she was a good egg. What is that? Hard-boiled, poached? She was scrambled. She was a challenge to live with. I don't know if you remember, but she was with someone, a woman who used to be our couples' counsellor, and I always felt so sorry for her. Eileen must have been incredibly—docile? forgiving? stupid? stoned?—because they were still together when Dree died. Losing a partner to death must be agonizing. Lord knows I have had my own worries I might lose you." Scout came off the nipple and Joe twisted to see Elliot.

Elliot squeezed her shoulder.

"Remember to love the one you're with, right?"

Ell made a noncommittal noise, said, "I wish I could touch you."

"I wish we could touch each other too, but it's five more weeks."

"I'm sorry you tore."

Joe nodded.

Elliot took Scout from her and burped her. "How's she been?"

You mean, the whole goddamned day when you weren't

here? "I took her out in the sun for a little bit. She had a screaming fit at some point. She gets herself so worked up that she just
becomes rage, and it makes me wonder what it was like in utero.
Did she feel no anger for nine months? What do babies in utero
do when they're mad? Because, holy heck, our girl can yowl."

"You ready for chow?"

"We could go visit Logan and Ajax." Joe laughed. Elliot
frowned. "Okay, I'm *kidding,* but don't you want to be a fly
on a wall? I would give a lot to hear what Logan is going to say
and if Ajax will say yes. She came over here and let me cry on
her shoulder a bit today."

"Ajax did?" A larger than expected burp came tunnelling
out of Scout.

"While you were with Scotia."

"I wasn't *with* Scotia."

"I thought you were going to be, though."

Elliot passed the baby back. "I want to spend more time
with Scout, but you've got her at your breast and all I have is,
I don't know, the top half of your breast and these flashes that
I know I shouldn't think are sexual. Your areolas are huge and
dark brown and your nipples are swollen and you look sexy,
and all I have are my inappropriate feelings about your tits, plus
the back of Scout's head, and then, you know, Scout's screams.
She doesn't have much awake time when she's not hollering."

Joe said, "She's a newborn."

"Aren't you glad that you still turn me on?"

"I don't want to turn you on, Ell. I just do not want to turn you on right now."

"Well, I don't get that." Ell's voice had gone remote, distanced, preoccupied; she fiddled with her iPhone, checking messages, maybe, moving to the window where reception was better

"Put your phone down," said Joe. "Please."

Elliot ignored her.

"Ell, please. No phones, not now, not in the middle of an argument." *Or whatever this is. A struggle.* Elliot didn't appear to even hear her. "Ell!"

"What?" Elliot looked up. She slipped her phone into her back pocket. "I want you. So shoot me."

"Blow you?"

"I said *shoot me* and you know it. Don't conflate the two. You always do this. With you it can't be, *My wife really digs me,* it's got to be some ulterior motive, some deep dark bullshit from the recesses of childhood. An orange is not an orange. I did not just ask you to blow me."

"But you'd like that, wouldn't you? You like to put your dick in my mouth, wouldn't you?"

"Oh, come on. Come on, Joe. Play fair. You're being an asshole." Joe said nothing. "Okay, fine. You already know you're right. I *would* like to see your lips on my cock! It would get me off. Those big tits? And so what? So holy hell, big freaking deal. I spent the day with a really hot kid who got me all worked up for my wife!"

"Just leave me alone."

"Be careful what you fucking ask for, Joe. I mean it, I'm warning you."

Joe looked sullenly at the baby without really seeing her. Then she looked up. "Are you threatening me? Are you telling me *watch out* because you have your finger on the pin? Because if that's what you're saying, you should fucking be *ashamed.*"

"Oh, don't you tell me what I should be. How about I tell you what you should be? Huh? How would you like that? Huh?"

Joe rolled her eyes.

"Be laconic. Go for it. See if I give a goddamned fuck."

"Maybe if I had a fuck left, I would give it to you so then you could give a goddamned fuck, but my fuck bucket, I am sorry to say, is completely empty."

"Good."

"Good!"

"Good!"

JOE

The next day, Elliot banged around in the kitchen, boiling things, *heating the very air,* thought Joe, and finally reappeared with steamed broccoli and breaded tofu. She carried a bowl to Joe on the couch without a word.

"Thank you," said Joe. "I have to pee. Will you please take your daughter?" She heard how she slightly inflected "your daughter." As in, *This kid is yours too, so fuck right off.*

Elliot accepted Scout without comment, but she wore her steely gaze: jutting chin, narrowed eyes. Elliot wouldn't be civil again for hours, and the most Joe could hope for was that she wouldn't be a total prick. Total prick would get on FaceTime and laugh her fool head off just to be annoying; total prick would blare recorded hockey games; total prick would slam out, and Joe would hear the boat engine.

Elliot shushed Scout and jostled her even though the baby wasn't fussing, while Joe stood watching. Scout did not focus on Elliot any more than she did on Joe. It was easy to feel worried: did the child have autism? Her mother had told her a story about how she had fallen in love when newborn Joe met her gaze; what did Scout's blankness signify?

It hurt to pee. A lot. Joe bent over her still-big belly and aimed a squirt bottle of saline water at the whole shooting match, but even so, it smarted fiercely. She felt like one big wound; everything ripped or torn or shredded and her uterus sore. Plus, she still looked like she was seven months pregnant, except the skin and fat were baggy, the infrastructure that had kept them taut gone. Which was not to minimize what was going on above her waist. Why had she thought breastfeeding was going to be a neutral experience? All those beatific madonnas with infants. If they were anything like Joe, their tits were orchestral; at one moment full of deep bass aches, at the next a string section of shrill violas and shrieking violins. Milk coming in was an utterly bizarre and unique experience. Once she'd assumed it would spill from her in a thin stream, but no, there were multiple milk ducts, and every milk duct had its own invisible hole. She was more spray bottle than faucet. And none of that happened without a dozen attendant physical sensations, the most predominant among them "let-down." *I feel a little let down. I feel a touch miffed, a tad depressed.* Let-down meant the milk genies snapped their fingers up under her clavicles and, all in a rush, the diluted sticky blue-ish stuff sluiced to the nipple and exploded from her body. It didn't come tidily on one side at once, oh no, evolution had not been that kind. The whole childbearing thing, as far as Joe could determine it, was a mess—she still wore thick menstrual pads, nearly a week after the birth. There was no lining to shed from her uterus, so she didn't really know what else there was, why the gushing— maybe she was bleeding from the wall where Scout's placenta had sheered off? Kind of weird that she could have all this—the torn clitoral hood, the blood, the milk—when she wasn't even related, biologically, to the infant she'd carried and now nursed.

And she missed Dree suddenly, with a strong pang. Dree

was so far in the hazy past that their relationship now seemed clean and easy by comparison.

She heard Scout start up.

Wasn't it a bit weird that the bio mom—MaPa, the resentful parent in the kitchen right now—didn't feel any small bit of any of this pain and leakage, any of the emotions? Okay, okay, maybe Scout *had* upset Elliot's apple cart. *Maybe.*

"Hey!" Elliot knocked. "Aren't you done in there yet? I can't stop her. Joe! We need you!"

Joe considered a way to mark Dree's death; she could float lanterns with candles out on the lake at night. She stood up from the toilet, long-suffering, annoyed, unwilling to do one solitary thing to help Elliot, even as, at the same time, she needed to rescue Scout, give Scout the solace of sucking. How did offering the baby a finger not interfere with breastfeeding while a soother did? Keeping an infant happy was logical, no matter how the parents got there. She threw open the door to her red-faced wife and her red-faced baby not two feet away. Tears sluiced down Elliot's cheeks.

"Is there a *problem?*" Joe said. "Is there a *reason* you're crying, Elliot?" She walked right past them.

"Don't be such a jerk, Joe," said Elliot, raising her voice above the baby. "So I admit it, I don't know what to do. Okay! It's hard work looking after a baby. Okay? Uncle. I don't know how to handle her. I don't want to handle her. I just want you to take her."

Joe leaned back against the kitchen counter and crossed her arms over her chest.

"How can you stand her crying?" Elliot said.

Joe lifted her eyebrows. "My ex just died, if you don't mind. Might I have a minute?"

"What do you want me to do?" Elliot asked. "Really, Joe, what? I've said I'm sorry, I've promised I'll never, ever, think of you sexually again!"

"Ha, ha," said Joe and gave her a withering look. She took Scout, but Elliot trailed them back to the spare room. "Big wide mouth," Joe said chirpily, and the baby opened wide, the adorable soprano mouth, and when Joe pulled her in, she latched on so feverishly Joe winced. Elliot sat on her knees beside them, her moist face pinched with regret.

Joe said, "I know I'm being pissy. We don't know what we're doing here. We're out of our depth."

Elliot took Joe's chin and lifted it so she would meet her eyes. The baby sent up wet, suckling noises. It was still hot, but a breeze had picked up and was wafting through the windows. Loons called out on the lake.

Elliot regarded Joe, expression inscrutable.

"Maybe we should have done this baby thing in the city with supports," said Ell.

"I'm just worried you want to be unencumbered. You do, don't you?" Joe began to cry herself. Again! She knuckled away tears. "You love Scout, but you don't love me anymore, do you?"

"I see you being vulnerable and afraid, and when I should be helping, I just want to vamoose. I know it's fucked up."

"It is kinda fucked up, Ell."

"But I can't help you beyond making food and keeping the floor vacuumed. I feel so clumsy. I just choose anything over confronting this." Her chest was caved in and she slid a hand through her hair.

"Having those things taken care of means a lot," said Joe.

"Being around that girl today made me see it. She was so vital—so skinny and agile and, I don't know, such a squealy *kid*. She just made me want to grow up."

"Dear god, please don't on our account," said Joe sarcastically, moving Scout to the other breast. She thought, *Dree is dead.* And, *What would happen if I just got in the boat with Scout and left?*

"You are the prickliest goddamned woman I know, Joe." Elliot heaved a dramatic sigh.

The laundry moved into spin cycle and the cabin shook. Joe put the now-nodding-off baby on the bed. "Okay, let me try again. I would love to come upstairs, Ell. Can we try?" Then she felt a prickle of real alarm. "But if we're co-sleeping, no alcohol, no drugs? You get that, right?"

"I am not about to endanger our daughter, for pity's sake." Elliot looked at her. "Besides, have you seen me drinking lately?"

Our daughter. Nobody could take that away. "I fully realize that was a skanky thing to say, but I had to say it, you know I did, because—Scout. Absolute and total sobriety so you won't roll onto her."

"Whatever," said Elliot. She carried in a rocking chair they'd stored on the porch and plumped it with a soft pillow, took Joe over to it, settled her down like a bird brooding eggs. "I'll just clean. Maybe that'll help."

Joe was uncomfortable in the chair, but she didn't want to tell Elliot. She wiggled. She rocked and the chair lightly creaked on its runners. *Creak, creak, creak.* If she used it regularly, that screech would go down in memory as the sound of breastfeeding. She was twisty and anxious. Why did they have to sleep infants on their backs? No blankets allowed. But swaddling, the encasing of an infant *in* a blanket, was encouraged, as if babies didn't flail, as if swaddles didn't pull loose and become, essentially, blankets.

Joe could already tell she was going to be chafing at the rules. *Play dates.* Was there a worse combination of words?

She thought again of Dree, poor wrapped-around-a-tree Dree. Dead, dead Dree. Joe wished she could go to the funeral to honour Dree's memory, to walk down memory lane, because there had been many good times between them as well as all the bad, and she could do with a little revisionism on how shitty that relationship was. It would be kind of wonderful to be with Dree's friends, some of whom had probably been their mutual friends back in Nanaimo, going to whatever ceremony a person like Dree might have planned, a wake, say, or even, who knew, a church ceremony, because she was always going on about how they didn't have enough spirituality in their relationship, enough religion, so maybe Dree got God, in the end, and would have a funeral in a church, the United Church maybe, or the Anglican. Truth was, Joe didn't know that much about Dree after they broke up. For a long time, she didn't want to know, and by the time news of Dree wouldn't have bothered her, she'd well and truly moved on. She knew Dree had worn feminism like she had the shirts she'd stolen from department stores—something to just pull on when it was handy. Dree had started a battered women's shelter, which was ripe, given that all Dree could say in her defence against her abuses when Joe left was, *I never hit you.*

Joe looked at her sleeping daughter, at the hand-hewn cradle, at the mountain of baby clothes on the change table, and she wished she could fly west. But she couldn't manage here alone, could she, let alone being self-sufficient on a plane, a ferry, and a rental car.

At least she and Elliot and Scout had *lives.*

Elliot had poisonous exes too, women pretzeled by childhood. There was Dahlia, and Denise, and Daria, the "Ds;" variously drunks, recovered drunks, and spendthrifts who put the "gas" in "gaslighting." There were the "Ps;" Patricia, Patrice, and Penny who all managed to be secret about polyamorous linkups, including with each other. There was Amy, who, according to Elliot, was a freakball who ran down the street after Elliot's car screaming *You narcissist! You narcissist!*

Everybody had exes, and the vast majority had unfortunately not moved to Texas.

Joe then had one of those realizations her mother must've had: *I have a baby. I am responsible. This will never end.* Joe's mother had decided, once, to quieten Joe by taking a drive. She stuffed Joe into a car seat with everything a mom needed to cart along in order to leave the house—soothers, diapers, Penaten cream, bottles, clean clothing, changing mat, warmer clothing, wipes—and drove through the rain-lashed late-night streets, hoping Joe would calm, car tires sounding on the wet pavement. Ten minutes later, she registered the quiet from the back seat and noticed that she, too, was more relaxed. She glanced in the rear view mirror to see whether baby Joe was asleep yet, but there was no baby. She'd forgotten Joe, in her car seat, on the kitchen table at home.

Why did people do this to themselves? It couldn't be explained by biology—or was it that simple, a sop against death, a chance to pass along genes?

"Come up!" shouted Elliot.

The extra day had made a difference in Joe's stitches. Upstairs, Elliot showed off the new nest—the far side of their bed, complete with barriers in case Scout rolled, a jerry-rigged change table, and all the supplies a newborn's mother could possibly need, including a portable kettle for quick cups of lactation tea.

"Ah," Joe said, "thank you, Ell."

Elliot said, clipped, "Welcome. But I might sleep downstairs if it's a racket."

"What about the mattress?"

"Don't leak tonight," said Elliot. "Not until I have a chance to get plastic."

Joe sat gingerly on the edge of the bed while Ell recounted all the things she had arrayed in the bathroom—all Joe's supplies, the baby's bathtub, the baby's "robe."

"I'm sorry I've been jerky."

"You've been really jerky," said Ell.

"You too, fuckface," said Joe, grinning.

"You're the fuckface." Elliot smiled. She tried, clumsily, to pull Joe into her arms. "I'm sorry for everything."

"I know," said Joe, "me too." While Elliot had her clenched, she looked around their bedroom like she'd never before seen it, had not fucked here, been ill here, snored and farted and spooned here. She felt marooned. Maybe being back in the city would be better, she thought. Then she thought of Dree again and felt that same catch in her throat.

Poor Dree. Poor dead Dree.

AJAX

They'd barely fallen asleep when Logan woke Ajax. "More adventures. Wake up."

"The rain stopped," said Ajax from the sheets.

Logan was dressed in shorts, a polo shirt. "Get out of bed, lazy head."

Ajax pulled the sheets over her head. "Fuck, Logan, go 'way. Lemme sleep." Logan uncovered her. Toby stood beside the bed panting, his red tongue lolling. He was almost sure to shake his head in a second and cover her with slobber. She closed her eyes.

"I have inducements," said Logan. They waggled the Sunday *New York Times*.

"Ohhhh, gimme," said Ajax, reaching. She got up on an elbow, frowned. "Did you just boat into Bracebridge?"

Logan laughed. "I have chocolate croissants, smoothies, coffee, strawberries, yogurt."

"Coffee," said Ajax nodding.

"Coffee for you in a thermos," said Logan. They threw Ajax's shorts at her. "Thick and strong. *Vite, vite*. Time, she is a wasting."

Ajax rolled out of bed; held her arms, shivering. "It's cold."

"It's beautiful, quit yer whining. Bring a coat."

Wrapped in a heavy sweater, the screak and slap of screen door behind her, Ajax followed her lover down to the dock: red canoe. Toby stayed on shore, whimpering piteously.

Logan paddled them over glassine waters in dawn's light,

quiet except for the liquid cuts of the paddle, drops falling, Ajax lifting her steaming coffee. The green-black shore was still shrouded in night, a cowl not yet pulled away for morning's breath, but the mist burned off the lake in the distance, small comforting sparklers evident on the water's skin as the sun caught. Ajax allowed herself the luxury of admiring Logan's forearms, their thighs, their face. Despite the sweater and the heavy borrowed parka, Ajax couldn't warm up; she shook and couldn't stop. Slowly they circled the island into the low-hanging sunshine, past stands of birch, pine, and hemlock now bright and dewy. Lily pads opened pink flowers. Geese flew honking overhead; two swans gave pissed-off hoots and swam away from the canoe.

"I canoe," said Ajax. "Can oe?"

Logan pulled the paddle. "Glad I yanked you out of bed?"

"Glad I'm finished turning fifty. Grateful for last week. The past months. Glad you're in my life."

Logan moored and climbed out, held the boat steady for Ajax, who smiled and said, teeth chattering, "Did someone say something about the *Times*?"

Toby was beside himself just on shore, wiggling his huge bum. Over breakfast, Ajax put her feet up on Logan's chair, while Logan put theirs on the dog.

"Let's go zip-lining," Logan said, looking up. "Want to?"

"Now you want to hang me on a clothesline?"

Two hours later, they were harnessed and helmeted on a rank beginners' course.

Logan said they loved being in the treetops where they could imagine themself an airborne creature. They loved the wind in their face, relaxing back off the line, even the self-rescues when they came up short at a platform and had to pull themself along, hand over hand. They loved the woody smell.

The course was too strenuous for Ajax even with a pro-phylactic nitro patch. Logan was solicitous, climbing patiently with her, waiting out her many breaks, sympathizing with her obvious bouts of pain, but was merciless regarding Ajax's fear of heights. On the suspension bridge, Ajax clung to the railing, and in the end, morbidly frightened, dropped to the boards, making the bridge jitter, and crawled back to the start, terrified.

"You good?" Logan asked Ajax.

"I am not good," said Ajax weakly, letting Logan pull her to her feet. "Also, I hate you."

"You'll remember this fondly."

"I won't." Ajax couldn't forget soon enough.

"I thought you loved nature."

"I love nature down there," said Ajax pointing at the ground, "where nature belongs. I do not like green trees and zips. I do not like them on this trip. I do not like them in a harness. I do not like them as an artist. I do not like green trees and zips. I do not like them, Logan, you drip."

"I'll make us capes for next time," said Logan. "We'll fly."

Ajax said, somberly, "There will be no next time."

But she gamely climbed a net like a spider, tip-toed across rolling logs screaming the whole way, and finally finished the course.

"Okay," she said when they arrived at terra firma.

Logan opened the car door. "Sit, baby. You were brave."

"*You* were brave. All I did was try to impress my bf."

Logan said, "I'm proud of you and duly impressed."

"I love you even if I do think you're an asshole. What else is there to do in these parts?" said Ajax. "Are we going back to the city?"

Logan said, "What did you do as a kid at your grandmom's cottage? I grew up in Paris, remember?"

"We could play board games."

"We have other games we can play."

Ajax squeezed their hand. "You can chute down my ladder anytime."

"I can't even think of all the things I want to do with you. I want you beside me all the time."

"Me too," said Ajax quietly, gripping Logan's hand. "I want that too."

They made love after they pulled up to the dock again without going inside—hot, itchy sex in the baking sunshine. Elliot and Joe could certainly see them, if they were looking, and this excited Ajax, and Logan's cock excited Ajax, and she gripped at Logan's ass, pulling them deeper, while in the trees, a raccoon mom and her kits wildly chirred, and inside Ajax pleasure percussed.

But a few minutes into it, Ajax had a suspicious feeling she was being punctured. A few more seconds and she shrieked for Logan to stop.

Logan laughed when Ajax stood up and showed them a bum full of splinters.

"Oww, oww, oww," said Ajax.

Logan flipped Ajax over the arm of the couch and picked out dock slivers.

"Fuck!" Ajax kept hollering. "That hurts, Logan, goddammit. Go easy."

"And it seemed like such a good idea at the time," said Logan. "How is it you didn't even notice, for christ's sake; you've got half the dock up your might-I-note-bruised bum."

Ajax stuck out her tongue. "You're on the bottom next time we do that, asshole."

"I was so *not* up your asshole, sweetheart. Hold tight. Don't wriggle. Maybe we should be thinking clinic, although, geez, you really are black and blue. That's making it worse because your tissues are swollen."

"Oww! No! No clinics."

"Well, Polysporin at least." Logan plucked, Ajax squealed, and Logan said, "This is going to be one of those relationship stories. Those *remember when you got slivers all up your bum* stories."

Finally Logan let her up, slathered in ointment with

a warning not to rub. Ajax pulled on a robe. "Fucked *and* plucked," said Ajax. "Kinda humiliating."

"That's not what you said about being over the arm of the couch the other night."

"*Va te faire fotre.* And your horse." The room smelled of oranges.

"My bride over the sofa arm ... nah-uh. It's going in the scrapbook."

"*I* keep the scrapbook, goddamnit." Then she realized what Logan had just said. "*What* did you just call me?"

Logan went down on one knee, pulled something out of their pocket, a ring box, square, navy velvet.

"Are you fucking kidding me?" Ajax said. "On bended knee? Get the fuck up. Get goddamn up, Logan. Do not do this." But Ajax was starting to laugh and cry at the same time, and when Logan handed her the box, she sobbed. She could see herself as if from the outside being proposed to in this stereotypical way—a log cabin, for christ's sake, French country chic, the beloved down on one knee—and it was goofy and absurd and her ass hurt a lot, the pain radiating down her thighs, but still, it was somehow perfect, somehow perfectly timed, and she knew that even though she was surely red-faced with embarrassment and pleasure—along with purple-bottomed—she was also full of love, the right kind of love, and a sense of safety and release.

"I want to marry you. Will you do me the honour of being my wife?"

Ajax opened the box.

JOE

Murderous dream of Dree attacking her, flailing arms and thuds. Tossing, sleeping, waking in a half-scream to Scout yowling. Joe stuck her nipple in the baby's mouth, but it wasn't enough; she fumbled a diaper change in the dark while Elliot snored obliviously.

Elliot threw her arm, glancing off Joe's face. Joe fretted anew about co-sleeping. She stared at the moon out the skylight as the baby suckled, baby-belly-round itself and as uncaring as dust. Jupiter hovered close to the moon, a sparkling engagement ring.

When Scout dropped off, Joe used the bathroom to change pads, slipped out of her sweaty bra and Jockeys, and had a shower. She imagined what Dree must have thought as her car went off the road. Dree'd had car accident after car accident when they were together; she went through cars like other people went through lovers. Not surprising a car wreck was how she'd die. When she was suicidal she threatened to slam her car into a brick wall, and Joe'd always wondered if her accidents had been dry runs.

Joe stared at the moon, missing Dree, loving Dree. She had angled after forgiveness for most of her years with Elliot but had not quite attained it. To get it now, when it was too late to communicate it, seemed faintly self-indulgent.

Nights, which had once been bastions of sensual pleasures — clean sheets, sex, tender spooning — were now feats of endurance.

Five-thirty a.m. and Elliot woke slowly beside Joe as the baby did, opening doe eyes and blinking.

"Good morning," Elliot said, frowning. Even teeth, the middle two longer. The privileged childhood of private schools and perfect dentistry always on display. Two long lines of worry between her eyebrows. "What time is it?"

"You slept through the racket," said Joe.

"Raccoons?" Ell shut her eyes.

"Scout crying." She pulled the baby onto her breast. Scout smelled like poop. "She needs a change, Elliot."

"I didn't hear a thing."

"That's what I'm saying." Piqued, Joe added, "Change her, 'kay?" She hated herself for making it a question.

"It's too early to get up." Ell rubbed sleep from her eyes, sighed.

Joe stripped Scout's onesie.

"Do you have to do that here? Can't you go in the washroom?" Elliot cracked one eye at Joe. "It's too freaking early and my stomach is still not behaving itself."

"Your sleep is not more important than mine. Change your daughter."

No one was sleepy after that.

Elliot was silent, then said a thin, "It's not even morning yet, Joe. Jaysus. You've got this. You're just being an asshole for the sake of being an asshole."

An asshole? Did you just call me an asshole? "Did *I* have a break? Who did the midnight feeding? Oh yeah, me. Who did the three a.m.? Oh yeah, *me*. Anyway, it doesn't matter if I *can* do this all myself—I don't want to, I shouldn't have to, and it traumatizes the heck out of me that you're not more interested."

Elliot took the baby. "Fi-ine," she said, the word elongated, the tone suffering. "Pass me the stuff then. If you want to take a chance on the baby catching this."

"Get your own damned supplies," Joe said and carefully made her way back downstairs into the spare room. She was shaking as she sat on the edge of the still-made bed.

The baby wailed, and Elliot came to the railing and yelled out, "Do you think it's possible you're just upset about Dree?"

Joe stood at the door to the spare room. "Don't try to make this about me, Elliot. As for Dree, she *died*, Elliot, for fuck's sake, what is it that escapes you about that? Dree *died*." She steamed. "What this is about is you being a pig!" She slammed the door and threw herself on the bed sobbing.

Elliot slammed the door upstairs.

Sometime later, Elliot tucked clean, sweet-smelling Scout into the guest bed and crawled in after her. While Scout ate, Elliot stroked her hair and trilled at her. "My little scoogly-woogly. My very own bitty baby. Does MaPa love her? MaPa is crazy about her girl." When the baby drifted off, so conked out that a lifted arm just dropped, Elliot transferred her to the cradle.

She climbed back in bed with Joe and drew her in close, murmuring apologies.

"Me too," said Joe, her back naked against Elliot's chest. She already felt contrite. It was not true that Elliot didn't like Scout; what a ridiculous, unsupportable thought. "Me too. So sorry."

They often made up like this, with a snuggle or sex or both, but no resolution.

It felt awkward and strange after so much baby-care for Joe to be near an adult whose body she knew so well it was truly an extension of hers. Joe felt her own clit twitch, unbidden, and then—she could have scripted this—the wide gulch of pain that yawned right afterward. Ell drew her bottom lip into her mouth, a sign of arousal that aroused Joe more; she thought ruefully of the things they used to do that they would miss now, as parents of a tiny one, things involving hooks and swings and door apparatuses.

Elliot ran her hands across Joe's breasts, whispering, "Gads, your tits feel amazing." The stroking made them let-down again and Ell squealed as they water-cannoned across her. "Oh. My. Fucking. God." Elliot pulled away, Joe mashed her hands on her breasts, but the milk still bubbled and dripped. Finally she took a nipple between her fingers and squirted Elliot on purpose. Ell shrieked and Joe laughed and Elliot laughed and they half-ran (Elliot), half-hobbled (Joe) through the house with Joe's spigot shooting a good ten feet.

"You're a nut bar," said Elliot, wiping off with a dish towel. "I'm all sticky, you maniac. I can't believe how crazy you are."

"Can I touch you, Ell? Can I fuck you?"

Elliot sobered and nodded.

And now Joe found what she could do—she could give.

She could let her fingers travel across Elliot the way she knew her wife loved to be touched, the way that, over years, she had learned to bring her off—quickly if she wanted, or slowly if she wanted that. The fool-proof way. She could whisper kisses across her neck, nibble her ear lobe. Bite her lips. The nipple rubs, fingers barely grazing skin, wetting her clit, rubbing it the way she most liked. By having Ell twist sideways, Joe could touch her clit and enter her without compromising her own stitches. Elliot was wet and her cunt was ridged and soft and went hard and tight against her fingers. Joe had a two-way strap-free strap-on she would love to use. She could think of it, dream about it, imagine it was in both of them now, and almost—almost—ignore her continual pain. Elliot was hot inside, her cunt pulling at Joe to go deeper, to fuck her harder and faster. Then she belled, inflating.

Out the window, Joe saw Logan and Ajax gliding by in a red canoe.

"Yes, yes, yes," Elliot said over and over. "That's it, yes, that, don't stop, don't stop." And finally, around Joe's fingers, she orgasmed, her cunt in waves and spasms.

After sex, everything seemed a little brighter—breakfast on the deck while Scout dozed in a rush basket, and Joe found she could sit, actually sit, without fidgeting or wincing from pain, albeit on a pillow, dipping toast into eggs and admiring the monarchs whisking through the flowers. She even tried a cup of coffee half-shot with decaf, although she knew it could keep the baby up through the night. It was going to be a scorcher; already, at ten a.m., the sun burned her bare toes. Bees lazily bounced up from the Ilse Krohn roses like slow yellow popcorn.

The quivering aspens shook lime-green leaves against the sky and made rustling music. Hummingbirds buzzed the feeder in territorial circles, angrily chasing off competitors. A blue jay landed on the railing to snatch a peanut in the shell Elliot had scattered. A monarch caterpillar inched across the porch railing, yellow, white, and black.

Joe felt much better. Much, much, much improved. Even without an orgasm. Just because Elliot had made her feel special.

Ell pointed out Logan and Ajax canoeing past and waved. "I wonder if Ajax said yes. She must have said yes. Who could say no to Logan?"

"Even you said yes to Logan once."

"They got down on their knees in this very living room and popped the question, but I was already leaving them then, and they knew it, and it was just a last-ditch effort to keep me with them. I don't suppose they really wanted to marry me. Queers couldn't get married then anyhow, not legally."

"Do you think it's a good idea, Ajax marrying Logan?"

Ell shrugged. "Can't say, really. Most stuff between a couple, it happens out of sight. It's entirely private."

"For both their sakes, I hope it's good, and lasting."

"Logan's really in love," said Elliot.

"Wasn't Logan in love with you too?"

"Sure, but we were poly. There were always other people in

the picture. Even after we moved in together, we had separate bedrooms because other women were coming and going."

Joe sighed in the sunshine. She felt warm, relaxed, safe. "Okay, but you loved each other."

"We loved each other. I still love Logan. Logan is easy to love, for me, but they're hard going for most other people. People like Logan in small doses. Even I like them in small doses."

Joe tried her hardest not to think of Logan, not to remember that long-ago fucking. "It's nice out here. Getting back into bed with you was a good idea." She waited a second. "So there's this thing, Ell. Can you sit down a minute? I kinda woke up thinking I should go to Dree's funeral."

"In BC!" Elliot dropped into a chair, legs spread wide, coffee cup balanced on the armrest.

"I'd like it if you could take me."

Elliot stared at the garden. "Getting back to the city, followed by a five-hour flight west, a hotel in Vancouver, a bus ride, a ferry ride."

Joe willed Elliot to understand, but the last thing she wanted was to instigate a fight. "Dree was the love of my life for a lot of years. I'd like to honour that."

Ell said, "I hated that woman."

"She didn't mean less to me because she was a scoundrel."

"I hated how she hurt you. She treated you like *ass*, Joe."

Joe thought of the fun she'd had with Dree, their jokes and laughter. She thought of how every summer day after work they'd hike down to the nearby lake and toss themselves in the water, and how Dree was always frightened there would be—something, monsters?—about to pull her under, and how she needed to be in a tube just to make herself stay put, and how the neighbourhood kids would exalt in dunking her. One night, Joe and Dree pulled their car up to the dock in fog, leaving the car lights running, and flew down the dock with their towels whipping behind them, shouting "Geronimo!" as they heaved themselves into sheer blackness. She remembered the surprise bio-luminescence, drawing in sparkling blues across Dree's back, kissing her fluorescent lips. Dree had acquired a cockatiel; they named him Faulkner, kept his wings clipped, let him flutter around the house when the cats were shut up in a bedroom. He had cavorted on Joe's shoulder, craning to clean her teeth.

"She was with someone, you know," Joe told Elliot, "after I left her. I can't imagine putting up with Dree for a week, a day, but, you know, she found someone who tolerated her antics"

Joe had wanted to take Faulkner when she left Nanaimo, even thought of suing for custody, except that it was the bad old days when queers weren't enfranchised to share property. Dree wouldn't let her—the cockatiel was nominally hers—and two years later, she heard, Dree left Faulkner's cage open at the same time as the front door, and the bird was crushed by a truck.

Not that Dree had told her. Linda had told her, much later.

How could Joe tell Elliot just how impassioned and full her life with Dree had been? How to say all the small accumulated things that make up a young life? She'd gotten her mechanic's ticket during that relationship.

Joe pushed her plate away. "It's not that Dree treated me well," said Joe. "It's that we still had a life together. Something we built as an ensemble. It was ours, you know, we made up its content and edges. We lived in it. Like you and I own this, all its benefits and flaws and complexities. Scout."

Elliot said, "Uh." Squirmed in her seat. "There's something I've been postponing telling you. There's something I need to say. I don't really know how to tell you." She looked at her lap, her face flushing, refused to meet Joe's eyes.

"Dear god, girl, you can't go that far and just stop." Joe laughed.

"Okay, okay. The thing is ... I can see this so clearly now with you saying you need to go to Dree's funeral. Joe, what I need to say is that—"

Joe dragged her finger through the remnants of egg yolk and licked it. She felt a titch of rising excitement. *I want to sell the cottage. I want us to move out west. I want us to go to Paris for a year.* "What? What?"

Ell looked briefly up. "I want to—you know. Stop."

Joe looked at Ell, the corrugations in her forehead, the dropped eyes, the slashed runnels between her eyebrows. "Stop what?"

Elliot drummed her fingers, said, "I want to stop. That's it. I want to stop."

"Stop," said Joe. And now she too frowned. Regarded Elliot

sitting in a simmer of—of what? A simmer of something. Now her excitement had turned to dread. "I'm not getting something here. What am I missing, Elliot?"

"I'm, ah … " Elliot knocked her fist on her leg.

"What are you trying to say to me? Would you please say it directly?"

Elliot shrugged again. "I'm wild about Scout, you know that, right? You know I love you, right?"

"Are you saying what it just occurred to me that you might be saying? Because, Ell, if you are, and you haven't even got the guts to say it out loud, I swear to god I will kill you dead."

Ell pressed her lips together—that obstreperous look of hers. The *I won't* look. The *You can't make me* look. "You are so hard to talk to. You scare me."

"I scare you."

"You're scary."

"Elliot, whatever this is, it isn't about me. It sounds like it's you being chicken. Use your words."

Elliot swung her head from side to side. "You're so patronizing."

Joe felt a sweep of hurt and anger. "Are you breaking up with me?"

Elliot stood up, shoved her hands deep into her shorts' pockets, mumbled, "Yes, Joe. I am, yes. That's it. Yes! Thank you! Exactly! I'm breaking up with you."

"You can't do that." Joe heard the shivery wave of fear in her voice. Her brain slid sideways, refusing the new information.

Ell picked up a peanut, bit into it, picked out shell. "I'm really sorry, is the thing."

Now Joe's voice went high-pitched and shrill. "What about Scout? What the hell will happen to Scout if she comes from a broken family?" Joe didn't believe in the phrase "broken family," because a one-parent household wasn't "broken," but where were her politics now? "We can't do that to her. Tell me you don't mean it, because, Ell, really, you can't mean it. Right? You're just—joking, I don't know. Joking with me. Bullshitting. Putting me on. You *definitely* wouldn't be this cruel. You wouldn't throw sixteen years into the trash." Joe didn't know what to do with her body. She paced and rambled. Her right leg kicked out—not at anything, shadow-kicking air. "Here I was already coming up with ideas to celebrate our twentieth."

Elliot pulled a finger along the porch wall. "I haven't been happy for a long time—you know this—and I'm not getting any happier now with the baby. It's like I want Scout, but I don't want you. I've exhausted myself trying to see how we can make this any better. You won't ever change."

"What am I supposed to change?"

"See? This is the way it always is with you. You think it's all me."

"Elliot, it is all you. Believe you me, it is all you. I've never once thought of separation."

"It's because of who you are."

"Stop dodging, Elliot. It's because of who you are. Pinning your troubles on someone else makes them seem more palatable."

"See? This is what I mean. This is exactly what I mean. I've had to live with this sanctimoniousness."

"But you just told me you love me. You just told me when I was fucking you," said Joe.

"That was mercy sex."

"Mercy sex?" Now her voice was shrill. Truly shrill.

"I felt sorry for you."

"You felt sorry for me," said Joe flatly.

"I must love you, Joe. I mean, we're married. You're not horrible most of the time, but meh. And more meh. The only time I *sort of* feel like I love you is when I look at you sleeping."

"Oww," said Joe. And then: "Seriously? Why did you just come around my fingers? Why did you let me fuck you?"

"You know ... I don't know. A kiss-off. Like I said."

A kiss-off ... "Is there someone else?"

"Scotia is not my lover."

"But someone? I would never—ever—do this to you."

"And you're not me, Joe—don't you get that? I am not you. It makes sense to me. It hurts me, of course, but it also makes sense, and right now—"

"*It* hurts you, or telling me hurts you? I'm wise to your tricks, Elliot. You could have just texted. Or wait ... texts don't go through up here. You could have sent Scotia to tell me. Or just ghosted me."

Prick, prick, thought Joe.

Elliot pushed at her hair again. "Right now, this minute, I admit it, I just feel relief, a great wash of relief. Look, I'll make sure you never want for anything. You can have the house in the city and I'll make sure it's free and clear, no encumbrances. You can come up here whenever you like. I'll support you and Scout, of course, in perpetuity. I promise never to leave you in the lurch. I am basically a good person."

I am basically a good person. Joe sagged, folding forward on herself, feeling as if her guts were about to spill and she was, just barely, holding them inside, said, "But this is ... Elliot, it's not fair."

"How could I be more fair? I've been talking to people who think—"

"You've been talking to people? I'm not the first person to know this?"

"And everyone thinks I am just too nice to you. You have a cushy life here."

Joe sank to a chair. "Please, Ell, reconsider. We're a team, a good team. We're mates. We work well together. I just had our baby, for crying out loud. I'm not strong. I can barely walk."

"See? You do this, this poor-me thing." Elliot sighed frustration. "You act like I've just said I hate a hundred percent of this, and Joe, it's just not like that. I see-saw back and forth. I have for years. Most of the time, though, I realize I just ... don't love you the way I should love you and it's not fair to you but—"

"*Years?* All that time I could have spent with someone who respected me and wanted to be my partner, but instead I got stuck with someone—had a *baby* with someone—who didn't give a damn? How is that fair? How is any of this *fair?*"

"I care. I care a lot. I love you, Joe. That's why I'm still here. I love you. I'm just not in love with you."

"You're telling me that I wasted the best years of my life on a loser? You're a loser, Elliot."

Elliot wrung her hands. "I could do a balance sheet and it would be fifty-fifty. Stay. Get out. Stay. Get out. Half the day it's one thing, and half the day it's the other thing. But my friends say—"

"Damn you! Damn you! You don't deserve me. You don't deserve us. Tell me something honourable or get the hell out! This is bullcrap."

"I just—You're not giving me a chance."

"You fuck other women! You have total freedom here as long as you talk to me about what's going on, so pardon me if I don't understand what I'm not giving you. What am I not giving you? What's making you miserable, Ell? Tell me how I'm failing you. Was the love utter *bullshit?* Is anything you said worth the carbon dioxide you expelled to say it?"

"I'm not leaving the island, Joe, except, you know, for a couple nights or whatever, just over to the mainland for a break. I'm not abandoning you with Scout. I'm not a complete shithead."

Joe laughed bitterly. "May I quote you? Wife leaves her spouse the week her daughter is born and, I quote, tells reporter, *I am not a complete shithead.*"

"I'm not leaving you in the lurch is what I mean. If you want to stay up here or in Toronto, either, I'll make sure I'm there or someone comes in to help."

"To help? What are we, Scout and me, a project to you? One of your fucking summer lists? Fix house siding, set up birthing pool, catch baby, live with family, make grilled cheese sandwiches, vacuum, let the wife I'm dumping fuck me?"

Elliot rubbed her face, her face that now seemed utterly transformed by her betrayal. "I'm just trying to have a reasonable conver—"

"I don't believe this," Joe said. "I'm in it, living it right now, and I don't believe it. Not one bit." The sun now seemed a menace. "And yet, yeah, okay, I do. I do believe this. Which is even scarier than not believing it. Because living with you these past years has not been a picnic. You've been evasive and private and paranoid and often not exactly loving, if you want to know the truth. And you live in the top two inches of life—"

"Top two inches of life!" Elliot repeated. "What's that supposed to mean?"

"I mean you're a cover with no book. A fan with no blades. A TV without a screen. You're a shallow person, Elliot."

Elliot back-handed her upper lip. "I am not a monster here, Joe. Really. I am the same Elliot I always was."

"If you were always a turd," said Joe, "I'd accept that."

"Joe, please stay rational," said Elliot.

"Rational? Damn, Elliot. How long have we been married?"

"I don't know. A long time. Years. Seven years."

"And how long have we been together?"

"Sixteen years?"

"Sixteen years, for heaven's sake. What's so important out there in the world that you've been okay without it for sixteen years, but now, just when I need you the most, you suddenly have to get out so badly you're willing to break my heart—and no doubt, your daughter's heart, even if she can't absorb that yet? Are we so unhappy together?"

"I am," Elliot said softly.

"You're not!"

"Don't tell me how I feel!" said Elliot. "Fuck, Joe! You're a bit insane, is the thing."

"But I've lived with you all that time, and if you were unhappy, it would have showed. It would have showed!"

"You aren't living in my mind."

Joe thinned her lips. "You have one?"

"See? This is what I mean! You're unspeakably cruel. People can't believe the nasty things you say to me!" Elliot kicked the table leg so cutlery scraped across plates.

"For fuck's sake, Elliot, we are *not* a struggling couple."

"*You're* not struggling, you mean. Don't presume to speak for me. You always do that. Every time you told people we were smitten—every fucking time—did you know I was dying a thousand deaths of embarrassment inside?"

Oww. Joe didn't even know where to put her hands. They migrated in circles around her head. *You were embarrassed of me? Embarrassed?*

"I was living with someone ... someone I was *ashamed* to be with. I deserve someone, I don't know, more educated. More on my level. Not a mechanic."

"You didn't just say that. You didn't just say something so repulsive and shitty."

Elliot sighed. "Living with you has been like living a quarter life."

Now Joe burst into tears. "A what? What did you say? Repeat that."

Elliot shook her head.

"A *quarter* life?"

Elliot ignored her.

"A quarter life?" How much had Elliot hated her? It had the sound of a comment she'd appropriated from someone else's mouth. All through their marriage, Joe could identify which were Elliot's self-generated thoughts, and the thoughts she had stolen from others. She usually could source who'd originally said them, too. But from whose brain had these particular bon mots issued? Not Elliot's, was all she knew. A quarter life? What wit thought that up? "Not a *half* life?"

"No," said Elliot firmly, squaring her shoulders. "A *quarter* life."

"How long have you been thinking like this? You were thinking like this when you asked me to marry you? You married me anyhow? You let me think everything was okay between us? For sixteen years? While trying to have—while having—a baby? Sixteen years you've been lying to me?"

Elliot shook her head in disdain, a bleak look plastered to her face. "What could it possibly matter *now?*"

"Whatever you've known all these years, I didn't know it because you didn't choose to tell me? So I have, um, maybe more than a little catch-up to play here. You've already done all the work, the emotional work, of leaving me. But I haven't done anything other than try to figure out ways we could get closer. The deck is stacked, and it's not stacked for me."

"Telling you things is terrifying, though," said Elliot beseechingly.

"Because of my rifle? Because of the knife in my hand?" Now Joe lifted a butter knife and held it mock-threateningly.

"Fuck off, Joe. You know what I mean. You roll your eyes. You sneer."

"I sneer and roll my eyes and that makes me terrifying, and consequently you thought it was perfectly legit to create and maintain a fake marriage? *Your* fear of confrontation makes what you did—what you're *doing*—excusable?" The soft morning scent of blooms opening to insects wafted toward them.

"I'll do right by you whether I want to or not, I promise. Other people won't talk me out of it."

"Uh-huh," said Joe. She kept sneaking peeks at Scout, thinking *Stay asleep. Be oblivious. Do not have this scene anywhere on your tiny retinas, in your tiny ear drums, transmitting to your infantile brain.* "Apparently, you're a seasoned pro at being a schmuck, Ell, but this crap is new for me. I promise I'll try to catch up, though, now that I'm cottoning on to the rules."

As if she had heard herself being thought of, Scout sent up a faint cry. Elliot snatched her out of the basket, bounced her. "Just don't poison my daughter against me."

"Don't even say something so completely, utterly idiotic." Joe shook her head. "I'm not the sociopath here. Are you sure it's your *home life* that's rotten? And not just you?"

"Stop railing! You're just pain shopping."

"*Excuse me?*" Joe thought she was going to wretch. Elliot was in therapy? Any therapeutic concept untempered by empathy meant precisely nothing.

"You just have an attachment disorder. That's all this is, your florid reaction, in case you want to know." Elliot said, "Who's MaPa's little strawberry?"

"You'll give her shaken baby, for heaven's sake, Elliot, don't." She dropped the butter knife.

Elliot didn't stop.

"Ell, I mean it. You could hurt her doing that." She added, "Scrambled brain." *Pain shopping. Attachment disorder. Florid reaction?*

"Leave me be," said Elliot. "It's not your business. She's *my* child."

Scrape of chair, orange juice glasses shaking. "Don't be a jerk."

Elliot held the baby high over her head, a heavenly offering.

"Give Scout to me. Don't mess around with a newborn."

"Joe, back off."

Joe grabbed the Quebec maple syrup in her hands and gave

the plastic bottle an unholy squeeze so it came out in a sticky stream aimed at Elliot's face. She dropped the bottle and grabbed Scout while Elliot sputtered and wiped at her eyes. "Get the fucking hell away from me and Scout, and I mean it."

Elliot went inside. Joe heard slamming, the shower, the front door slam, the boat engine.

Joe undid her nursing bra (*wide open mouth*) and pulled sticky, messy Scout mid-cry onto her nipple, wincing. Joe shut her eyes. *This is not happening, not happening, not happening.*

AJAX

Ajax said yes.

Her simple silver band excited her on some still-vibrating level. At lunch, Ajax realized all their talk had now evolved (*or devolved?*) into wedding chat. What did they want? Who should be invited? Big or small? Where? Who would stand up for them?

Logan said, "My mother tells me I can't get married until she's dead. Toby here"—they dandled the big dog head—"says he gets to be my best man."

Ajax had made egg salad sandwiches for lunch. "I would have expected more from your mom."

"Not so much the supporter of queer rights. She has never been okay with me. To the extent that I hide myself—not binding when I'm around her—it's because I don't want her to comment."

"I was once shunned at a women's centre I worked at for being gay. Which was, and I quote, a 'lifestyle more suitable for the city.'"

Logan sighed. "It's probably the trans thing. If I was just a lezzie ... She despises what I am. Every skirt I wore, I wore for her."

"But won't it please your mom to see you launched and happy with someone as she grows more frail? It's very powerful, the act of witnessing love."

Logan harrumphed.

"I've been at dozens of our weddings. Straights *speak*

weddings. Love is love is love—people understand that when we show them." She laughed and looked at her ring. "I've seen surly parents changed, although maybe it was just alcohol speaking."

"She won't come," said Logan.

"Hets can destabilize our relationships by treating us like crap." She didn't quite grasp Logan's relationship with their mother: highly entangled, both doting and acrimonious.

Logan picked up their sandwich, fooled with the lettuce, smiled. "Small or big wedding? Private or public? Toronto or Vancouver?"

"The Bahamas," said Ajax, without hesitation. "Where I grew up."

"Can we get married on the beach?"

"I scattered my mother's ashes there. We'd have to take the kids, and the grandkids."

"Expensive."

"And your mom."

Logan scoffed.

"Your mom," said Ajax more insistently. "She'll come, I'm sure, when push comes to love. "

Logan closed their eyes, said they doubted it.

Later, as they were prepping dinner, Logan joked about just calling their friend the lawyer and having her plug their numbers into DivorceMate software right away instead of waiting, and Ajax erupted into laughter. "Oh god," she said, thinking of the painful divorce she herself had tucked in her past and how lower-income earners were inevitably fucked over, "are we completely insane?"

And then she thought, *I'm the lower-income earner again.*

Logan said, "Stats would insist we are."

"Half of all marriages don't work, but really, that means half do," said Ajax.

"Thank you, Pollyanna," said Logan. "Maybe they do, or maybe those are mostly lives of quiet desperation."

"You're such a cynic," said Ajax. "And yet, I just did not for a *second* see that proposal coming. How the hell long have you been planning it? And why didn't you propose when you had the flower petals scattered around the bedroom?"

"I planned it for years, baby. Since you were a mere chick of forty-nine."

Logan uncorked champagne, the pop echoing across the lake. "To us."

Ajax raised her glass. "I guess this, um, implies that we're, um, considering a committed relationship?"

"I'll drink to that." The barbecue puffed, slow-cooking the ribs. Logan slathered on sauce.

"With, you know, cleaving unto one another." Ajax scratched a bite.

"Yup."

Ajax said, "Like, practically speaking, I guess one of us is moving?" *Meaning me*, she thought. *Who else?*

"Do you really wanna be on the phone every night till six a.m.?"

"Nah, so done with that," admitted Ajax. "Or I guess we don't have to live together."

"I've put in twenty years looking after my mom. I don't need to hang around Toronto any longer, in case you want me to come in your direction."

"Still, you don't get to suddenly say, 'Sorry, gig's up, Ma, I'm leaving. You're eighty-three but I've, you know, had it. I'm pushing off now.' She's going to need more of you as time goes on, not less. That job ends when she ends, really."

"You've got a kid and soon a grandkid in the Bahamas, and a kid out west. What would you prefer?"

"You've got Lake Ontario," Ajax said, but actually had to stop herself from laughing. They had a faux-beach downtown park with sand poured over concrete some ten feet above the water. The dog beach was lame. Ajax put her head in her hands. "I mean, I can paint anywhere." She rented studio space from an art school in Vancouver. "I can't believe this, Logan. I can't believe this. Did you really *propose?*"

Toby barked.

"See? Even he's happy. McIntyre, let me ask you something. Do you feel celebratory?"

"Honey, this is one of the happiest days of my life." Ajax got up, removed Logan's champagne flute, and took Logan's hands. "It didn't even occur to me that I was going to have something like this in my life again; I certainly didn't see it being with you. I mean, we've known each other for a hundred years and nothing happened before now, and you've always been a bad boi."

"But it means I kind of know you. I've been aware of you over time."

"I had outrageous fantasies of marrying you before we even slept together." She shouldn't admit that, she thought, but then she thought, *Why not? Dreams can come true. Even for old people. Even for people in my straitened physical condition. Or not,* she thought.

Logan grinned big, rakish hank of hair falling into their eyes.

"We need to get you a ring, too." Ajax ran to cut a piece of yarn from the pull-down on the blinds, roped it around Logan's finger, kissed the top of it.

Logan beamed and touched Ajax's face.

"We can figure all this out later. You're right that there's nothing saying we can't continue doing this long distance, at least until we know what we want."

"But I miss you, miss you, miss you."

Ajax moved her chair closer to Logan at the barbecue.

Logan said, "I know. I waited all my life and now I'm still waiting. The ribs are done."

Ajax served the ribs with corn and new potatoes with chives. "My friends do it," she said. "Vancouver to France, back and forth."

"You're more or less free to move to Toronto; I'm more or less free to move to Vancouver. It's different than having jobs that lock us down. I can do what I do wherever. One of my former partners has a kid I like in Vancouver."

Ajax stared at her ring finger, rapt. "Did I say thank you for this perfectly simple ring?"

Logan said, "You thank me a lot. I like that."

"I'm grateful a lot."

"I love how you take care of me, Ajax."

Their eyes met—*I love you passionately*, they said.

Ajax went for dessert—raspberries they'd picked out back. They were half white and not really ready. Ajax put on "Koop Island Blues," danced, pulled Logan to their feet, and that was somehow it, officially—silver band, champagne, yarn ring—they were engaged.

JOE

Joe curled into a fetal ball to nurse Scout; the sights and sounds normal, the smells of baby powder and urine commingling normally. How had she just landed in the middle of a breakup without even having realized anything significant was wrong?

Gone. Joe was numb. She pinched herself and felt nothing. She flicked her cheek, registered a faint sensation. She realized how many times Ell had come up to the cottage alone over the past couple years. Why? Why had she done that? Joe just wanted it to make sense. And this made no sense. Was it too much to ask that it make sense? Ell, ditching her wife with a newborn on an island, taking their only boat. Come Monday, Logan and Ajax would surely be gone, and what if, at that point, something went awry? What if the baby got whooping cough or an allergy, or god forbid Joe became too ill to feed her, and the landline went dead? This was how jeopardized she now was.

She could hear Ell's voice in her head: *You catastrophize. None of that will happen. You're giving yourself horror movies.* Her wail in response: *But it could!* She had to plan for the possibility, remote as it was. Apparently, no one else was planning for her welfare.

If Elliot wouldn't, didn't, couldn't — even so, their welfare still mattered. They still needed income, a home, food. She had tremors from the weight of her vulnerability.

Surely it was just a case of horniness — Elliot's clit pointing like a retriever in some hunter's field? She'd come back home, she would!

By noon, the sun had long since boiled the maple syrup that had spilled on the patio stones. Maybe Joe should pack—ask Logan to help—go back to the city, to their house in the Beaches, to lick her wounds and be where she had friends, family, support? She looked around the cottage that Elliot and Logan had built pretty much by hand. The plush couches, the crude pine dining table, the worn Persian rugs, the chandeliers. She'd thought it was hers. Wasn't it hers? Scout had been born here. The birthing tub was still up against the wall in the guest room.

She thought back to Logan and Elliot's breakup. How had that come down? Elliot had been draconian, hurtful, parsimonious, had kept the cottage that Logan'd helped to build. Logan sued, succeeded in getting half the island, but that was all. It was different then; in the bad old pre-rights days, Logan had been lucky to get that much recognition. But now queers had rights and obligations. Elliot would have to split things fifty-fifty.

Joe, thought Joe, *you are extrapolating. Do you know a single thing about separation?* She didn't. When she and Dree split, Joe walked away, period.

What Joe had loved had just turned to dust.

Every time Scout sent up a whimper, it jolted Joe, whose mind was madly calculating money and how much she had access to, even on charge cards, and when she could go back to work, and who would watch Scout, and whether Elliot was going to be a shit—a *shit*—with the divorce. *Divorce.* No. Divorce? She meant separation. She would never divorce Elliot. She believed in Elliot, believed she'd do the generous and right thing without a fight. Elliot was honourable. Wasn't she?

Maybe Elliot had confided in Logan?

Nearly supper time, and she didn't know where the day had gone. Joe's stomach growled, and there wasn't any Elliot around to dish out food. Scout was soaked and poopy, from the smell of things—had Joe even changed her today? Somehow Joe had turned on the air conditioning, and now she shivered. What had just happened? *I kissed Elliot here*, she thought. *Elliot and I wrestled here. This is where Elliot proposed.* Joe left the baby shrieking in her cradle and walked outside—aimlessly, in a fog—through the ants and wasps into the flowers wishing they were opium poppies strong enough to put her to sleep.

Logan and Ajax were fucking on the dock—it sent her back inside. Goddamned love.

Back inside, she examined Scout as she changed her. Elliot in her lips, her nose. "I'm so sorry, Scout. I'm so sorry," she whispered. Joe had already let her daughter, not a week old, down. *You have another mother, Scout, but she doesn't live with us.* There had to be another woman! When did Elliot meet her, and why hadn't Joe suspected or noticed?

She'd wanted to bring their daughter into a good world, a world where avarice and greed and hatred didn't win, where corporations weren't gods, where icebergs weren't melting, where climate change wasn't alarming, where at least, at least, her parents were good at heart. But maybe it was cruel to have a baby at all in this garbage globe. She hadn't thought much about that, had she, when the procreation hunger swept over her?

They said you couldn't know the fullness of love until you had a baby. She got inklings of that now, this love for which she would lay down her life.

Would Elliot really fight for this baby?

Joe could go to Logan's, barge in, say, *Hey, Elliot left me.* Oh god, she could not.

She could not intrude on a romantic weekend with this news. She rambled into the kitchen and boiled instant noodles and ate them out of the colander at the sink. She checked her phone, but Ell hadn't called.

She walked the house, opening closets. *Coat, still here.* She wrenched open Elliot's underwear drawer: *All new.* She ransacked the drawers of Elliot's dresser, in which half the clothing was new, still creased. *What the fuck?* She shook drawers onto the floor. Receipts tumbled in a paper rainstorm. Receipts, she saw, for flowers (she hadn't received), for dinners at restaurants (she hadn't gone to), for jewellery (she didn't own). Twenty receipts, thirty, forty. And a wad of cash, fresh twenties and fifties. Ticket stubs for concerts (she hadn't gone to). Tickets for museums and art fairs (she hadn't attended). Then an e-ticket for a trip to Rome. Upcoming in November. No mention of a co-traveller.

She went to check Elliot's Facebook, but she'd been blocked. Elliot's email, but the password was changed. Elliot's desktop — but there seemed to be no clues.

Wow, she thought. *Wow.*

It wasn't a dream. This was really happening. Tectonic plates had been shifting, and Joe had been stupidly oblivious. Elliot had moved from love and admiration and a sense that it was the two of them against the world into ... whatever this was, estrangement. Hatred, maybe.

Shouldn't there have been an earthquake first?

AJAX

They'd slept entwined at night — they'd found each other during sleep instead of rolling into the shadows. But now Logan stumbled into the late-night living room where Ajax had marooned herself on the couch. "What's up? Come back to bed."

"I'm sick, honey," said Ajax quietly. She was curled up behind Toby. It wasn't *I have a cold, I might have the flu, my tummy's upset.*

Logan sat on the armrest, stroked her hair. "Honey, tell me."

Ajax's voice came out whispery. "Do you think we can get me to a hospital from here?"

"Fuck," said Logan.

Ajax was thinking logistics, 9-1-1, choppy boat rides, helicopters. Rescue. Was there even a hospital up here? Of course there was a goddamned hospital, there had to be, but was it any fucking *good*?

"Were you gonna wake me up?"

"Yes. No. I don't know. I love you, Logan," she said. She coughed. Couldn't stop.

"What's going on, Ajax?" Birds chirped — morning even though it was still dark.

"I suspect it's atrial fib. It's not a really good thing." Her voice was weak, her pulse as she felt it thready with thuds. "But not fatal, either. I mean, I'm not going to fall over dead on you."

Logan squeezed her knee. "I'm going to get my phone." They were back in an instant. "I can take you in my boat."

"Joe's alone over there with an infant. I saw Elliot leave. We can't take the only boat. She has to have access to a boat, Logan." She tried to talk, a few strained words at a time, a suck of breath. "My heart feels like a horse is kicking me inside." She patted Logan's hand. "I'm short of breath. Very tired."

Toby heaved himself up and slinked off the couch, came to Logan, his collar clinking.

"Have you tried nitro?"

"Yeah, couple times, not that it would do anything for this. Can you do a stroke assay? Listen to if I'm speaking intelligibly, if I can extend my tongue left and right, if I can lift both arms together with my eyes closed, if I can smile without it being lopsided?" Ajax moved through the steps herself successfully. "I'm a little numb on my left side, so there might be a bleed in my right hemisphere. Or maybe it's nothing, just me sitting here imagining symptoms. But we should, uh, probably get me out of here to be on the safe side."

"Yeah," said Logan, dialling, talking to the emergency operator, going through symptoms, offering their coordinates.

Ajax rocked, her face turned toward the window, conserving her energy for breathing.

"Help is coming. Okay. They say lie down in case you get faint, and we need to get some clothes on you." Ajax was naked under a blanket; Logan shooed the dog down, got her up to dress her in track pants, and led her back to the sofa. Ajax coughed; Logan propped her up on pillows.

Ajax asked them to sing.

"You're going to be fine."

"Sing," demanded Ajax, coughing.

Logan sang quietly — bluesy love songs, lullabies. Soft, comforting songs. Sat on the floor, held tight to Ajax's hand while Ajax drifted in and out. "Don't you die," Logan whispered. "Don't you goddamn die the day I propose to you."

Early dawn; there were robins in the yard, pecking for worms as the newly woken sun rose; poppies bent from the weight of dew, the grass silvery. They squeezed Ajax's hand.

Ajax felt drifty, spacey, only half connected to reality. Then she thought, *It sucks worse for Logan.* Then she thought again, *Should I call my kids?* "Call Joe, okay, so she's not freaked by the ambulance?"

"Okay," said Logan. Ajax's eyelids fluttered. "What's your cell phone password so I can call the kids?"

Ajax opened her eyes. "Don't call them. Not necessary at this stage. Find out if there's something to worry about first."

"Honey, your cell password."

Ajax told them, "If this goes sideways, tell the children I couldn't have asked them to be better people." She looked into Logan's eyes, held the gaze tight. Had a coughing fit. Logan sat her up, pounded her back. Ajax smiled weakly, but her eyes were closing. She was sliding somewhere, sliding away.

Logan said, "Baby, you're going to be okay." They sang.

Ajax's eyes fluttered open. A robin found a worm and tugged it from the ground, red belly glowing. Logan phoned Joe, said they'd explain later, told her where the boat keys were, asked her to take Toby to her cottage.

"And the grandkids," said Ajax suddenly, her eyes opening. "I have the best grandchildren!"

Logan sang "Too Darn Hot," just to shut her up, belting the tune.

When the water ambulance arrived, two paramedics took over Ajax's care, giving her oxygen, switching her to a gurney.

"Take my ring," Ajax said, lifting her oxygen mask, holding out her arm to Logan.

The ring that had glided on so easily now slid off and was pocketed. In the boat, in the ER, Ajax heard Logan telling the paramedics they were married. "She's my *wife*."

Ajax was immediately transferred to an available bed.

Logan and Ajax watched the atrial fibrillation on the ECG monitor, crazy-assed tracings with no rhythm, a two-year-old's scribbling, a heart rate of 180. They did tests and dispensed a blood thinner, a medication Ajax had long resisted because of the potential that she might, as she described it, "spring a leak." She'd had two instinctual evasions through her years of being sick: first, open heart surgery, which meant a broken sternum, and second, blood thinners. She'd eventually given in to a modified version of the first. But warfarin meant a continual and strict regime of measuring levels, multiple changes in dosing and considerable risk. The problem with not using it was that a chaotic atrium could throw a clot and cause a stroke.

Ajax had an IV taped to her hand; a bag of glucose hung beside the bed. "Tired of hospitals," she said.

"Baby, how often you been hospitalized lately?"

Ajax counted on her fingers. "Nine surgeries? Plus a few stray times landing in ERs temporarily."

"And you wonder why you're tired all the time?"

"I'm tired because my left ventricle doesn't work," she said. "And lots of my medications cause fatigue, and I've been pushing myself with you."

"Still."

"Glad you said we were married. It gets you access. I wish you *were* my spouse."

"Right now, I just wanna take you home so I can get you back to the city."

"They're not making admitting noises," said Ajax.

Both of them watched Ajax's heart going in and out of rhythm. "You feel better?"

Ajax shrugged.

"You were right that it was A-fib."

She looked at Logan. "Life in the fast lane with a heart crip. How come the heart crip crossed the road?"

"I give up."

"She thought she saw a salt shaker." Ajax drummed her fingers on top of the blanket. "I'm enough sick that I need to be here, but not enough that I *want* to be here. Discharge, discharge, discharge."

Logan sang to Ajax—French and German lullabies they

said were from childhood. The ER crashed along around them—nurses, the screech of curtains, intercom, paramedics, doctors, gurneys whipping by, *Code Blue, Code Blue, Code Blue.* Somewhere in all of this, Ajax's heartbeat returned to sinus rhythm. She looked less ashen.

The neuro resident arrived to do a stroke battery. Logan sat off to the side while Ajax was put through complicated paces. "You're lucky again," the neurologist finally said.

"Yup," said Ajax resignedly.

"I don't think you had a stroke. If you did, just another TIA." She put her hand on Ajax's leg.

"*Another* TIA?" said Logan; they had to ask what it was. Transient ischemic attack, mini-stroke.

Ajax grimaced.

"Possibly past TIAs," said the resident and scratched her head. "See how her face is lopsided? She's been hospitalized for stroke before, she said."

"Ajax, you never said that."

"*Arguably* a stroke," said Ajax, shrugging. "It's why I smile in photos, to even it out."

Logan said, "Doc, is she sick or not sick?"

"The A-fib leaves her high risk for stroke. Several doctors have tried to impress that on your wife previously, from what she tells me."

The doctor tapped notes into an iPad. "One of these days, Ms McIntyre," she said, "one of these bullets is going to find you."

Ajax sighed.

"You really should be dead." The doctor frowned down at her.

"But I'm not dead."

The doc said, "But you should be."

Logan said, "Um ... "

"It's impossible that you have your history and are still alive."

"And yet..." said Ajax.

The neurologist shrugged.

Ajax scowled. "Don't push me into the grave yet, okay, just so I fulfill your statistical expectations?"

Logan said, "Yeah, come on. Does she look dead to you?"

The resident's boss came in. "We're going to release you, but we want you to stay on the warfarin, and see a Toronto cardiologist. You have to have your blood monitored every two days until we get your levels right. I'll send a consult note to your GP, and here's a referral for the bloodwork and the cardiologist. He'll see you immediately."

"No CT?" asked Ajax. "No cardioversion?" Cardioversion, a little trick they did with heart shocks.

"We can't do cardioversions here. If you're still in A-fib when you get to Toronto, go in again. Your atria are reset, it looks like, and the digoxin will help — but if you have symptoms again before you go, we want to see you back, and you need to promise to have your levels monitored for toxicity."

"Yes, yes, of course," said Ajax.

The resident passed Logan a stack of prescriptions, the tinkering they'd done to her current medication regime. "You can help," said the neurologist to Logan. "Make sure she complies."

"Compliance definitely being her strong suit," said Logan.

"Am I under any restrictions?" Ajax said.

The doctor said no. "Crisis averted," he said sternly. "But consider this a warning."

"I'm sorry I tanked our perfect weekend." Ajax felt glad to be heading back to the cottage for solace.

"What's up with the previous stroke history?" said Logan behind the wheel. "Seems like what you tell them when I'm gone to get coffee or whatever is a bit more informative."

"I just get into more details, is all."

Cows, horses, sheep, trees, fields. Driving in Ontario reminded her of car-sick drives when she was a little kid and her family flew up from the Bahamas to visit her grandparents, and of her father, dead now more than thirty years and impossible, anymore, to make real. "I was bike riding down at False Creek, and I started getting numb on one side. In Emerg, they noted I had measurably less sensation on the one side of my face. Personally, I think it was related to TMJ, which correlates to a spot in my upper back, because it often makes my face go numb. The hospital and I had to agree to disagree. I was supposed to do follow-up in six months, but I never did."

"TMJ?"

"Temporomandibular joint—the jaw hinge." She smiled. "The part that gets sore giving blow jobs."

They grabbed a water taxi back to the cottage. The sun was already slacking in the sky, tired with noon, but even so, the day showed no signs of cooling down. As they lurched across the water, Ajax lifted her chin, dropped her head back, and closed her eyes in the wind, relieved not to have been admitted. Or cardioverted, for that matter. Just a private second to cherish life.

"I'm scared," said Logan, shouting over the motor.

"Honey, don't be scared now." But this is how it went— when the crisis passed, emotions barrelled in. "My ticker is ticking. Regularly. It's all good."

Ajax had once told Logan never to love her. Not ever to fall in love because of her health; she'd made sure Logan knew its dangers. But she'd also said, *I'm not strong enough to resist this, so it's gonna have to be you who stops us.*

Logan hadn't stopped. Logan didn't even seem to be stopping now after the hospital, though Ajax would always hold a half-worry that they might want to someday because of medical issues. She was fully aware that lovers could turn on her midstream, walk out, walk away, close their hearts, be finished.

Looking at Logan in the boat, their hair blown up in a messy cockscomb, Ajax couldn't help it—she was still crazy in love.

The boat pulled up, bumping on the rubber tires. They heard Toby barking at Joe and Elliot's.

As they watched the boat pull away, Ajax undid her pj top, slipped out of her bottoms. "Fuck," she said. As in, *It's good to be home.* She dove in. Submerging was perfection; she could feel the hospital sluice from her skin in sheets. She stroked out far, for ten or fifteen minutes, swam back in past a life preserver floating near the dock, and climbed out satiated and streaming with water.

Logan passed her the pajamas, wouldn't look at her.

"Logan, shit, honey, it's over. Hit 'play.' We're back. Pretend it never fucking happened." Ajax shook her head, pounded her skull to unblock her ear.

"The inconvenience of you almost dying, you mean?" Logan said, voice cracking. They turned away, seemed embarrassed.

Ajax touched their shoulder. "Hey, sweetie. I'm sorry. I didn't mean to make light of it. I was just ... pushing it away, getting past it. I don't expect you to—"

Logan jerked free, walked away.

Ajax trotted after them as fast as she could go. *Don't run,* she thought. *Rest your heart.* "Logan! Wait up!"

"No," said Logan, turning on the pathway above Ajax. "No. You don't get to say, 'Logan, get over it.' You don't get to say that. I just fucking found you, Ajax. You don't get to *die.*"

"I'm sorry," said Ajax, tears welling. "Please, I'll—"

"You don't get to be fucking sorry, either. Sorry doesn't hold water; sorry is a paper bag with the bottom torn out. Sorry gets me absolutely nowhere. Are you standing there telling me you've been going through this for twenty years, that your *kids* have, that your *lovers* have? Watching you almost die and then not dying and going on like nothing fucking happened?"

"Well, yeah," said Ajax, pulling her shoulders back, squaring herself. "Yeah, I guess I am, actually."

"Fuck you, then, because I can't do this. I *won't* do this." Logan trembled.

"Logan, don't," said Ajax. "I'm sorry I hurt you. I didn't do it on purpose."

"Really, don't do this? Really, subject myself to this *bullcrap* for the rest of my life? I'm sane, right?"

Ajax nodded reluctantly. "Sure."

"So why would I do this?" Logan pulled the ring from their pocket, held it on their palm, and as Ajax reached for it, tossed it onto the path behind Ajax, who yelped as it rolled into the bushes.

"Go fetch," said Logan bitterly.

"Logan—You love me, I know you love me. This is what you want—to stop? To stop *now*? Or do you want me to get down on my hands and knees and crawl into the bushes to find your love?" Ajax started to cry. Her ring, her beautiful ring. She'd worn it for *maybe* twelve hours. Ajax grabbed Logan's arm. "I try not to give in, you know. That's all. Not to give in."

Logan twisted away. "Oh, fuck you, Ajax. Not give in? Do you have any notion of *how much* you minimize? Nuts to you. Nuts to this whole screwed-up circus. You and your goddamned medical acrobatics." They swept their arms from side to side to ward Ajax away. "I don't care. Don't you get it? *I don't care.* You're sick. You're not even *well enough* to be my wife."

Ajax pulled back, hurt. "That's a horrible thing to say. It might be true, but it's a horrible thing to say."

Logan stomped up the path. "It's over, Ajax."

Ajax plodded after them, bypassed them inside the cottage, climbed into the shower, showered slippery-fast, scrubbing at the ECG glue stuck on her in circles, yanked on shorts and a T-shirt, jammed her other clothes into her suitcase. She couldn't stop sobbing. She needed Logan to take her out of here in the boat and get her back into the city—or maybe she could ask Elliot. She'd stay with friends while she figured things out, till she flew back to Vancouver.

Logan showed up in the doorway. "So last night when I found you, were you going to wake me up so we could get help?"

"Don't talk to me."

"No, I mean it. Were you just going to let yourself die?"

"They didn't do anything to me in the hospital, Logan. They didn't save me. My heart just went back into rhythm. I don't agree with you about this. As far as I'm concerned, we should be celebrating because I'm okay, but never the fuck mind. Never mind. You threw my ring away. Just take me back to the city. I want to go now, right now."

"And if your heart hadn't?"

"Who cares, right?"

"That's so fucking awesome of you, really. So *kind*. To just sit there in the middle of the night, after I'd just proposed to you, waiting to die."

Ajax slammed her suitcase shut. "Really? Because *you're* some kind of medical role model, Logan? You, who told me you've never even had a pap? You, who don't even know if you're in menopause? You, who had your last mammo when? You want *me* to change? Then you change and get your gynecological business looked after. People get gynecological cancers. You take goddamned chances with the boi who's going to be my whatever-the-fuck-you'll-be—my *husband*—every goddamned day. So don't you be giving *me* lectures about how to perform medically." She hefted her suitcase, shoulders heaving, tissue pressed to her face.

Logan grabbed her.

"Let me the fuck go. You can't ever—ever, *ever*—touch me during a fight. That's fucking off the table, and I am so not kidding."

Logan released her. "Give me your suitcase. You are not spending the morning in ER and then carrying around a suitcase."

Ajax said, "But it's okay to toss my ring in the bushes. That stress will be just ducky."

"Fine. Have it your way," said Logan, setting down the suitcase with a clunk, wiping their hands.

Ajax whirled. "*My* fucking way? You're moronic if you think this is *my* way."

"I don't want to break up," said Logan.

"'It's *over*,' you said. To quote ... um ... you. And throwing my ring? That wasn't breaking up? That and four-and-a-half bucks and I'm good to go at Starbucks."

"Okay, then," said Logan spreading their arms. "Maybe I was a jerk. Maybe I shouldn't be mad."

"I don't want to live with a jerk. I need a person who respects me and treats me *well*. Who doesn't use their fear against me. That's immature and hurtful, and, you know what, anyway, *fuck you. Fuck* you."

"Fear? Who wouldn't feel fear? You diving into that lake?

What if you never came up, Ajax? What if you went under and I couldn't do a goddamned thing to rescue you? You swam out a long way."

"Well, throwing a life preserver out twenty feet would probably not have worked." Ajax blew her nose. "I am not a fucking china doll. How many times have I been hospitalized? A reasonable guess?" Her face prickled with anger.

"How the hell would I know? Thirty? Fifty?"

"So how the fuck many of those times did I die?"

Logan pressed their lips together, threw up their hands. "Okay. Okay, I get your drift."

"You don't, though. I won't be made a prisoner of this disease or my disability—either by me or by you. I already can't dance. I can't really walk. I can't carry shit. But I can swim because I can float when I need to stop moving, and I can kayak and lift weights because those only use half my body at a time. I can fucking go to Whitehorse and see the northern lights. I can go to Churchill and see polar bears. I can go on a safari in Africa or take art lessons in Bali. What I can manage, I can do. Okay? Got it?"

Logan nodded.

"You can cross streets, but I should stop you because you might get run over? I mean, I get that it was visceral for you today. Scared is reasonable. Being an asshole to me because you're scared is not reasonable."

"I can't lose you," said Logan, sinking down. "Please, Ajax."

"Then use the goddamned words *I'm sorry*. For fuck's

sake. Show me you even know what a turd you just were."
Ajax sat down, took Logan's hand, softened. "Don't make *me*
lose *you*. Don't call it quits, you fucking wimp. Step up instead.
Apologize. Show me you understand why that's needed."

"I shouldn't have thrown the ring," said Logan.

Ajax rolled her eyes. "Ya think?"

"I'm sorry I said you weren't well enough to love. I'm
just—" They backhanded their hair, the rakish curl tumbling
back down into their eyes. "I'm—you know—sorry. I'm sorry.
Sorry I was a pig."

"Don't do that to me. I don't deserve it. I want my ring
back, too."

"Right," said Logan. "I'll find it, I promise, before we leave
here." They sighed. "You are cavalier, though, right, you have
to admit. If you hadn't—"

"Whoa, mister, stop right there. Are you about to say I
provoked that abuse?" Ajax's eyes went wide. "Because, oh no,
no-no. Where have I heard that before? Oh yeah, in the bat-
terer's handbook." She felt her atria kick, told herself to stand
down. "Okay. I agree I could die. But I didn't die." She took
a deep breath. "Do you know how much angina I have, how
often my heart squeezes from lack of oxygen, how many times
I've squirted nitroglycerin in my life? Like 100,000 times. You
go through that a hundred times a hundred times, and yeah, it
doesn't have a huge impact anymore. *Don't get admitted, don't
get admitted, don't get admitted*, that's maybe all the mantra I
have left. And I get to be a complete person even though I'm

disabled. I get to have a life, Logan! Don't turn me into my disease. I get to laugh and swim and fuck and—"

Logan ran the back of their fingers up the side of Ajax's face. "I want to feel things," they said, "but then when an emotion starts, I just go cold instead."

"I know," said Ajax. "I see it happening."

"Are you really okay?"

"I'm really okay. I'm okay, honest." Why did Logan go cold? And how would their arctic heart play out over time? Ajax needed to think. She needed not to be swept back into infatuation.

Logan said, "Your blood thinner is horrible."

Ajax did not like to think of the rat poison circulating in her bloodstream now—did not want to contemplate the bruises that were going to pounce across her skin. Spankings were most likely out; bondage too—it was good the doctors hadn't seen her bottom. But she wouldn't tell Logan that: need-to-know basis. Reality jerking at their reins—she'd spool that out slowly.

"I love you," said Logan. Their eyes got moist.

"Be more respectful next time," Ajax said, almost coldly.

"Yeah," said Logan. "I agree. One-hundred percent, I agree. That was completely uncalled for."

Ajax reached to thumb a tear from under Logan's eye. "I get that you have this really strong need to feel in control. I don't mind that. If you need to do the driving, that's fine. If you need to change the lightbulbs, knock yourself out. If you need to do all the cooking, I can even handle that. I have a huge tolerance for that after living with the ex. I'm a very patient person. But I demand respect, and I ask that you behave civilly when you're angry. I'm not even talking about yelling here, though that too—I'm talking about verbal content. It's a bottom line issue for me, Logan."

"You deserve that."

"I do deserve that, that's the thing. I was not respected in my last relationship."

Logan said, "I didn't want the same kind of relationships I'd been having; I'd decided just to pack it in. No more dating. And then you showed up and my whole world tilted. I want to be with you, McIntyre."

"I want to be with you, too."

Logan leaned forward and took Ajax's hands. "I want to marry you. Tomorrow—today if we get back soon enough. I don't want to wait. I know I want to be with you. I know I don't want you flying west again without being my wife."

"Logan—" Ajax stared at her fiancé, flummoxed. "I haven't even got a ring, not to put too fine a point on what a jerk you were. Plus, our families."

"We don't have to tell them. We can do it over again when they can be with us. This can just be for us, Ajax."

"It's a public document. And anyway, how the hell do you think my kids would feel if they found out I got secretly married to someone they hadn't even met? If I were them, I'd be plenty hurt."

"I want you right now."

Ajax looked out the window. Conifers reached green arms. In the meadow, the corn poppies tossed red heads, the sun velcroing itself to the tiny hairs along their stems and buds. A field of carmine tissues dropped by the sad and hurt.

Logan kept touching Ajax's face. "I love you to bits."

"I'll be here for a long time to come," said Ajax softly.

"I'm hot for you, baby," said Logan.

Ajax nodded.

She knew that Logan regarded vulnerability as female, but still they stepped out of their shorts, their cock, and stood before Ajax. "I love you," Logan growled, and pushed Ajax down onto the bed. "Oh god, I love you."

She moved Ajax's hand to their wet.

Ajax was all clumsy touch—unsure of the territory. Unsure of Logan's comfort level.

"Yes," Logan said. "Yes." And pressed Ajax toward them. Gripped her shoulders.

Ajax swept her fingers across Logan's clit—brought moisture forward. Logan took her wrist and pressed her inside. Ajax felt the corrugated walls of her lover's vagina, stroked their "G" spot, fucked them hard when Logan wanted that. Fucked them up to her hospital bracelet. Logan slung their legs over Ajax's shoulders and jigged their own clit until they burst.

"Jesus Jesus Jesus," Logan said. "I am not supposed to like that."

Ajax scooted up the bed and rested her head on Logan's shoulder. "Good?"

"So good," said Logan, voice guttural. Logan made a noise—surrender. Their legs were frog-open and forgotten. "Fuck, fuck, Ajax. I forgot it could feel that good. You are a shining star."

"You always touch your clit when I fuck your ass," Ajax said sleepily.

Logan shook their head. "I—I'm on my belly; I didn't even realize you knew that. It's just what I can do to finish when the visuals aren't on."

"Look, baby, we don't ever have to do it again."

"I loved it," said Logan turning to look at her, their eyes wide and vulnerable. "But I don't know how you can do it all the time."

Ajax rolled off Logan's shoulder. "I just open to you, is all. I want you as deep in me as you can go. Because I love you. Because I trust you."

Logan drummed their fingers. "I'm most nude when I'm strapped. That's just how it is for me. But, like, I liked what you did enough that it's gonna fuck me up."

"How fuck you up?"

"When I get into the shower with you without a cock? I'm gonna think I'm a girl again," said Logan. They stuck their arm in the air, had Ajax feel up their biceps. "Thinking I'm a girl fucks me completely up."

"You're not a girl," said Ajax firmly. "You're a boy."

"I'm a *boy*," said Logan.

"Think of cunt for you as inverted cock," said Ajax. "Think

of it as having your cock fucked inside out. Me fucking the inside of your cock."

Logan laughed. "Yeah, yeah." They sat up, pulled on gear and gaunch. "I survived it anyhow. Intact, or at least happy." They undid Ajax's T-shirt, ran a soft finger down between her breasts. "You."

"I guess I'm a pragmatist. I'm a fan of capitalizing on what I have," said Ajax.

"Yeah, I've noticed. I love your skin. It's the colour of toasted nuts."

"It shows every scar."

"Scars should always show. Scars are honour badges." Logan lifted their arm, showing a slash they'd got years ago after falling off a horse. They reached over. "I'm putting my finger here, Ajax, and all I can think about is whether your heart underneath is working okay, not that your nipples are inches away."

"It's never working okay. But it's a trooper," said Ajax.

Logan flattened their hand.

Ajax put her hand on Logan's crotch. "I put my hand here, and all I can think about is that it's you—whatever *you* means. I don't think 'girl.' I don't think 'boy.' I don't think, is this person going to transition?"

"What if I did?"

"I would help you in any way that was possible for me. I hope you know that. You can just feel free to be you, okay? And I will do my best to stay me?"

"Stay you and alive," said Logan.

"Okay," said Ajax. "And we can have whatever kind of sex makes sense to both of us. We can change it up, or we can keep on doing the same old fabulous stuff we discovered at first."

"I'm all for variety, in theory," said Logan.

They smiled at each other.

"I'm especially for getting my ring back."

Logan swatted her. "I was a jerk. I'll get you another one."

"I don't want another one. I want that exact one. The one you gave me when you proposed."

JOE

Joe was up all night railing and howling to everyone she could conjure—family, Linda, Toronto friends—and distractedly caring for Scout. Scout must have sensed the dis-ease, because she cried disconsolately, forcing Joe off the telephone.

Late into the night, Joe woke—was it waking? Had she nodded off?—to the sound of a boat engine. She went to the window, saw red lights growing more distant in the fog above the lake. If it was Elliot having second thoughts, realizing the devastation of her actions, she'd changed her mind about coming in.

Joe discovered a phone message from Logan saying they'd had to go off-island and asking her to watch Toby. Toby, the drooling giant. The small horse of a dog.

Now that she concentrated, she could hear Toby howling. She padded across the dewy grass to rescue him, brought him to her place with some chow, and, after feeding him, spilled out a knuckle bone for him to gnaw on and scrape. His enthusiastic tail could have taken out a six-year-old.

The early dawn was clear, with heat lightning. Joe imagined Ell standing arm in arm with whatever woman she was with, looking up at this same fulgurating sky, seeing different things than Joe was seeing—shooting stars, maybe, promise and beginnings in each flash. Maybe they weren't even up now; maybe they were tucked in bed together, post-coitally spooning.

Joe, though? Joe made it all the way through to Monday without sleep. And Elliot stayed gone, with all her cruelty left behind to boomerang around the cottage. *I'm not in love with you. I should have left you years ago.* Maybe it was sinking in, but it still didn't have as much power as the older things between them: Meeting and falling in love. Laughter. Connection. Dancing. Gardening. Fucking. The fertility lab. Scout!

How do you take what you built together and aim a wrecking ball at it? How do you cause someone that much pain and call yourself reasonable? And why not turn it around and make it right?

Somehow Joe paced her way to Monday afternoon telling herself to *just stop, just stop, just stop.* She looked at her wrists with longing, her baby with detachment, her rafters assessingly. Struggling from bed yet again, she remembered that Elliot, the cad, had done pretty much this exact same thing to Logan.

The heel.

The turd.

Using poly to link up hard with a new girl, breaking poly's boundaries. Long ago, Joe herself said, *Elliot, go home and clean up your mess. If you want to be with me—if you want to get serious with me—then go fix things at home however you have to do that. Resolve things.*

I can't, Elliot had said. *I can't hurt them like that.*

It's not respectful not to tell them the truth.

I don't want to hurt them, but I just don't have the juice for Logan anymore.

You're hurting them now, Elliot. Pretending they're causing this disruption, when it's you? Telling them you're somewhere

else when you're with me? Do the honourable thing. Tell Logan.
Leave them if you need to. But you can't stay where you are,
living with them and loving me. Logan's been making life choices
based on believing you. Leave them or consign me to obliv-
ion—your choice. And if this ever happens to us at some future
point, please, let me be the first, not the last, to know. Promise?

Elliot had crossed her heart.

Ha! How could Joe have forgotten that? Elliot was entirely
self-absorbed, without compassion or insight during that
breakup. She'd thought the rules of good behaviour didn't
apply to her. In the end, she'd dropped Logan like Logan had
never existed, and for years after that, even well into the time
Logan was building on the island, she'd kept their feud going,
stubbornly insisting that everything that was actually her fault
was Logan's.

What a primo assaholic—and Joe had been put on notice
then, hadn't she? She had to know identical behaviour might
be coming her way.

If Ell could walk in right now and wind time back so that
the things she'd said vaporized, would Joe welcome her?

Other than to let Toby out, Joe stayed locked up, not eating,
barely keeping water down, nodding off with Scout at her
breast, and bolting awake in a dream state where she'd forgotten
the crisis and believed, for a split second, everything was fine.
Everything *had* to be just fine, because she couldn't handle being
a single mom; she couldn't manage *that*—she'd never wanted to
have a kid alone. She felt a buzz of protectiveness for Scout, and

as she fed her, promised that she'd keep her safe and happy; she didn't have to go and live with her other mommy, she didn't.

She kept trying to get it to make sense: *Ell left me. Ell left me, Ell left me, Ell left me.*

I promise I will keep you safe, Scout. I promise I will be your mommy no matter what happens with Elliot.

She finally slept out of sheer exhaustion, though she kept startling awake.

Joe was more dishevelled with each passing hour, but she picked her slow way down the path and across the flagstones and knocked politely at Logan's door. Logan came up behind her from the dock, mud on their knees, twigs in their hair. Toby thrashed his weapon of a tail, excited to be home.

Joe thrust Scout into their arms.

Logan said, "Joe, whoa. Not a good ti—" but Joe had barrelled inside. Logan followed her in, brushing off their knees.

Ajax, fuzzy-slippered feet up, lifted a wan hand in greeting. "You look like hell, Joe. Come over here and tell me."

"You can't be here right now, Joe," said Logan firmly. "We're on our way back to Toronto." They exchanged a warning look with Ajax.

"Elliot left me!" Joe said, windmilling her arms.

Logan said, "What are you talking about?" They held the baby out like Scout's diapers were stinky.

Joe grabbed the baby back.

Ajax struggled to get up. "No! Oh no!"

"Don't you even think about getting up, Ajax," Logan remonstrated.

"Why can't Ajax get up?" Joe looked around. "How did the proposal go?"

Ajax sank back down. "We're engaged!" She lifted her left hand, ringless. "Theoretically, there's a ring."

Logan sank to their knees in front of the couch, dug in their pockets, and pushed a silver band onto Ajax's finger.

"You're filthy, Logan," said Ajax, beaming, giving them a kiss. "Tell us about Elliot, Joe. What the *fuck?*"

"Congratulations!" Joe bent to kiss Ajax's forehead, lowered the baby into Ajax's reaching arms. "Congrats! How wonderful! Congrats, you old dog," said Joe to Logan, shoulder-punching them. "I'm thrilled for you."

"We're pretty happy about it," said Ajax.

Logan scowled. "You mean Elliot's off somewhere? She left you here alone?"

Joe said, "No, I mean she walked out on me. On us. I don't know when. Yesterday?"

"I know we're talking Elliot here, but she wouldn't do that."

Joe shrugged. "Hours before, we were fucking." *I screwed her brains out,* thought Joe.

"That's what she did to me, too," said Logan. "She fucked me when she was about to tell me she was dumping me. There's someone else, right?"

"She alluded to it. Vaguely. Possibly." Scout began to root

on Joe's shirt. "If I stop to think about it, she's been very distant. She barely seems to care about Scout."

Logan said, "If Elliot hadn't dumped me, I wouldn't have found Ajax."

"You're coming back to Toronto with us," said Ajax. "We're not leaving you up here by yourself, Joe, no way."

Joe looked at them and realized something was very off. "What's going on, you guys? I mean, besides the fact that you're getting hitched?"

They gave her the medical update.

Joe fed Scout with tears streaming down her face. *And she thought* she *had problems.*

AJAX

As they bucked across the lake toward Logan's car, Joe leaned back against Ajax's knees with the bundled baby, white as the froth on the wake, belongings piled high around her; Ajax and Logan were taking her back to her city house in the Beaches — where, with luck, Elliot hadn't set up shop.

Everything was freaking Ajax out (quietly, quietly, so Logan couldn't tell): Elliot's duplicitousness and abandonment, her own engagement, Logan and whether Logan would be, long-term, dependable. Thoughts sped through her mind triple-time. *Face facts*, she said to herself. She was a genderqueer woman engaged to a maybe-transitioning guy. Logan's cunt was a relic from an accident of split cells; in lowering their cunt onto Ajax's mouth, in calling for Ajax to fuck them deeper and harder, had Logan felt surreal? The answers could wait; for now, Ajax was happy they could touch each other's sore, bruised parts and claim it as love.

The Mustang's top was up to protect Scout; Joe half wept, half slept slumped beside her car seat. On the other side of Scout, Toby hulked, his head mostly dangling out the window. Ajax craned around frequently to see if they were okay. *Define okay*, Joe thought, *with a massive dog goobering on your baby's head.* Ajax watched the scenery slide past. *Stop whining and get on with it. You've been sick before. There's plenty to be happy about. You're getting married! To a person you adore!*

And you have less chance of a stroke! More chance of a bleed, but less of a stroke.

Dropping Joe off at her house was hard, but she wouldn't agree to come stay with them. "We'll call you," Ajax called, blowing a kiss. "I'll be thinking of you every second."

Logan was obviously itching to get Ajax inside. From the parkade, Logan steered her firmly toward the apartment and bed, tucked her in, and took Toby for another walk. "He needs some roughhousing," they said. Ajax drifted off into a dream of jogging; Logan was keyboarding beside her when she woke the next morning.

"You don't by chance have your divorce certificate with you, do you, sleepyhead?" said Logan. "We need it for our licence."

Ajax, still dreamy and warm, rolled into her lover's arms; Logan put the computer aside. Logan hugged her, kissed the end of her nose. Ajax said sleepily, "Where's the fire?" Meaning, *I didn't die. Would we be doing this right now if I wasn't sick?*

Logan popped out of bed to feed the dog; the aroma of canned dog food and kibble wafted in. Logan jumped back in bed and said, "You don't want to get married anymore?"

"I get that we shouldn't wait to have a ceremony in the Bahamas, but I still want my kids there, a bit of a proper occasion. And I think Joe and Scout have to be there, if not Elliot. Symbolically, new life, right? Plus Joe needs company right now. Joe is going to really need the heck out of us." Ajax threw back the covers and they gasped. While she was sleeping, she had bloomed with blue roses. Bruises, dozens if not hundreds, regrettably easy to distinguish against her still-grey skin.

"Ajax, sweetheart, what the hell?"

"Oh, fuck goddamnit. Pass me tissues." Ajax rolled from bed, bleeding from her nose. Even with a wad of tissues, blood dripped around Ajax's fingers. "More, more! Fuck!" She tried to catch the overflow with her legs, but she bled on the bed, the carpet. She daubed ineffectually at her legs. She watched Logan's face grow horrified. She ran to the bathroom, saw what looked like slaughter in the mirror—blood tears, blood everywhere—threw back the shower curtain, dropped herself into the tub, and sat there stunned and freezing, shivering with goosebumps. She pulled down a towel and wrapped herself in it. She'd read the stats on hemorrhaging from blood thinners; big chance, especially in the first month. Twenty percent of people who landed in the hospital died within a week. And there was gangrene, necrosis, amputations, strokes—not one of those a word she wanted to utter around Logan, but every one of them a word which Logan might soon hear. The good news was that her stomach didn't hurt and she wasn't vomiting; there were no signs of internal bleeding, so far. *Touch wood*. This was just what they called "nuisance" bleeding.

Logan called 9-1-1.

"I knew I'd hemorrhage. I *knew* it," said Ajax, tilting her head back. "Why didn't I listen to myself?"

Logan draped a blanket over her. "I would have made exactly the same decisions."

"But I knew better. My instincts are usually good. I can't fucking be on these drugs."

Logan tried to mop up Ajax's face, but the blood continued to pour from her nose and tear ducts.

"I'm so cold, Logan," Ajax said, shutting her eyes.

"Help is on its way, sweetheart."

"My left arm is tingly," said Ajax, opening and closing her hand, wiggling the fingers. She looked at her fiancé. "I knew I should walk away from you. I didn't think it was going to get bad like this, not for years; I thought I was basically okay, or I could work on getting better, anyway. I did all the right things to get better, honey, so we could have a life together."

"This sucks, but you don't suck. Your left ventricle doesn't work, is all. When I met you, you felt like total shit, and you kept on trucking anyway. I'd have you out walking, you'd be limping, and you'd be trying to distract me so I didn't see you spray nitro, or you'd be wearing a patch I didn't know about, and you'd be coughing, and I honestly didn't know what that meant, but you just kept on going as if you were perfectly okay. Which you were not. And you were *happy*."

"Well, I *am* happy," said Ajax. "Also fabulous at hiding illness. Years ago, when I came out, other people were busy hiding that they were queer, and I was perfectly up-front about it, but that I was a heart crip, no way, that was my deep, dark secret."

"Weird girl," said Logan softly, stroking her brow.

Ajax looked at the tub, felt squeamish and faint. "Well, at least we know I have a lot of blood."

The buzzer went. "That's the ambulance."

"Your mom is going to give you such a lecture," said Ajax.

Ajax was pre-triaged in the ambulance and admitted. Her left arm wasn't getting circulation, so the nurses checked for skin necrosis and gangrene, rolling her over in the cot every five minutes.

"All this from a little rat poison?" said Logan. "My little rodent."

Ajax laughed.

Logan kissed Ajax's cheek. There was dried blood caked in her hair, crusting her eyes and the corners of her nose and mouth.

Ajax surrendered her phone with the kids' numbers again. "This time, I don't think there's any choice. You gotta call."

"Have they said when I can take you out of here?"

"CICU, baby. Cardiac Intensive Care Unit. I'm admitted. It'll be, you know, days. Maybe you had better call Joe, too. Joe will be wondering what happened to us. I told her we'd bring lunch by today."

"Honey. Honey, I can't stand this."

"Can you grab me another blanket? There should be an oven somewhere for heated ones. And if you could bring me decaf and edible food, I'd really appreciate it. Yogurt and fruit in the mornings?"

"Hon, if your kids are flying in anyhow—"

"I don't think they need to *fly in* for this." But Ajax thought, *Twenty-percent fatality rate.* And then, *They do.*

"I'll fly them in and as long as they're here, let's get married during Pride. Why not get married at the Dyke Parade?"

Ajax burst out laughing—because she'd done exactly that at a long-ago Toronto Dyke March to the ex who hurt her. This coming Sunday would have been their anniversary. The laughing started her nose bleed anew; she was laughing and snorting when a nurse rushed in with ice and a vitamin K boost and made Logan leave.

Logan turned at the curtain. "What a complete moron your ex was, I just have to say."

"Out," said the nurse and held the compress to Ajax's face.

Barrelling toward catastrophe. Doctors, nurses, techs, janitors swishing filthy mops, doctors again, shift changes, staff turn-over. IVs, MRIs, CTs, bloodwork, bruises, spelling out the jargon for Logan: IV = intravenous line. MRI = magnetic resonance imaging. CT = computed tomography, multiple combined X-ray images. Fear = fear.

Backrubs, neck rubs, right hand rubs. Reading Audre Lorde and Marilyn Hacker. Slumping through bad TV. Waiting, waiting. Visitors, a thin stream; Joe with Scout and updates every day; Logan's mother Ruth, grudgingly, and none too friendly; Ajax's old high school friend, Denise. Calls and texts from Bahamian relatives and friends, Vancouver relatives and friends. Simone and Vivi, her daughters, calling day and night. Waiting for something to happen, the gangrene to spread, the doctor to order debriding, to say it was time to operate and restore blood flow.

Her hand turning red and black. Learning what dry gangrene was and how there was every likelihood that she had contracted it—a ten-percent chance of their diagnosis being wrong. Being glad it wasn't wet gangrene or gas gangrene. Watching a nurse draw a black magic marker line across Ajax's palm to see if it spread or declined past the border. Thinking it was spreading. Thinking it was abating. Thinking it was spreading again. Talking to everyone Ajax knew from BC on the telephone. Hogging the computer when Logan brought it in. Worried about herself; worried about how haggard Logan was looking. Neither was getting enough sleep, enough good food. Ajax was probably drinking too much coffee and definitely not getting adequately clean each day. She was fretting too much and worrying about hospital-acquired infections. The ward around her rattled with efficiency. This, at least, was good news. The sicker one got, as she knew, the quieter things were.

Logan said, "I say your name everywhere I go. 'Ajax, Ajax, Ajax.' I get pretty convinced I can cure you by the sheer force of thinking you well."

Smells of bleach, of antiseptic soap, urine, shit, blood, perfume, body odour. Things undefinable. Magazines chewed up with age, water glasses with bendy straws, pull-up taupe trays, bed bars, call buttons, heart monitor stickers that itched, blood pressure cuffs that squeezed too hard, IVs that stung at the puncture site and up the vein. Hospital-green walls. Fluorescent lighting. Noise and never a second's privacy.

Falling more helplessly in love.

"You know when I first realized that I was going to marry you?" Logan grinned. "Remember? I was drunk, stumbling home from Veronica's Grill. I was on the phone to you, and I said, *I'm gonna marry you.* And you said, *No you fucking aren't. I wouldn't fucking say yes even if you asked me.*"

Ajax laughed, asked Logan to raise the head of the bed.

"I knew then. Because you were mouthy; you talked back."

"Ha! Well, shit, I'm still talking back."

Logan sighed, sank on to the edge of the bed. "Thank god you are still talking back."

JOE

If Elliot thought of them at all, she probably imagined they were still at the cottage. Joe'd left her messages—*Please, Elliot, reconsider, Elliot, please please please I beg you*. And, *Take your narcissism and stuff it where the sun don't shine. You're the cruelest person in the world and I hate you! I hate you!* And, *No, no, I'm sorry, I didn't mean it! I love you!*—until her box was full, with no response. What would Ell discover if she went back? A missing wife and daughter, dirty diapers still in a pail.

Joe hadn't left a note. Because, *fuck Elliot. Go to hell, Elliot, and take your handbasket with you*.

"What am I going to do?" she wailed to friends.

One said, "But Elliot was looking forward to the baby! She told me so, over and over!"

Another said, "But Elliot is crazy about you, Joe. There's something you're missing."

"But don't you guys—aren't you guys the poster kids for dyke marriages, actual functional, working dyke marriages? If you guys break up, what does that mean for the rest of us?"

"Did you *do* something? What did you *do*?"

One of Elliot's lovers said, "You kicked her out."

And Joe said, "I did what?"

"Elliot told me you made her leave."

"I didn't make her leave; she just left."

"She says it was you. If you wanted to keep your marriage, you have a pretty weird way of showing it." One's grasp of so-called "truth" was often just whose story reached you first, Joe realized. "You can't expect things to just go back to normal after that."

Joe said, "You talked to Elliot?"

"Of course I talked to Elliot. Five or six times."

"She's *okay?* God! Where is she?"

"Joe, I know you have a baby, and it makes you moody, but Elliot's not wrong about you being over-dramatic."

"Just tell her I want her to come home. Will you please tell her that for me? She's not picking up messages."

The friend said, "I'm not comfortable being your go-between. I don't want to get in the middle of your fights."

Joe sighed. "We didn't have a fight. We didn't have an anything."

"Well, don't drag me into your whatever, your *nothing*, okay? If you have to know, Joe, I support Elliot in this, okay? I'm on Ell's side."

There were sides now?

To Linda, she said, "Ell is all mixed up for me now with Dree, and it's like I don't even know, half the time, which one of them is dead. No, no, that sounds stupid. I mean my brain is refusing to process any of it."

"I don't blame you," said Linda.

"I can't come back for Dree's funeral," said Joe. "Obviously."

"Of course," said Linda. "But I know you wanted to."

"Put a flower on Dree's grave for me, okay?'

Hours collapsed in an exhausted, wet blur—tears and urine

and breastmilk. Joe's mother came by to help with pragmatic matters—fed Joe lunch, did laundry and shopping, prepped easy dinners of salads and cold cuts.

It was hard to talk about the breakup with people who hadn't been supportive as the relationship unfolded. *Yes, we fought this hard for the right to marry. Yes, we asked you to put aside your qualms and attend our weddings. Yes, our marriages are still not perfect. Because we're just like you*, thought Joe. *The same hopes, the same fears, the same fights.*

Her mother said, "You always defend her. And Scout is hers."

Not that Joe hadn't thought the same thing, but she was offended.

"You're the one stuck doing all the work while Elliot's off gallivanting—"

"Stop that. Scout's my baby too. Just as much my baby."

"I never understood your arrangement, you girls."

"You didn't—don't have to, Mom."

"Well, I don't. I'm just telling you that I don't, and nobody else in the family does either."

"Okay then. Mom, the important thing is, I'm really grateful for your help. And … um … I think we can manage just fine without it."

"Ha!" said her mother.

Joe felt almost as much shock that Ajax was fighting for her life as she did that Elliot had left her, which had come to seem, in the space of a couple of days, almost inevitable. That Elliot had left Scout, though? Still there was radio-silence, as if, in fact, Ell had not walked out, but had been removed by aliens.

By her people, thought Joe snidely.

Then, after three days, Logan played (in the hospital cafeteria, far out of Ajax's hearing) a rambling message they thought that Joe deserved to hear, about a guy, Steve, Elliot's "true love," and about how Elliot had finally figured out that she was "not gay after all." And the message concluded after a long pause: "So, yeah, um ... also ... I'm preggers. Don't tell Joe."

Scout tucked deep into her baby wrap. Clatter of knives and forks. Sliding plastic trays. Chairs scraping. Heads bent over lunches that probably no one tasted. Weak light coming in through high, dirty windows. Staff laughing. Shell-shocked relatives of patients, occasional outright sobs.

Adrenalin swept through Joe's body. A guy. Steve. Elliot "preggers." A guy. Steve. Elliot pregnant. Elliot pregnant! Suddenly Elliot's nausea made sense. Joe looked intently down at Logan's phone as if Ell might appear from it like a genie, then passed it back to Logan without comment.

A guy. Steve.

A baby.

Joe wracked her brain to remember any such Steve. Who the hell was Steve? A Steve up north? Was Steve the reason for all the trips to the cottage? Had Steve fucked Elliot in their marital bed?

Logan said, "Elliot would be the first person to condemn someone else acting exactly like she is."

Joe grunted, some noise in her throat that made people from another table look up.

It seemed Elliot had made a decision about the separation some time before she clued Joe in. And Elliot had been on about some guy in her office. Some guy named—? Joe couldn't remember, but she didn't think it was Steve. She'd mooned around the house for months, sighing. "I just *love* Gerry. Gerry's so amazing." Or maybe it *had* been Steve—*Steve is so amazing.*

"Elliot's pregnant?" Joe screeched. "How did I miss this? She's been throwing up. My wife's been seeing a dude, and I didn't have a clue? How many times over the years has she told me she's wanted to go back to men? I am so dense. I am so freaking dense."

"No," said Logan, "you're trusting, and that's a good thing even if it doesn't feel like that right now."

"Gullible."

"You aren't the one in the wrong here, Joe."

"So much for Elliot, open and honest poly practitioner, eh? My wife was *pregnant* while I gave birth to our kid? When we were together the other night, a thought flickered through my mind about her gaining weight, because she had the littlest pot belly, and she's never had one before, but never, ever, did pregnancy cross my mind. Why would I think that? She's not even that fertile according to the doctors. No wonder she's been moody. No wonder she's been off eggs. And beer! Logan, do you know this guy? Steve is going to be the father of Scout's sister or brother." She wrapped her arms tight around Scout.

Logan shook their head. "I know I should tell her about Ajax, but I just can't deal with her right now."

"Did she really think you wouldn't tell me she's pregnant?"

"She probably knew I'd tell you. Then she doesn't have to, right? Chicken's way out." Logan drummed their fingers, glanced behind them.

"Did you know something, Logan?"

They brushed back their hair, squeaked their chair over the tiles. "Joe, what if Ajax loses her hand? What if the gangrene spreads?"

Gangrene. It hit Joe again, a speeding bullet. *Gangrene.*

Sleeping with Logan had finally been supplanted by reality. Now Joe thought, *Just let Ajax survive.*

"She's going to lose her hand, I guess," said Logan with finality. "I have to come to grips with that." They drummed on the table. "*Grips.* I just said grips."

"I'm sorry," said Joe.

Logan shrugged. "Fuck."

"Fuck," said Joe quietly.

"Her kids are arriving later."

"Do you need me to go to the airport?"

"I promised Ajax I'd pick them up myself. You just go home and, I don't know, try to cope with what Elliot's left you to cope with. Knowing Ajax, she'll probably appreciate the chance for a nap."

"I can't change anything," said Joe sorrowfully. Scrape of chairs, clatter of trays being emptied.

"No," said Logan. "You can't. I can't, either."

"Maybe seeing her girls will make Ajax rally?"

Logan jingled their keys. "She didn't even want me to call them. I didn't call them when we were up north. I'm guessing they'll have some choice words for me about that."

"I think she hates freaking people out." Across the room, someone dropped a tray. Clattering of dishes, coffee cup smashing.

Logan looked at Joe. "I hate that she's freaking people out, too. I would give a whole lot to go back to *before*."

"Before would be an excellent place to live."

But it was harder than Ajax imagined to get well. When she was still hospitalized three days later (*deaths in the first week*, thought Ajax), and the docs on their two p.m. rounds had confirmed that there was no longer any doubt that this was dry gangrene (*gangrene!* thought Ajax), she lost spirit. Life got harder not easier with age, with fewer opportunities for holding out for hope. Offers of psychiatry from the hospital were politely declined. "I've been dealing with this disease for twenty years," she told the nurses. "It's not a shock. I can manage." She could manage, but perhaps not now, not right now, not in front of all the intrusive staff. If she was going to be cut off at the knees (as it were), then she was going to do it in the loo, sobbing into toilet paper.

"Glass half full of bullshit," she said, looking at the floor, wondering again about hospital acquired infections often contracted in washrooms. She had watched the cleaning staff with their filthy black mops swishing germs.

Okay, okay, there was love, love with spikes. (Yes, the doctors had checked her all over, including her bruised ass, had questioned and delivered a lecture about how she could not afford ... how she should not be ... how she would need to be more careful, given her blood thinners. "But I am not on warfarin anymore, right? Didn't you take me off warfarin?" Grudgingly, scribbling notes, they admitted they had.) Loving Logan was not going to be a peaceful ride, she understood that, whether the subject was sex or not. And maybe she was grateful for that, because what woman of fifty would want an uncomplicated partner, a life without colour?

She had strong, independent children and step-grandchildren. And her painting.

Was she really going to move to Ontario?

What it was, though, for all its insanity, was a life going forward, a life with a future. On the other side, there was this confounding, blasted illness that had dogged her heels for most of her life. Some people didn't reach thirty-one, the age at which she had been felled. There was that. Many people had more pain than she did.

But between interruptions for needles or assessments or sponge baths or meals or tests, she had nothing to do but lie in her bed and stare at her yellowing nails and blackening hand with its Sharpie-boundary, waiting for the gangrene to come on worse or retreat. To stare at the innocent-looking non-perfused arm or the rest of her blighted body that barely worked or the blankets or the ceiling tiles or the pages of books she didn't even realize she hadn't been reading until twenty pages had gone by.

Logan dropped off Ajax's kids, who were, besides jet-lagged, uncharacteristically sombre. Ajax tucked her hand under the covers. Simone from the Bahamas, the event coordinator, pregnant with Ajax's first natal grandchild, and Vivi, Ajax's IT baby with the wild shocks of purple hair, were both slump-shouldered and dull, with sharp small blades of worry sparking periodically in their eyes.

"It'll be okay, I promise," said Ajax. And thought *Ha ha ha ha ha ha.* "Sorry you had to meet Logan at the airport. Honey?" she said, patting Vivi with her right hand. "This is not all doom and gloom. It's just a set-back, is all. Did someone tell you this was some lost cause?"

"Mom, I flew in from *Vancouver*," said Vivi. "What the fuck else would it be? They want to amputate your *hand.*"

"It's just my left hand."

"It's just your *left hand?*" said Simone. "Well, shit, I guess I'll fly back to the Bahamas, then."

"I mean, it won't kill me. Yes, it's a drag and all, but ... not fatal." She thought a moment. "You girls sit down."

Vivi began to cry, her curls shaking. "This is horrible."

Her children seemed bleached by the insipid green walls, the green curtains on their tracks around the bed, by fatigue, by worry.

"This is so fucked up," said Simone. Simone had eyes the colour of turquoise, but in here they looked grey. She had straightened her hair and pulled it severely back from her unlined face.

"I know," said Ajax.

Vivi sighed dramatically and said, "Well," and yanked tissues from the dispenser.

Simone said, "Oh, Mommy."

"I'll be out of here soon," said Ajax. She reached to touch Simone's belly. "Simone, tell me about the baby."

"A girl," said Simone with a wan smile. "We just found out. So you have to not die, Mom, because I need you to be at the birth. I need you in my daughter's life."

"Congratulations," said Ajax. "A girl, wow. Due date in October?"

Vivi said, "We only have girls."

"October seventh," Simone confirmed.

"I look forward to it," said Ajax.

Vivi said, "We so have to get you better."

Ajax said, "There has been some heartening retreat of the, uh ..."

"Don't be stoic."

"Yeah," said Simone. "For once I agree with Vivi. Don't be stoic."

The girls left after a short visit. Ajax fatigued easily in company—even with her own children. *When to stop fighting for more life?* she wondered. At some point, so many pieces of her would be carved off, there'd not be much more than a spine left. Big scar down her right arm from an arterial transplant. Gouged-out breasts. Scar under her left tit from open heart surgery. Scar on the top of her thigh from same. Numerous numb patches. Scars dotting her body from a runaway allergy to a prescription. *Where to draw the line?* wondered Ajax.

The next day, when Logan arrived at the hospital, Ajax had

turned for the better, and the doctors had removed amputation from the equation. Ajax felt the difference as the antibiotics dripped slowly into her, her hand perfusing. "Maybe you slept on it wrong," a doctor opined about the bad circulation. *Yup. That's where I've come to*, thought Ajax. *Slayed by sleeping wrong.*

Her hand was affected halfway up her palm, the skin shrivelled and sucked dry, and her fingers were still numb, but the docs concluded they'd probably caught it early enough.

Logan got pissed off in a way they hadn't been when amputation was on the menu, and ranted about a lawsuit.

"Hon, forget it. Nobody forced me to take warfarin," Ajax said. "Just get me out of here. Look, can I just be supremely happy about not losing my hand for one second here, please? May I just be really glad that I'm not leaking from every pore any longer?"

When Simone came in, wreathed in smiles at the news, she said, "Mom, we flew all the way here; you could at least have the decency to die."

Vivi said, "Yeah, I brought my best mourning dress," and kissed her mother's forehead, her purple curls falling on Ajax's face.

Ajax laughed. "So, um, look, while we're, uh, you know, gathered here together ... "

Logan said, "Your mom and I are getting married!"

Ajax beamed.

Silence. The noises of the hospital went on around them, the intercom, patients coughing, nurses talking, bleeps.

Vivi said, "But she's our *mom*."

"And I'm going to spend my life looking after her," said Logan.

"Wait just a goddamned second, the bunch of you," said Ajax. "I am *not* feeble. I'm planning to look after myself, thank you very much, and look after you lot, as well." She regarded her kids' stricken faces. "Logan and I weren't expecting to feel this way, or so soon, but we do."

"Mom, you're covered in bruises!" said Vivi. "And they almost just cut off your hand."

"But at least I don't have A-fib anymore, right?" She laughed, but no one else did. *Yet,* she thought. *She didn't have A-fib again* yet; *she'd probably need ablation surgery to treat it.* "Right?"

Simone shrugged and Vivi crossed her arms over her chest.

"I know it's hard, you guys, all of this. I've put you through a lot with my medical crap over the years. But I love you, and we're not asking your permission, only inviting you. I really want you to attend my wedding."

"Mo-om, *another* wedding?" Vivi whined.

"When is it?" said Simone.

"Just be happy for me, okay, girls? I know you're concerned, but I'll be okay. They said I'll be fine."

"O-kay," said Simone.

Vivi nodded and said, "Sure. As you can see, we're stunningly happy, we pair of sisters."

"Well, it wouldn't kill you, you know, to support us," said Ajax. Logan sat down on the bed and Ajax bumped over her legs to make room. "Why bet for this to be a mistake? You don't know any more than I know, or Logan knows. We might be about to do something that will be really great for us. It's possible. Fifty percent of marriages make it."

"Are those *gay* stats?" asked her eldest.

"I support you," said Vivi and elbowed Simone. "We both do."

"Yeah," said Simone reluctantly.

"Saturday," said Logan.

"Saturday's Mom's anniversary," said Simone. And then, pointedly, "To our *other* mother. Our *actual* mother."

"No, listen, definitely not Saturday—yuck," said Ajax. "But we'll do it soon so you can be with us. Okay? You'll come? Say you'll come?"

JOE

Joe spent an hour sobbing in a lawyer's office for $450, Rebecca's hourly rate, telling Rebecca that nothing made sense, and that as far as she knew, Elliot had been perfectly happy.

"Okay, not perfectly happy," said Joe, patting Scout, sniffling, "but not *unhappy*. How did we go from long-term couple to an acrimonious divorce without passing *go*?" The lawyer said it often happened; one spouse made plans to move out and didn't mention it in order to gain the upper hand.

"But that's cruel!" Joe said. "I don't want to have to think she's a shit-head when I've just spent the bulk of my life being crazy about her. How can this just happen unilaterally, and I get no say?"

"You have to defend yourself," said Rebecca, passing Joe a list of documents she'd need to prepare—three years of tax returns, bank statements, investment information, real estate holdings, health records, marriage certificate, duration of her maternity leave, and Employment Insurance. "And, remember, you'll have two children."

"Two children?"

"Elliot's child will be born while you are still married, so you will be its other mother."

"Oh my god. Are you kidding me?"

Rebecca shook her head.

"Scout's hers, biologically!"

"Where the law is at all dicey on that, it comes down on

your side as the mother who carried. Of course Elliot will be expected to contribute to her welfare. We've received notice that Elliot intends to sue for shared custody."

"*Excuse* me?" Joe pinched her leg just to force a sensation that wasn't fear.

"Given the infant's tender age, there are likely to be adjustments until she's weaned."

"No!" said Joe, half standing. "No! My daughter and I aren't adjustments. How is my life falling apart without me having any say in it? I'm married! I want to be married! It's not fair that Elliot can just drop us. This is our life we're talking about. This is everything we are. This is our future. She can't just kick us aside like we're garbage."

"I'm sorry. I know it's hard. But the law says that indeed she can. Do you have keys for the cottage?"

Keys for the cottage?

"Because the law says that what Elliot brought into the relationship stays with her. Of course there will be modifications because of the time you cohabited—you'll get half of the increase in value during your relationship. Her lawyer is advising her to have the cottage locks changed. And you should do the same with the matrimonial home."

Cohabited? Change the locks? Matrimonial home?

"She wants to clear out her things. I have three dates that will work from Elliot's side. You need to pick one and vacate your premises for three hours."

"But who says what belongs to her?"

"You should do an inventory."

Elliot's voicemail remained full. She'd blocked Joe on Facebook and Twitter. Joe's only means of communication was by letter, so she sent a bulging, plaintive letter to Elliot's office marked "Private and Confidential," begging Elliot to reconsider on behalf of their child—their children, if you considered Elliot's pregnancy a child. *Elliot, pregnant! Elliot, with a guy! Elliot, gone! Elliot, fighting her in a court battle that her lawyer warned her was very likely to get ugly before it was resolved!* What was the point of battling it out and making lawyers rich? Joe asked. Couldn't they just agree to split things equitably? Couldn't they just remember their vows? Couldn't they just remember their promises? What happened? she asked in her letter. What did I do wrong? Was it something I said? Something I didn't say? Something I did? Something I didn't do?

Did you fall in love with him?

Were you plotting to leave me the whole time?

Were you even a tenth of the person I thought you were?

She thought of all the dozens or probably hundreds of times that they'd resolved problems with shy grins and laughter. The fun they'd had. Their jokes with language—the times they'd cracked each other up learning German. Their trips, their gardening, their renovating. Was a mid-life crisis automatically worth heeding? Was whatever this was for Elliot—a psychotic break?—more important than the jewel of their marriage? Was she really so naïve as to think her problems would be solved by leaving—that she wouldn't take her discontent, her inability to be satisfied, with her? Didn't she know that any woman's, any man's, halo would tilt within six months, and she'd be right back where she'd been with Joe—living in reality? The problem Elliot was having was inside Elliot.

They had been each other's backbones, each other's blood, each other's hearts. They'd supported each other through every kind of life event. Why on earth was Ell willing, eager, to toss it all aside now? Maybe Elliot needed to turn Joe into a pile of shit in order to make it possible for her to walk away.

Joe asked Logan to be at the house while Ell was there, but also asked them to stay after to pick up Joe's pieces. When Joe knocked—on her own door, no less—Logan let her in. Almost everything had been taken—the antiques, the dishes, the cutlery, the furniture, the rugs, the art.

"What the fuck?" said Joe. The baby was in her Snugli, sound asleep, her neck slicked with sweat, head kinked at an odd angle. Joe couldn't stop touching things—door frames, countertops, door knobs. "Did you talk to her, Logan? Did she say anything?"

"She had movers and she directed them from room to room. She didn't say anything personal to me the entire time. Didn't even really look at me."

"She's actually doing this, isn't she?" said Joe.

"Please don't ask me to explain her." Logan kissed her

forehead. "Any fool could see the mistake she's making. Any fool would love you."

Joe followed Logan from room to room like a hurt puppy, tail between her legs, mewling. In her office: "She took my desk?" In their bedroom: "She took our bed?" She slumped against the wall as Scout woke. "Jesus. Did she leave anything? They took this in three hours? Without packing?"

"She hired specialists."

"There are people you can hire to move you out when you're leaving your wife?"

She just said, "Take it all."

"Christ," said Joe. "Can I get something, a court order? Where the fuck am I supposed to sleep?"

"She left the crib."

"I see that," said Joe.

"And your books. I guess they're your books."

"They're my books," said Joe. "But fuck a duck, Logan. Taking everything is legal? What the hell am I going to do?"

She knew what she was going to have to do. Temporarily, until she got furniture, she was going to have to move in with her mother.

AJAX

Ajax was released from hospital two days after Simone and Vivi's arrival with her left arm in a sling. She was gobsmacked that being hospitalized had run her so far down; even though all she wanted was to cuddle up with Logan, alone, without bars on the bed, without hospital personnel around, she was tired to her bones and crawled into bed to sleep straight through until the next day, when Logan woke her up to feed and water her.

"Honey, I don't know if I can go out," said Ajax, peeling a banana in the kitchen. Toby thumped his tail beside her. "Where are the children staying?"

"I've got them in at one of the hotels I'm building," said Logan. "I offered a room to Joe, too, but so far, she says no, she's fine licking her wounds at her mother's place where she can get help with Scout."

"Poor, poor Joe," said Ajax. "Divorce is a cruel business."

"She doesn't even know how she can pay her lawyer," said Logan. "Elliot cleaned out the accounts, and when Joe's lawyer asked Elliot's lawyer how Joe was supposed to survive, she apparently just said, *Really not my business.*"

"Not her business? What, does she think Joe can pull money out her asshole? You can't support someone for all those years and then take a pass. What kind of cretin would even consider financially dumping someone in need? Support may be inconvenient, it may leave you hurting for cash, but I'm sorry, only a mega-creep would try to hold it back."

"I don't think Elliot thinks. Because otherwise it would occur to her: *Can't work, completely dependent on me, mothering my daughter*. But no."

"Cruelty is not on. It's only fucking money. God, if you have it, share it. Make sure the people you love—"

"She says she doesn't love her."

"People's needs don't vanish because you did."

"Well said."

"Ell is a douche-canoe."

"Don't get riled up," said Logan.

"I really wish there was such a thing as fucking karma. I would like to see people get theirs. Joe's a reasonable person. Couldn't Ell have sat her down and said, *I've fallen in love with someone else?*"

"She's always felt entitled. She thinks that no one else's troubles matter. She had breast cancer back in the Pleistocene epoch and therefore seas should part for her."

"If I got an iota of the special attention for my cardiac disease as Elliot got for a cancer long gone ..." Ajax sighed. "I'm so tired."

"Go nap. There's time before dinner."

"I'm just fed up with what turdy shit-heads people are."

Toby had flaked out near the foot of the bed. Ajax stared down at her hand. She could still make out the magic marker line, but her fingers weren't yellow, just scabby and rough, the skin peeling back to red skin underneath. She'd lost three fingernails, which hadn't hurt.

"I want to see the kids, but maybe just downstairs at Le Lapin, because I'm going to need an early night."

They met Ruth, Logan's mother, and Joe at the restaurant, sat outside on the patio with Toby tied to the railing. You could see right away that Joe had been crying; she passed Scout around.

"She's so adorable," said Ruth.

"Isn't she sweet?" said Ajax, baby-cooing. Logan twisted in their seat. They yanked their ball cap off, crammed it back on. They ordered vodka tonics, two, while Ajax and Ruth sipped Sauvignon Blanc and Joe a nursing-friendly lemonade.

Ruth was in her eighties, but easily functioned as someone younger. A retired professor, sharp-tongued, and brusque, she was perplexed by her "daughter's" life choices.

Ruth said to Joe, "It's a pretty stupid time to break up your marriage, don't you think? I remember having this one"—she pointed at Logan—"and I couldn't have done it alone. Of course, Erika was forever a handful. That never stopped."

Logan made a disgusted noise, wouldn't look at their mother.

"Who's Erika?" Joe said.

Ruth pointed at Logan.

Logan said, "Mother, please stop. Just stop. You know my name."

"I'm doing fine, thanks," said Joe.

Ajax wondered what it would have been like to grow up with censorious Ruth as your mother

"You think you are," said Ruth. "But you're on what? Week

two? You just wait." She looked from Joe to Ajax, reached over and poked Ajax's arm. "I told my Erika not to get involved with you. She wants to rescue you. You're a poodle to her, Ajax. To my daughter, you're just some dog from the pound she took home. She'll be sick of you before you can snap your fingers. I know. I've watched her all her life."

Logan tossed back their drink, grabbed the other one, drank that back too.

Ajax reached for Logan's thigh under the table, squeezed it. "I don't need rescuing by Logan. I've been rescuing myself for twenty years. Fifty, if you count more than just the time I've had a bad heart."

Ruth made a sucking noise. "Erika didn't even go to work while you were in the hospital."

Joe said, "Hey, now. If your husband or kid was in the hospital, would you go to work? It's not different because we're queer, you know."

"The words you young people use." Ruth ordered more wine. "I don't have to have this conversation."

"Mom," said Logan, stopping Ajax with their hand. "You don't get to be nasty. Whether you like what's going on here or not, Ajax and I are—goddamn it, Mom." Logan pulled off their ball cap, threw it on the table, moved Ajax's hand up to kiss it. "We're getting married. Actually, we're getting married tomorrow at two p.m. on the lakefront." Their voice rose and almost squeaked as Ruth's face crumpled. "You suspected this was coming."

Ruth turned back to Ajax. "Ajax, you would do this to my girl? You're ten years her senior. You're—whatever you are. Dying. You would steal my daughter's life from her?"

Ajax kept her voice firm, low, steady. "We'd like you to be there with us."

Ruth pushed up from the table. The heat pressed in like a suffocating pillow.

"Mom, sit the hell down. I've been in the same building looking after you for twenty years. Don't you want me to have a chance at the brass ring? Don't you want me to be happy?"

Ajax saw her children approaching, pushed up and waved.

Logan said, "Mom, just lay off. This is supposed to be a celebration."

"You'll be crawling to me by Christmas saying you made the biggest mistake of your life! And don't say I didn't warn you! I warned you!"

The girls looked questions at Ajax as she hugged them.

Logan stood up, held chairs, said, "Mom, these are Ajax's kids, Simone and Vivi. Girls, this is my mother, Ruth."

Ruth bitterly said, "Erika, how many times have I told you not to get married until after I was dead?"

Ajax slapped her good palm on the table. "Can't *someone* celebrate with us?"

"I will," said Joe, raising her lemonade. "You bet Scout and I will be there."

Ajax said, "We're really over the fucking moon; we're happy. Can't you please, please put yourselves and your worries aside, and just be with us? You're all right, of course; it might not work. It might be a huge honking mistake. But who knows? It also could be fabulous. And Ruth, it would mean the goddamned world to Logan if you'd get over yourself and show up. Just *show up* for your kid."

"Whoa," said Vivi, putting up her hands to ward her mother off.

"Look, we brought bubbles," said Simone, swirling her index finger. "Mom's getting married. Woo hoo." She pulled out small white bottles for everyone, blew a bubble.

"Well, I'm for it," said Vivi. "Why not bet on love?"

"Thank you, Vivi. You show up for us tomorrow, Simone, Ruth. Now, I have to go to bed. C'mon, Logan, come upstairs with me."

Ruth said, "*I'll* leave."

"*We're* leaving," Logan said. "I have to walk Toby. You all stay here and talk about how horrible it is that the queers have found true love. We'll catch you on the downside." They threw cash on the table to cover the drinks.

"You okay?" Logan said to Ajax as they walked away.

"No," said Ajax. "You?"

"Not very," said Logan.

JOE

Joe and Ajax's daughters were left at the table with the bottles of bubbles and the trickling stream of pedestrians beyond the small, hedged fence.

"I'm going to take Mom and Logan some food," said Simone, standing and rubbing her belly, a gesture familiar and comforting to Joe. Simone gave Vivi a kiss on the cheek. "I'll catch you in the morning, sis. I'm going to order and then get this weight off my feet."

As they watched Simone disappear inside Le Lapin, Joe thought, *Could I have a glass of wine to pump and dump?* She turned back to Vivi, who regarded her across the table with a frank gaze, startlingly blue eyes under her frame of purple hair. Scout slid off Joe's breast, sound asleep, and Joe worked to fasten her bra and get her top back together.

"I'm sorry about what happened with your wife," said Vivi.

Joe held the slumberous baby and fiddled with the salt shaker. Vivi seemed to Joe to be surrounded by sparks.

Vivi's melodic tone dropped. "Maybe I shouldn't have said anything, but Mom told us. She just walked out, without any warning?"

Joe said, "I've heard rumours that life goes on. Two years out, they say, it's as if nothing ever happened."

Vivi shuffled in her chair. "You're staying at your mom's?"

"I have a house, but I guess you heard what happened there.

My ex—" She could not get used to ex'ing Ell. "She pretty much cleaned it out."

"That's shifty," said Vivi.

"Well, I'll miss things, I guess, is all. According to her, what's hers is hers and what's mine is hers because I'm the *noncontributing* spouse."

Vivi stuck out her tongue; Joe noticed a piercing. She found herself wondering where else Vivi had piercings.

"Is there legal recourse?"

Joe transferred Scout to the car seat now taking up one of the spare chairs, rocked it to settle her. "Apparently, the law doesn't care about what they call household goods. But it's a gesture of bad faith that will probably go sour for her in court," said Joe. "As if I ever imagined a woman I trusted completely and was crazy about would sue me." Joe sighed, then bitterly laughed. "But I'm so sick of talking about my situation." She twirled ice in her empty lemonade. "Let's talk about you."

Vivi grinned. "I do a boring IT job in Vancouver; how do you think my life is? I need to shake it up. Go back to school, move somewhere, rattle it somehow, get the lead out."

Joe smiled. "I guess I meant, how's your romantic life?"

"Ah," said Vivi lifting her glass, laughing. "Well, that would be a different story."

The waiter came by to take their order.

"I fuck women now, I guess is the news. Mom doesn't know. I'd say I came out, but I don't think it's called coming out if nobody much knows."

"Congratulations," said Joe. "That's big."

"I was bisexual, but then when I got to my twenties, I don't know, something changed in me, and I realized I was with men for all the wrong reasons. To fit in. To ease my way. As a reaction against having queer moms." Vivi shrugged. "They thought I was gay since I was tiny, so I always balk at confirming it for them."

"I like your mom," said Joe.

Vivi said, "We're lucky in that regard, I think. I don't know how Simone is going to stand being in the Bahamas and so far from Mom when she has the baby."

"As much as mine drives me around the twist, I'm grateful for her. Especially now."

"Our other mother, Hope, can really be a dick, a lot like your Ell. Worse, probably," said Vivi.

"Oh no."

"She disavowed us after the breakup and pretended we weren't her kids. Went around in the world as a person who didn't have children. Puts on a good front, but that's all it is, a front. They had a messy breakup, and Mom didn't get what she should have. I learned that money is power. Mom was bouncing from one medical emergency to another, and Hope exploited her disability. No basic human empathy. She went unglued when she realized Mom was going to have open heart surgery—but not out of worry—out of anger because it meant Mom might not die as soon and she could be stuck supporting her."

Joe extended a hand for Vivi's.

Vivi started to cry. "Oh, look at me. Two drinks and I'm making a scene."

"You're worried for your mom," said Joe. "That's reasonable. Maybe now, in the face of this crisis, you're just letting yourself start to feel things."

Joe stroked Vivi's hand, astonished by the unlikeliness of the contact. Vivi was almost a replica of her mother—wide-shouldered and radiant with intelligence, but bruised around her eyes, stressed and sad. "I'm sorry it's been hard for you, Vivi. Hope sounds horrible."

"The appalling thing is that she doesn't even know it. She'd charm you if you met her." Vivi pulled her hand away and swabbed at her eyes, but barely broke the gaze, and Joe didn't either.

Their meals came; Joe tucked into Coquilles Saint-Jacques with her stomach growling. "She's strong, your mom. Maybe things will get better for her now. They'll get her an operation for her fibrillation and get it under control. Logan is smitten; I've never seen them like this."

"Mom's awesome, really. Ask her to show you her work sometime. She shows at Wilderness Gallery here." Vivi poked at onion soup.

"That's across from the AGO, right?"

"Yup," said Vivi proudly. She wrinkled up her nose. "I hope Mom does find some happiness. She works like a dog. If she had even a dollar for every hour she's devoted to her craft, she could pay off her mortgage."

They finished their meals in companionable silence. It was cooling off, and Joe covered Scout, tucking the blanket up around her ears. She asked Vivi if she wanted to move inside, but Vivi said no. "If it's all the same to you, Joe, could we just go back to my hotel room and continue our chat?"

"Um," she said. "I have ... um ... the baby." *I have Elliot,* was what she was really thinking, quite desperately, *I have Elliot!*

"We can talk around Scout."

"Um," said Joe, thinking *talk, just talk,* but still a wash of nervousness overtook her. She reminded herself that she needed human companionship—she needed to be out in the world. A little subverted lust would not be a bad thing, except maybe for her stitches.

An hour later, Joe was nursing Scout in Vivi's nondescript hotel room in an uncomfortable chair and had called her mother to say she would be out late.

"Did you ever sleep with anyone else while you were married?" Vivi asked. She had sprawled across the bed, leaning on the heels of her palms. "Or was it only Elliot?"

"I did, once," said Joe, "but I never told Ell, which violated every letter of our agreement. It was right at the beginning, before we had really cemented things." She flushed as she thought again about Logan, and then her breath stalled as she realized, *This is Logan's almost-wife's daughter. How do you spell incestuous?*

"Tell me more about you," said Joe. "You know all too

much about me, given the week you arrived, but your mom hasn't told me much."

"I was with a guy for a lot of years. A fundamentalist who maintained that I was going to Hell while he and my step-daughter were going to Heaven. He was a liar, a cheat. He'd been convicted of fraud. I was a total hermit with him. Now I'm forcing myself out into the world—I'm trying to see how many things there are to do in Vancouver. Beach volleyball. Biking, hiking, caving. Bungee-jumping. I went to Africa for a couple months."

Joe stood up with Scout, who was starting to complain, and held her the way she'd seen a doctor hold babies on YouTube to stop them from screaming. Scout settled and her eyes flickered closed. Joe gently transferred the weirdly contented baby back into her car seat. "I'm sorry."

"I was young. I didn't know I could have a life," Vivi said, pushing back her fizz of hair. "I didn't realize there was a whole world outside that hotbox of marriage."

"There's a life outside marriage?" said Joe ruefully. She thought she might cry. She thought about dead Dree, for whom there had surely by now been a funeral of some kind. A woman who had loved her was no more than dust now. The enormity of the world outside her marriage already overwhelmed Joe, and she hadn't done a thing to prepare for that enormity except remove her wedding ring when she unpacked at her mother's place. Now she rubbed her thumb up and down on her index finger where the ring had been for so many years, then had to force herself to stop, to lay her hands flat against her legs.

"It hurts, is all," said Vivi. Tears wetted her eyes and spilled over. She grabbed tissues. "I'm only a year out of it. I'm sorry, I'm sorry."

"No," said Joe, getting up, crouching beside Vivi, putting an arm around her, "don't be sorry. Please. I'm just as sad as you are. Maybe that's all we get to be in this life, broken. A bunch of broken people betting it all on a vague dream of future happiness."

Vivi inclined her head onto Joe's shoulder and said that she was pretty sure Joe was wrong. "It gets better."

"It gets better," said Joe. "It gets better. I believe it'll get better. Someday it may even stop hurting. But the place where Ell lived is a vacant canyon inside of me."

"I know," said Vivi, reaching for Joe's face, running her finger across Joe's lips. "I know exactly. Can we lie down?"

"Yes," Joe whispered. She confided the ways she was out of commission. The faint scent of lemon as she buried her face in Vivi's hair. She knew her breasts were going to leak, but she forgot to be anxious about it, and before she had time to analyze what was happening, to ask herself if it was what she actually craved, whether she'd regret it in the morning, whether it would change her friendship with Ajax, with Vivi's *mother*, whether it was breaking a bond with Elliot that she wasn't ready to smash, whether Vivi was the woman she wanted to hold, these unfamiliar shoulders, these breasts—these breasts! She'd missed breasts! Was that cruel to admit? — they were beside each other, Joe smelling her own milkiness, smelling Scout. They read each other, maps of forgiveness and solace and lust, removing clothing, touching, their fingers conduits for surprise. When Joe met Vivi's gaze full-on, she caught her breath and had to flick the light off to escape the intensity. She let her fingers run across Vivi's skin, across her nipples, feeling the areolas wrinkle, the nipples harden. She kissed Vivi, the sensation burning across her own lips, a line of fire. Vivi tasted of red wine; Joe's tongue felt the metal stud in Vivi's mouth, warm, round. It made her clit twitch. Vivi's lips were traps. She didn't stop kissing her. Joe touched Vivi's damp face, let her fingers tangle in Vivi's purple curls.

Vivi climbed on Joe and sat astride her, leaned forward, her hair tickling Joe's face. Where Elliot had been swarthy, earthy, bound, Vivi was a bird, hollow-boned, about to launch into flight.

Air.

AJAX

The next day was pouring rain, a deluge with thunder and lightning. Logan and Ajax woke early, and Ajax pressed herself hard back into Logan.

"Your arm," Logan said, pulling away.

"Never mind my arm," said Ajax. There was no way she could get on hands and knees, but like this?

Logan rolled away.

Ajax made a disconsolate noise.

"Lube," said Logan, laughing. "You know you never need to ask twice."

"Ah," said Ajax and rolled onto her back grinning.

"God, I love you," said Logan, the squirt bottle in their hand. They put a fingertip on Ajax's chin. "I love you, I love you, I love you! You scared the fucking *shit* out of me this week, girlfriend."

Ajax grinned ruefully. "I know, but think of this; tomorrow you get to call me 'wife.'"

"Whoa—wife. My wife." Logan wrapped her tight in their arms. "My wench."

"Want me to call you husband?"

"Hmm ... Not sure."

"I'm really sorry about what happened," Ajax said, pulling away so she could see Logan's eyes. "Sorry for you. All of it. The arrhythmia. This." She lifted her arm in the sling. "No second thoughts now you know some of the crap that can happen?"

"I'm just glad you're going to be okay." They trickled their fingers through Ajax's hair.

Ajax snuggled in. "Will you rub my clit? I just about went mad in the hospital, I was so horny for you."

Logan touched her until Ajax arched her back, until she moaned. Logan said, "Baby, you don't need lube."

"I do if you fuck my ass," said Ajax, turning so her gimp arm was on top.

"Baby," said Logan, slipping their wet finger inside, wiggling it against Ajax's anterior wall, the back of her clit.

"I'm gonna come if you do that," said Ajax groaning.

"Come with me instead." Logan slipped a condom on. "Where do you want my cock, baby?"

Ajax had pins and needles in her bad arm and checked to make sure it was suffused. When it had been compromised, it was a very dark red; now it was blotchy. It pulled her away from sex. "In my asshole, in my asshole."

Logan pushed in an inch, met resistance. "Do you want it? Say it. Tell me."

"Logan, make me hurt *so* good." Pushing her ass toward Logan. "Really, really slow, honey," said Ajax, savouring it. Ajax couldn't last, not after her anxious, bored, hospital-bound days. She was ravenous; she pushed back hard onto Logan's cock. "Fuck, fuck, I'm already coming, Logan."

"I'm coming too, baby. I'm coming inside you." Logan ground themself in deep, and Ajax cried out.

Ajax's orgasm still thrummed vaguely in her toes and legs

when something else, something new, started to suffuse her. At first she just thought, *Cool,* but in another minute it was clear to her that it was something a lot more meaningful than just her orgasm's afterglow moving up into her abdomen and chest, moving into her head and down her arms. She didn't have the words for it—the closest she could get was that it was a full-body pre-orgasmic state, except it lingered, built, and instead of reaching toward climax, it reached instead toward her love for Logan. She felt it concentrate in her belly just above her naval, and it moved out to the edges of her skin and past it, in her imagination, concentrated light.

As quickly as it washed through her, it vanished.

"I wish I had something better to wear," said Ajax. Simone had gone out to find something, anything, black slacks and a tank top, which Ajax had pulled on when she returned. Logan wore shorts and a pressed white polo shirt. "You're sure we want to be this casual?"

"You're a knock-out," said Logan, leaning on the doorframe.

"Can you go see if your mom has a white scarf I could use as a sling? Or look, here's Joe. Send Joe."

Kisses all around.

Vivi was mere steps behind.

There was an air of frantic gaiety.

"Morning," Vivi said, and when no one was looking whispered in Joe's ear, "I brought flowers."

"Where on earth did you find peonies at this time of year?" asked Ajax, beaming. "Where's Simone?"

"Here I am!" called Simone from the hallway.

Logan put a collar and bow tie on the dog, who didn't protest.

Vivi pinned a boutonniere on Logan.

Logan came back into the bedroom shrugging their shoulders, smiling, passing Ajax a scarf, helping her rig it as a sling. In a perfect imitation of Ruth, they said, "'You want me to treat this day like it's something special and you're wearing shorts, Erika? Please go put a dress on.' I wouldn't say Mom's what I'd call overjoyed, but she's meeting us in the lobby."

"Do you have the licence?"

"Licence, check. Bride, check. Children, check. Mother? Check. The officiant's meeting us there. Honey," said Logan, kissing Ajax's neck, turning her around. "You're going to shatter mirrors this morning, you're so beautiful."

Ajax gave herself a stern talking-to: *Not a kid, for god's sake. Calm the shit down. No fretting yourself into A-fib.* She started to cry, but they were tears of happiness.

"It's okay," said Joe. She took Ajax by the shoulders. "I am incandescent with joy for you, Ajax McIntyre. You are going to have a brilliant marriage. You can so do this."

Simone handed out mini-cameras and the little jars of bubbles. "Take lots of photos, everyone, because we don't have a photographer."

"Mom, you look stunning," said Vivi.

"She's perfect," said Simone. "Here, Vivi, take some pictures."

"I feel better today," said Ajax, wiggling her fingers. Today was the first day she'd been able to freely move them. "Apparently, I'll need my ring finger today. Oh, Logan, I am just crazy over the moon about you."

"Come be my wife, then, gorgeous," said Logan, kissing her forehead.

Joe wore Scout in the Snugli, leaving her free to hold hands with Vivi. If anyone thought this was unusual, no one commented.

Ajax took a big breath.

Logan took her elbow.

And they walked toward it, whatever it was.

A beach. A lake. A marriage.

Life.

ACKNOWLEDGMENTS

Thanks to Gladys, LL, Uggy, Martin, Leah, and Margo—for enduring love. Thanks to Hezah for 'douche canoe' and to my many friends who shared their stories of queer inseminations. Thanks also to my precious ones: Meghann and Sarah. Thanks to Davina and Naiya for becoming my new favourite people. A nod from my heart to my gay son, bill bissett.

Thanks to my sisters-in-lit, especially Eden Robinson and Brenda Brooks.

Thanks to Mary Bryson, Leah Macfadyen, Cornelia Hoogland, Patricia Young, and Tanis MacDonald for their generosity and friendship.

Thanks, Shelagh Plunkett, for the wide-ranging writing chats, Shelagh and Kari Szakacs for taking me to a cottage in Quebec where my characters, had they been real, might have hung out.

Thanks to Janice Stewart for putting the posit in position.

I'm grateful to Tom Cho, Jackie Wykes, the gang, and Historic Joy Kogawa House for hosting Shut Up and Write sessions during the writing of *Weekend*.

Thanks to Alice Anderson of FOITS fame, and to the people on social media who sustain me. I write knowing you have a hand on my elbow, propping me up.

I wrote *Weekend* for Arsenal Pulp Press—not at their behest, but because of my own appreciation for their titles over the years. *Just a little love story*, I told myself, *what could go wrong?*

A lot did go wrong, and Susan Safyan and Clara Kumagai were instrumental in fixing those things. Thanks to the rest of the team at Arsenal Pulp Press: Brian Lam, Robert Ballantyne, Cynara Geissler, and Oliver McPartlin. I appreciate all the work the team does during the lengthy process of seeing a book into the world.

The phrase "What we talk about when we talk about love" is taken from Raymond Carver's story of the same name.

I am grateful to the BC Arts Council and the Canada Council for their continued support.

Jane Eaton Hamilton is the author of eight books of fiction, non-fiction, and poetry. Her story collection *July Nights* was a BC Book Prize finalist, her poetry title "Body Rain" was a Pat Lowther finalist, and her story collection *Hunger* was a Ferro-Grumley Award finalist. She is a two-time winner of the fiction prize at the CBC Literary Awards. Her most recent book is the poetry collection *Love Will Burst into a Thousand Shapes* (Caitlin Press). Her work has been published in the *New York Times* and *Salon*. She lives in Vancouver.

janeeatonhamilton.wordpress.com